Accidental
Healer

Accidental Healer

Tales from the Afterworld

Book 2

V. K. Pasanen

Copyright © 2024 by V. K. Pasanen
IngramSpark Paperback Edition
All rights reserved
ISBN 979-8-9882654-9-8

Editor
Marie Anne Cope

Cover by
JDandJ.com

If you enjoy this novel, show your love and leave a rating and review on Amazon. For those who wish to continue the journey, subscribe to my website for a free gift with more to come.
www.vkpasanen.com
v.k.pasanen@vkpasanen.com
v.k.pasanen@talesfromtheafterworld.com

This book is a work of fiction. Names, characters, places, and incidents are either figments of the author's imagination or used fictitiously. Any resemblance to actual persons, living or dead, businesses, companies, events, or locations is purely coincidental in the reality of the author's imagination.

Welcome back to my tales from the Afterworld.
Now that you know who I am,
I will take you back
to where the end began.
I touched upon it without knowing
in my final work as a mortal,
but only scratched the surface.
My soul was young,
and I was still unaware
of all the machinations
driving events behind reality's curtain.
Nor did I have the all-knowing eye,
without which this work and
warning wouldn't have been possible.
My hope is that this labor of penance
will help the dying Afterworld
grasp the how and why,
we reached this precipice—this Ragnarök.

I will not return to these tales as a major player
until the dark clouds of Apocalypse
fill the skies of my former reality.
That is not to say I don't play a role.
That role will become evident
as will my guilt in everything that transpired.

N. Reaper

One

Time? Day? The Hole, Helix Eternal Laboratories Main Complex, Undisclosed Location.

Mary DeMure's eyes crept open to dim light and a familiar smell of mildew and rat pellets. *Welcome back to consciousness. But for how long?* thought the former Green River College student. She sat up on the dingy mattress and shivered as she studied the out of place antique desk in her gray-block cell. She wondered if its drawer still contained the one finger twitch out of hell she passed on the last time she was here. She also wondered if she was all who remained. What sadistic torments did the mad general have for her now? She eyed the drawer again. *No. Not giving him the satisfaction.* While there was breath in her lungs, she would claw to life until he put her down or his corpse was melting in her hands.

She suddenly realized her tongue was glued to the roof of her mouth. *So thirsty*, she thought and grimaced at the rusty sink next to the corner toilet. She remembered its fetid water and retched. Unlike her first stint in the Hole, nothing in the water could harm her now. Dr. Evil and his whore bitch had made her immune to everything except death. But even death was harder to achieve compared to the day Louis and his team abducted her from Walnut Hill, Washington. *How long has it been?* She wasn't sure. At least a year, maybe more… or less.

She glanced at the desk again. The lock disengaged, startling her to her bare feet as her fingers curled like talons and her feral glare burned into the gray metal door. More of the General's men were about to be dead. How many? She hoped all but one. And while she wanted to take it slow and anything but easy as she had the orderlies, she was going for the gusto this time—maximum kills, motherfuckers.

"It's me," came the sweet voice of the only motherfucker she didn't want to kill.

She shook her head and relaxed her talons. She regarded her blood-caked fingernails as the door squealed open.

Louis Suerte entered in a white hazmat suit with an M4 Carbine dangling around his neck. An air pistol was in his right hand.

She smiled at the tan, handsome face of her abductor who she'd fallen for—lock, Stockholm, and barrel.

He didn't smile back. "Could you all wait outside?" he asked the others.

The other guards laughed and the one with the Aussie accent heckled, "Better Teflon your pecker for that one, mate."

Louis shook his head and pushed the door closed. "Fuckin' asshole," he muttered.

"Why are you here?" she asked.

"You're being *released* along with the five who survived yesterday. The General doesn't feel you're *worthy* of Caine's *gift*. But he did want it done outside—he thought it would be nice for you to see the sun before we cut off your head. He said it was the *least* he could do since you made it this far."

"Well, ain't that fuckin' sweet."

Louis dropped to a whisper. "Hey, I got a plan. But you have to trust me. Do you trust me?"

"Yeah. Of course, I do."

"Good. I have to make this look good." He curled his lips into a charming smile and lifted the pistol.

Two

Mary stirred and awakened from a dreamless slumber to find herself jostled back and forth. Her mouth was gagged. She heard the rumbling roar of a heavy truck engine. She tried to move but thick chains pinned her to a gurney. Even her head was fixed so her gaze remained on the beveled army-green canvas above. Her hands were covered with something thick and warm enough to make her palms sweat. The General's guards weren't taking chances and Louis was making it look good—*too good*. She hoped she hadn't let her heart lead her head into an easy slaughter.

Her eyes shifted left. She saw Louis's face behind his hood's shield. Her gaze shifted right to a second guard but saw only the top of a hazmat hood. She felt a gentle tap on her shoulder and her attention returned to Louis.

He gave her a reassuring grin and shushed her with his lips. He scooted around the gurney and sat by the other guard. "Snake, huh? Why do you always play that stupid game?"

"What the hell else is there to do?" he asked in a subtle southern drawl without looking up. "It keeps my mind off this fucked up job. I just wanna get'er done, then contract's up. Then I'm off to Disney World or wherever the hell else I wanna go. I gotta forget this year, or at least try."

Louis stole a glance at Mary before she heard the distinctive discharge of an air pistol.

"Owww, bitch. What the fuck, Loui…" the other guard said, lifting his face for Mary to catch his shocked expression before Louis's arm came around the man's neck and his hand pressed the flexible shield over his mouth. The guard kicked several times then went limp. Louis laid the man out of her sight. He nodded at her and raised a peace sign. Only the driver and a passenger stood between them and a possible life together.

She heard retching sounds and felt violent rattling and kicking beneath the gurney. A mouth fountain splashed its contents against plastic, and then came the choking.

Louis's eyes went wide. He lipped, *"Oh, shit."* He swiftly unlocked her chains and head restraint. He made sleepy hands, and cocked his head to one side.

She closed her eyes.

He whispered in her ear, "No matter what happens, you go to Arizona. In your pocket, there's a map to our ride and a compass—I know you know how to use it. Everything else is in the Land Rover. You have to find the medicine man. He has the power to cure you. After that, there's a place I can take you where the General won't find us. And…and if you can forgive me, I'd like to stay there with you. I'm… Goddamn, I'm so sorry… I mean, for everything. If this mortal shell doesn't survive, just know that I love you, and I'll always be watching over you."

Louis spoke into his comm which Mary had never actually seen. "Hey, something's wrong with Charlie."

The driver stopped the truck, and Louis hopped out the back.

"What be the problem, mate?" said the asshole Aussie.

"Hell if I know," said Louis. "He was just there playing that stupid game on his phone then he starting seizuring or something. He never said anything about having epilepsy."

"That's 'cause he doesn't, mate. Never woulda got the contract," said Aussie Ass as he hopped into the back leaving Louis out of sight. The guard wasn't wearing a hazmat suit. He was dressed in standard-issue black and white camo with a black beret topping his smooth brain dome. A second guard joined him who was likewise unprotected.

"Blimy, Louis, why didn' ya take off Charlie's hood?" said Aussie Ass as he knelt to do just that. His beret dropped from sight.

An air pistol discharged twice. The second guard turned with a startled expression and dropped hard on the truck bed.

KREW-KREW.

Mary's ears rang as she shot up. Aussie Ass was facing away holding a smoking Glock. She couldn't see Louis. She clenched her teeth.

Aussie Ass wheeled around, pointed, and fired at Mary's head.

Sound died as vapor mushroomed from the barrel. An orange arrow cut a line toward a spot between her eyes. She cocked her head sideways and the bullet floated past and hit somewhere behind with the sound of one hand clapping. She removed her welder's gloves.

The guard's face was nearly frozen in stunned betrayal. His half-lip snarl was rising and beginning to show clenched teeth.

Mary dodged a second floater as she bounded to her feet. Her chains slid off and dropped to the ground. She tore off the gag and head restraint and threw it aside as she plunged a fist through the man's face like her sensei in Seattle had taught her.

The Black Beret's nose caved in, and his eyes popped from their sockets like space rockets lifting off. His head whiplashed back, carrying his body with it, lifting him off the bed. He rolled backward as slow as ketchup and flipped out of the truck.

Mary was on the tailgate before the man landed on Louis, whose eyes were set on the sky. Aussie Ass's body slow-sprung off him like a mattress and rolled face down beyond his body. Mary saw two black holes in the white over Louis's beautiful heart. She looked up. No sun. Only gray clouds above the pine and fall-colored birch trees.

Time caught up with the soon-to-be-dead man. Astonishingly, he was still conscious after the brain pulverizing blow and had rolled around and onto his knees. Blood bubbled from his nose crater. He blindly groped for his gun, gasping as crimson streamed from his face and his eyeballs dangled.

Mary's hands shimmered blue as bee sting static made her wince while watching the man endure his last seconds this side of Hell. She tried not to look at Louis but her eyes refused to obey. The sight of shattered hopes and dreams made every muscle burn. She felt like she might explode like some of the others did—some of the ninety-nine who'd never see the sky again.

She looked at the dying Aussie Ass. He would be dead from the punch before the Touch did its thing. But this was too quick, and he deserved *so* much more. A lunatic chuckle escaped as tears trickled. She grinned and laughed in discordant spurts as the Black Beret found his gun, gripped it, then relaxed and crumpled sideways. The bubbling paused for several seconds and returned for an audience pleasing double ruby gush.

She turned to the unprotected guard tranquilized by Charlie. She watched the man's chest rise and fall, wiped her eyes, and grinned.

She looked at the welder's gloves but they were too unwieldy for what she had planned. She removed the guard's gloves, taking care not to brush his skin with hers. She rummaged through a pack for a vial of reversal and epinephrine and several syringes and shoved everything into the coat she'd worn the night of her abduction. She reached in the pack once more for a camouflage t-shirt and wrapped it around her mouth and nose.

She stripped the guard, found a rope, and hog tied him, leaving plenty of line. She hopped out and yanked him from the truck. He slammed to the ground and didn't stir, not that she expected him to. She waited and when she saw his chest rise and fall again she dragged him into the woods.

Three

Mary's face twitched. She dropped the last syringe on the ground, then wiped her crimson-caked hands on her blood-soaked shirt, coat, and jeans. She located and unfolded Louis's map. It was reddened but still readable. She twitched again and thought of the once unthinkable, savage cruelty her hands had just delivered—not that this was the first time… but what she did to that man… this, this was... She used to be a good person before... She would've never… but she did. Her breathing was thready and shaky with nasal wheezes. Then her eyes moistened in memory of Louis and his reassuring grin. She had to focus and bury what she'd done—what she'd left in the forest. Louis would not die for nothing. She would find his medicine man and then she would finish this.

She studied the map and found her bearings with the compass. She was somewhere in Colorado and there was an X on a remote road. She suspected it marked the spot where the truck had stopped. There was another X several miles away along another mountain road. She followed the winding line on the map that accounted for every hill and valley and eventually arrived at Louis's Land Rover.

She looked through the window and saw the packs that contained what she'd need for the drive and/or hike to Arizona and beyond. She looked at her reflection in the window, then at her clothes, and thought of Carrie after the prom. She liked Sissy Spacek in *Coal Miner's Daughter*, but no longer cared for *Carrie*, or Stephen King for that matter, especially now that her life was like a horror novel. She wanted happy stories, fairy tales. She was more of an *It's a Wonderful Life* kind of girl, anything to take her mind off life's bottomless abyss. But even *Ahh, shucks* Jimmie Stewart reminded her of someone she'd lost.

She regarded her blood facial then looked to the ledge next to the SUV. It was a sheer, thirty to forty foot drop to a creek where she could clean up. She wasn't up for the hop down, so she scanned for an easier way, found one, and descended quickly.

She was sticky and soaked to the skin like she'd bathed in the man's blood but couldn't remember certain parts of her crime that were already blackening. She peeled off everything and hid it under rotting, moss-covered limbs, then scrubbed away the gore as best she could in icy water she was used to.

She ascended the bank dripping dry and barefoot, slicing her feet more than once. She hardly noticed, since even major lacerations would heal rapidly and infection wasn't a problem for anyone with the Touch of Pestilence. She glanced down. Everything she'd touched had wilted and was already being reclaimed by the soil.

She rummaged through the packs in the Land Rover and found fresh clothing and got dressed. Most of it was cotton. Luckily the Touch had no effect on plants and animals that were already dead. She got in the cockpit and saw a Timex watch in the console next to an empty *Texas A&M* travel mug. She grabbed the watch. It told her it was near noon, *SAT 9-1*, and that it'd been eleven months since she'd seen her home outside Seattle. She put on the watch, found the keys under the sun visor, adjusted the seat and mirrors, and started the vehicle.

She navigated the Land Rover at a slow jogging pace up and down deeply rutted roads. She paused every so often, glanced at the map, and checked her compass to keep from getting lost before she reached something paved. When she did, she pulled over and examined the map. The next Xs were over Grayson and a smaller town to the south called Packer City. From there, Louis's line led to mountainous roads and high passes that would be slow but still passible this early in the season, but the skies were gray and she could smell rain. That'd be just her luck—bad as usual.

She scanned for easier routes, but the General would be monitoring them. His *Typhoid Mary* had broken her chains and was on the loose. He'd be pissing himself and pulling out all the stops to capture and contain his prototype. No. She had to trust Louis's plan and forge ahead and hope she hadn't wasted too much time.

She pulled out the second map. It was a sturdy laminate of the four corner states with a line drawn to Canyon De Chelly. On it Louis had written, *Find Manycows*. Her lips trembled. Another wave hit her and she started sobbing. It was a few minutes before she could see straight, and when she could, she snorted, wiped her eyes, put away the map, and pulled onto the road.

Four

7:00 p.m., September 1, 2007, Grayson, Colorado.

Mary reached the outskirts of the next X near dusk. Just as she passed the city limit sign that boasted a population of 5,491, the SUV made a funny sound that wasn't very funny to Mary. She didn't know the first thing about cars, other than how to drive them.

She chewed her fingernails and pleaded, "Come on, baby. Hold together. Please, hold together."

Halfway through town, smoke began pouring from the hood as the engine made a grinding noise. The SUV kept rolling until she passed the *Leaving Grayson, Colorado* sign. The grind suddenly stopped, and was followed by a dreadful death rattle.

"Oh, fuck me," she said as the vehicle drifted to a stop on a shoulder inside a small canyon across the highway from a nearly dry river bed. She got out and lifted the hood and coughed as she fanned away smoke, and then gazed cluelessly at the maze of metal, plastic, and rubber.

An orange Jeep CJ7 pulled in front of the Land Rover. She glanced over and hoped the driver would continue on his way since she wasn't wearing gloves and her face was uncovered.

True to her bad luck, the old man got out and approached her. His face was kind and reminded her of her Peepa (her granddad's nickname she gave him before she could remember).

"I see you're stuck," said the old man.

"Yeah, my car overheated."

"I can see that. But don't you worry, now. I'll get you some help. Or if you're headed my way, I reckon I can give you a lift if you need one."

Mary paused to consider her options. With the General's reach and time on his side, they were very limited.

"Ma'am. Ma'am," the man said, raising his voice slightly on the second ma'am. "You okay?"

"Yeah, yeah. I, I'm sorry."

"It's okay. So, where you headed?"

"I need to get to Packer City."

He chuckled. "Well, it's your lucky day. I'm headed there now. Just got back from Breckenridge." He reached for something.

Mary flinched.

He pulled out a wallet and flipped open to a picture of a baby wearing a powder blue jumper. "This here is my great grandson, Henry. Cute as a button, huh?"

She kept her distance but leaned to see. "Yeah. He, he's beautiful."

"Well, come on—let me drive you. Rain's a comin' and you look plumb tuckered." He paused. "You don't look too sure about me. I understand in this day and age. But I can guarantee you, I am as harmless as a ladybug."

Even if he wasn't, that wasn't what worried her. "Okay, I'll get my stuff." She did, but first she tucked her shoulder length blonde hair under a beanie and covered her mouth and nose with a wrap-around face mask. She slid on her jacket, and zipped it to her chin covering all visible skin except around her eyes. She wished she still had the jacket she discarded. It had thumbholes. Without them, there was a chance her wrists might be exposed. Maybe she was being paranoid, but in her current state, she was primed and lethal. She put on leather snow gloves and pulled the coat sleeves over the gaps.

The old man raised an eyebrow and had the look of someone that might think twice about picking up a stranger in distress. If so, he didn't say anything. He just asked, "You cold? I mean, it is a bit chilly, but you sure are bundled up."

"I'm not good with the cold, " said Mary as she threw Louis's pack in the back and got in the Jeep.

"Okie smokey. Well, then, let's go. Oh, and I didn't introduce myself, my name is Melvin Anderson. And you are?"

Mary thought of a news reporter named Julie and a town in Oregon. "I'm, I'm Julie Springfield."

"Well, Julie, do you have any family in Packer City?"

"No. Just a friend there," Mary said as she glanced out the window.

"Well, you just tell me where you want me to drop you off, and I'll get'cha there."

Mary felt a hand pat her wrist. She pulled her hand away and saw that her sleeve was bunched exposing her wrist.

"Ahowww," the man howled like a child as he gripped his hand as if he'd touched lava. He looked confused as he rubbed a swiftly blistering palm.

"No. No. Please, no. Damnit, no. I'm sorry. I'm sorry," she whimpered.

Mr. Anderson's eyes widened like he was seeing something that wasn't there. He began to shake and his teeth chattered. Blisters spread up his arms and soon covered his neck and face. He gasped for breath then fell forward and the horn blared.

Five

Dusk, Saturday, September 1, 2007, Mama Maria's Southwestern Bar and Grill, Packer City, Colorado.

Ex-Army Ranger Ryan Mender kissed his wife, Suzanne, and ruffled their son Alex's tight curls at the rear exit. He couldn't believe Alex was nearly seven and felt blessed to soon be celebrating it after January's scare. And oh, did they have plans for his second birthday party at his grandmother's namesake.

Suzanne inhaled contentment. He could almost read her mind after a decade and eight wedding anniversaries, the last by far their happiest, even though it began with him in the hospital bed. It was the morning after the miracle of his bloodline drove Alex's leukemia into remission, and according to everyone who witnessed it, resurrected him from the dead.

She panned the packed restaurant and asked, "Hard to believe, huh?"

"Yeah," he said as he wrapped an arm around her and squeezed and enjoyed all the happy faces. Alex looked up at him and he fought to keep his eyes from misting.

Fifteen months had passed since they opened the doors of the newly named restaurant. Before that, it was called *The Old Prospector*. It had been a town landmark for over a century, and before it was respectable, an old dance hall/brothel in what was Hells Acre in the old mining town.

Alex tugged on Suzanne's coat. "Can we go? I left my Harry Potter book at Hogwarts. I was getting to a really good part when we left this morning."

Hogwarts was what Alex called the Watchtower where the Mender's had lived blissfully since Spring 2006 (minus the previous fall). That was also when they bought the old restaurant that'd been an important part of Ryan's life since his first visit with his granddad, Edwin, and his white uncle, Mel, the summer before he started kindergarten in Grand Junction.

"Okay, okay. We'll go in a minute," said Suzanne. "Now Ryan, if the new cook needs any help, don't hesitate… Never mind. Don't call. No point. You need to head up to Denver next week. I don't like being out in the boonies without a sat-phone."

Alex looked at his shoes. "I'm sorry," he said.

She looked down. "Don't be. Accidents happen. Just be more careful next time," she said concerning his last conversation with Nana Norine and Gamba James, which ended with the satellite phone plummeting to the base of Tower Rock.

Ryan chuckled. "Well, Suzanne, you know what they say. You can't always have your castle and your cell coverage, too."

Her eyebrows rose with her droll expression.

"Alright, alright. I'll head up to Denver Monday morning."

"You promise?"

"I promise. And I also called WORLD Net. They can't send anyone out to fix the internet until the fourteenth."

"Are you kidding me?"

"I wish I were."

"Dangit." She sighed as the front door swung open.

Scrawny Eugene Lee walked through the door with his usual scowl, threadbare red mackinaw coat, ratty faded jeans, and favorite boots that were coming apart at the soles. He was a Vietnam vet and cantankerous racist with a chip on his shoulder larger than Sisyphus's stone. He was far from lovable and loved by only one person that Ryan could think of. That was his wife, Charlotte, who ran the most popular coffee shop in town, which was the only coffee shop since no one counted *The Greasy Spoon*. Eugene was also Brigham Norsworthy's nephew, the deceased former resident and builder of the Watchtower. Eugene let it be known that the Watchtower should've been his by right since he'd been the caretaker for the dozen years after his uncle's stroke. Moreover, Eugene considered himself a Packer City founding ancestor since his family had lived in the area through thick and very thin since its founding. He made no effort to hide his bottomless resentment toward his uncle's spoiled children after they sold the castle out from under him to the *hoity-toity* Menders.

"Well, gotta go. Have fun," Suzanne said with a grin. She pecked Ryan's pursed lips and was out the back before Eugene uttered his first vulgar word for the night.

Six

8:30 p.m., Mama Maria's Southwestern Bar and Grill.

"Tone it down, Eugene," Ryan said for the final time. "You're making my patrons uncomfortable." He was beyond sick of Eugene's backhanded comments and slurs meant for Lei Tran, one of the town's two physician's assistants, who was there on a date with his girlfriend and coworker, Marcy Green. Tran had moved to town a year before the Menders and since then Eugene had seemed hellbent to remind the world what he thought of Asians whenever Tran was within earshot. To Tran's credit, he always ignored Eugene, but the old bastard was on an unusual tirade tonight. Ryan was fed up putting up with his racist crap, small town or not. And he didn't give a damn anymore who Eugene's uncle was or who his great grand honky-ass might've been either.

Eugene scowled and redirected his rancor. "Some... some war hero you are, big man. You ain't seen shit like I saw in 'Nam. Damn gook bastards. Wished we'd killed them all. All that shit in Almawt Lilkifaar... everybody with half a brain cell knows it was all fake. Made for TV bullll-shit. I don' care what you or anyone else says—it was fake news from the deep state. Yeah, you were jus' a dupe for the military industrial complex my Uncle Brigham warned us about. Like that overhyped wannabe Nathan Miller... yeah, you two sure did grease Cranston's asshole for Adamson. Now look where he is. Good job, soldier boy."

Ryan grinned as his nostrils flared. He thought of fluffy bunnies but they kept growing sharp, pointed teeth that could easily rip his fuckin' throat out. He cracked his neck one way, then the other. He looked at Saint Mom on his shoulder and said, "Yeah, Eugene, you're done here tonight. And, and don't bother coming in tomorrow or any time after that. You hear me?"

Eugene's bloodshot eyes widened and he exploded into a chain of expletives that began with, "I'll tell you when I'm motherfuckin' done, boy. I've been coming here since before you were sucking on mama's hoity toity tit."

Ryan was about to release his fluffy bunnies when the earlier forbidding skies opened up and thunder rolled out with a deluge that made it hard to hear anything else Eugene said as he continued to invite death. He was tempted to grab the bastard by his britches and throw his bony ass out the front door. But again Angel St. Mom suggested he call Charlotte to drive him home, if not for Eugene, for everyone else on the road. Ryan called but the barista extraordinaire refused. She was in the middle of a *Beverly Hillbillies* marathon.

Ryan peered out the front window as unruly skies refused to behave and ankle deep rivulets streamed along the roadside toward Grayson Highway's two lanes. It was closing time, and oh, how he needed Eugene gone, or, no lie, he was going to kill him. Still, he hated sending everyone else into weather.

He huffed and looked over at the bar. Eugene had pulled out his emergency flask and was gulping away as he goaded Ryan to say something or make good on the threat in his eyes. "I hate to do this, but I gotta close up. You guys come back soon, except you, Eugene. Get out of my restaurant, now."

Eugene flipped him off.

A few minutes later, Ryan stepped outside and sighed as he locked the doors. The last regulars and a few late-season vacationers ran through the flood to their vehicles. He looked at the door and thought about the mess he'd left. *Fuck it, I'll get it tomorrow*, he thought. It'd been a long day made longer by a few hours with Eugene. Now, he wanted to get home to Suzanne in time to tuck Alex into bed.

Rain pattered like machine gun fire on the copper awning as he rubbed his clean-shaven braincase. He tightened his lips, ground his teeth, and glowered at Eugene as he swayed back and forth and stumbled every few steps. He sunk in a rivulet, tripped, somehow caught himself, then tried to act like he meant to almost eat shit.

Ryan wished Eugene had but silenced the blazing devil on one shoulder and listened to Angel St. Mom again and hollered, "Hey, Eugene. Let me give you a lift home."

He clumsily waved him off and said, "I dun need no Ga-damn ride. I can drive jus' fine." The rest of what came out of his filthy mouth was unintelligible.

Ryan shook his head and clenched his fists as his nostrils flared. He inhaled through his nose, pulled in good thoughts, and exhaled the desire to pummel the insufferable bastard.

He grit his teeth as Eugene navigated growing puddles with the skill of a drunken martial artist, slipping and sliding every few steps before he arrived at his rusted red pickup truck looking like he'd taken a dip in the big lake. He opened the door, stepped up, slipped, and almost fell again. Once his bony butt settled into the lumpy, weathered seat, he rummaged for keys. He found them, narrowed his eyes, and stilled his swaying head like he was trying to make multiple keyholes become one. After a miss, he found success and slammed the door. He cranked the engine. It sputtered before limping to life. He stepped on the gas. The pickup lurched forward and almost hit another patron and a vehicle. Ryan opened his mouth to warn but the patron had a middle finger ready coupled with choice words for Eugene.

The curmudgeon U-turned and splashed a second patron with muddy water. He hit the gas, kicked up mud and gravel, then swerved back and forth to the highway. He turned north without a California pause as his worn tires spun. The Ford fishtailed and disappeared around the corner.

"Goddamnit. What a piece of shit. Fuckin' Eugene, say goodbye to *The Old Prospector*. You won't be darkening these doors again," Ryan said as he rubbed his stubbly chin and Eugene's irritable engine faded into the stormy din.

He hurried to his white F350, jumped in, and glared at the restaurant through a renewed cloudburst. He thought about Eugene's antics and seethed with tight fists. *Fuckin' Eugene. Fuckin', fuckin' Eugene.* He couldn't get his Goddamn words out of his head because he was partially right. That's what made Ryan's stomach turn every time he saw his old commanding officer on TV whenever a word was needed from the Chairman of the Joint Chiefs of Staff. But the part that wasn't fake was the hole left inside him. He thought about the tattoo on his right arm and the eleven initials inked below the tan-bereted skull that had incorporated a bullet scar in its forehead. Ryan calmed himself, rubbed his lips, then said each name, trying to remember something other than the dead faces for the ones who still had faces. "Roderick Williams. Toby Almaraz. Jesus Gonzales. Riley Jameson. Thomas Jones. Max Iverson. Stan McConnell. Ricky Mendez. Benny Roessel. Geno Simmons. Kyle Wheeler." His lips quivered. All he saw was body bags. "Damn, I fuckin' miss you guys," he said and started weeping.

He breathed deep, wiped his eyes and cheeks, then started the engine, and headed toward Grayson Highway. He turned south without looking as his mind wandered. He saw headlights. An orange Jeep swerved and barely missed his truck. The driver continued toward the Howard Creek Bridge. Ryan knew the vehicle and the license plate. It was Uncle Mel's, who he'd known his whole life and couldn't remember driving anything else.

A week earlier, his granddad's old friend had left for Breckenridge to visit his son and hold his first great grandchild. Uncle Mel said he'd be back that weekend, but Ryan didn't see where he needed to be in this weather other than at home, and home was the other way. He suspected he might be heading to the Watchtower and his guess proved right when Mel turned onto Lake Hotchkiss Road outside town and sped up. "Going my way, I see," Ryan said with a sniffly chuckle and a head shake. "Must have pics burning a hole in your wallet. But I sure do wish you'd slow down. We ain't going nowhere."

Ryan's face tensed. That didn't make sense. Uncle Mel had never visited at night and didn't like to drive in the rain, and especially not in this shit. And since they'd moved to the area, he'd only been out to the Watchtower three, four times, maybe? They'd told him more than once that they wished he'd come out to the castle more often. But why come now, when it'd be safer in the morning after church?

Ryan felt sick as the Jeep neared Lake Hotchkiss. Melvin was taking the winding curves faster than the vehicle should in the present weather, or any weather. "Maybe that's not you behind the wheel." Melvin was never reckless and always drove below the speed limit. That is unless he was drinking. Yeah, his pop had told him stories about Uncle Mel. But to Ryan's knowledge, he was a teetotaler and had been for years thanks to Grandpa Edwin, who gave up the drink years before his fellow commando. "Hmm. If that's not you, then who's driving your Jeep?" he asked as the CJ7 continued along the northwest shore.

He slowed and followed at a distance until the Jeep's lights disappeared around a curve. He wasn't concerned about losing the classic. If it was Uncle Mel than he would catch up with him at the Watchtower and ask what the hell was he thinking driving like a bat out of Breckenridge. And if it wasn't him, and someone had stolen his baby… well, he knew the area, and if the driver didn't, they'd find themselves stuck on one of two dead-end roads or a poorly maintained wagon trail that led to Nutmeg Pass. While the driver had a Jeep, the pass was slow and difficult in the best of conditions. Tonight, it would be slippery and death-defying. The driver would have to turn around if they didn't get stuck or slide into oblivion, and Ryan knew where to wait in case the driver didn't.

Seven

9:17 p.m., September 1 , 2007, Southwest of Packer City, Colorado.

Mary looked in the rearview. She could barely make out the truck's light that'd been tailing her since she left town. She exhaled and lifted her foot from the gas. She ground her teeth and chewed a fingernail. She tasted old blood and spat.

Her gaze fell on headlamp reflections off streams crossing the road. Rain bombarded the lake to her left. Lightning streaked from towering thunderheads, revealing a mountain dotted with pines and aspens that sloped steeply upward to the right. The rain let up suddenly. She forgot everything for a second as she beheld the mountain-cradled lake bathed in moonlight seeping through fissures in the clouds. A bright flash. A loud crack. Her gaze shot back to the mountain as a tree exploded into flames. The downpour resumed and the fire was dampened. Her attention returned to the road where a horned elk stood in the headlights.

She swerved left, right, and slid left. The Jeep hit the loose shale on a steep slope. It flipped forward, whipping her head into the steering wheel. The Jeep missed a tree and landed upright in the water.

Eight

Ryan heard tires screech, metal scrape, and the crunch of loose stone before a splash. He rounded the bend. A rare Wyoming elk dashed in front of the truck, then twisted toward the mountainside. He swerved left and hit the elk's moving back half. The right headlamp went dark as the animal whirled into the ditch.

He hit the brakes, and the truck slid a few feet. Once stopped, he eased the truck to the brink. He flipped on the hazards and left the one working headlight shining bright.

He opened the glove box and found his tactical knife under a holstered Glock. He hopped out, shoved the knife in a back pocket, and started down the steep embankment. He slipped and caught himself on a blade of stone and sliced his left palm. Blood flowed, but he gave it a glancing notice and focused on the vehicle's submerged lights as it eked toward a steep drop. Its engine burbled, and the headlights went out.

He slid off his jacket and tossed it on the rocks by the lake's edge. He removed his belt in one fluid motion, and secured it around his left forearm. He strode through the frigid water, then swam a short distance to the Jeep which was now completely underwater. He grabbed his knife and dove. He shattered the window with the glass breaker. Uncle Mel wasn't in the driver's seat. It was hard to make out who was, but even in the dark with blurry underwater vision, he could make out a petite feminine form whose head rested against the steering wheel.

He reached in, pushed the unconscious lady into the seat, and grabbed the seatbelt with his sliced hand. Using his awkward right, he sliced through the belt. The knife slipped from his hand and fell between the seat and door. He grabbed the lady's arms and pulled her free as the vehicle tilted and rolled into the underwater valley. He locked his arms under her armpits and kicked to the surface. He continued kicking until he touched bottom, and then carried her petite frame to the shore.

He laid the lady on shale at the shoreline. The rain fell hard and washed away blood trickling from a large gash on her forehead. She wasn't breathing.

Ryan swept blonde hair from her face and cleared her throat. He began CPR and felt a pleasant burning sensation in his hands and lips. Then his mouth began tingling uncomfortably like he brushed his teeth with Icy-Hot. He shook it off and continued intermittent breaths and chest compressions. He felt dizzy as the stinging sensation spread over his face, neck, chest, up his arms, and down to his feet. He tried to break the lip lock, but a jolt, like grabbing a live wire, plunged him into full-dark. A pinpoint of light broke the black and grew like a train rolling toward him as if he were tied to a track. The light hit him and his senses cleared. Snippets of someone else's memories followed. They belonged to the woman.

Her eyes were sunken. She was frail as a rail, shivering, coughing, and curled up on a thin, dirty mattress in what looked like a gray-stone prison cell.

The cell morphed into something else. The young woman suddenly appeared healthy and bright as she sat alone on a bench surrounded by trees. She was reading an open textbook as students weighed down with books and backpacks hurried past.

Ryan tried to focus on her face and found himself standing in a church filled for a funeral. The younger version of the woman was crying over an open casket containing a senior gentleman.

The scene changed again and the man in the casket was alive and walking up a steep sidewalk on a rainy night. Seattle's Space Needle towered in the background. The grave-faced man continued to an apartment building with a secured entrance. Used needles were scattered at his feet. A homeless man near the door had a hand out. The gentleman gave him a five dollar bill, then punched in a code. He opened the door, stepped inside, and climbed two flights. He moved down a hall with deliberate speed and stopped at apartment #313. The man looked angry as he knocked.

No one answered.

He unlocked and opened the door.

Sitting on the floor was a young girl, no older than three or four. Her face was filthy, as was her pink dress.

Her head turned. An instant smile lightened the scene as deep blue eyes came alive. She screamed "Peepa," and ran to the man.

He picked her up and turned her head away from the open bedroom door. He peered inside. On the bed was a woman and a man who looked as if they'd been dead for a few days. Both wore tourniquets, and each had a syringe hanging from that arm.

The gentleman's ire melted as he held the girl and wept. He looked up and around as if someone was watching.

Ryan was in the apartment, dripping water and blood on a well-stained emerald carpet.

The elderly gentleman glared at the intruder.

He wanted to look away but couldn't escape the bottomless abyss in the man's pale blue eyes. The man nodded. No words needed to be said. His eyes revealed the scene. Ryan knew what the man required of him and it was a request he wouldn't... he couldn't refuse. Or could he? The gentleman left with his granddaughter and locked Ryan inside the memory with a dead daughter and her decaying boyfriend.

He returned to the lakeshore in the pouring rain, and his heart ached as he desperately worked to save the little girl in the pink dress as the gentleman's eyes prodded him on.

He broke the lock and shook his head. The tingling and burning dissolved but he remained dazed. He regarded the woman's face and felt a compulsion to mend her and protect her at any cost. *What the fuck... I gotta get some sleep,* he thought.

The woman coughed, spat water, and coughed again. Her eyes shot open, and she kicked him in the balls. He grimaced and tried to catch his breath. Before he could, the woman slammed her palms into his chest, sending him airborne into the water. He inhaled lake, then popped up hacking in time to see the woman frantically scurry up the embankment at unnatural speed.

He held his crotch and sucked in enough to croak, "Stop! I'm trying to help you."

The woman ignored him and was out of sight when she passed the edge of the road. He heard frenzied movement up the mountain, and seconds later, foot-patters faded into raindrops.

He shook off stomach-churning pain as he wondered if he'd still be able to give Alex a brother or sister. He suspected a rib fracture or two and his left hand was still leaking. He stepped from the water, grabbed his jacket, wrapped the gash, and struggled bow legged up the loose rock with his good hand, fighting through splintering pain caused by deeper breaths and slight twists.

He assessed the truck damage and almost sighed but gagged on fetid air from what the elk left behind. He tried to not double over as his chest expanded a little too much. He held his breath as he shook his head. The bumper's right side was bent, and the grill was totaled. Feces splattered the left side like mud. Fresh blood, fur, and pieces of skin caked the busted headlamp and radiator bug guard. He heard death rattles from the ditch. He went to the glove box and unholstered his Glock.

Nine

Mary paused and let time catch up.

KREWwww—KREWwww startled her and echoed through the wind and rain. She looked down from a large rock as blood, tears, and raindrops flooded her face. She could barely make out the shadowy silhouette limping back to his truck. She hoped he wasn't hurt too badly, but it didn't matter. He'd be dead soon like Mr. Anderson. What surprised her was that he wasn't already writhing on the ground. At least the mangled elk wasn't suffering anymore. She only wished she had his gun to do for him what he did for the animal.

She watched the truck's one headlight disappear as she shivered and her teeth chattered. She needed rest and something to eat before continuing, but her cash, gear, supplies, and Louis's maps and compass were now at the lake bottom.

As terrible as the day had been, this was far from the worst of many since her abduction. At least now, there was a glimmer of hope that she might get her life back, but first, she had unfinished business. She had to focus. She had to get to Arizona, but she didn't know where to go from here. She wished she could go to the police. Tell them what the lab had done to her and the others. She wanted the General and his doctors to fry for their crimes and for killing the man she loved, but the law wasn't an option, especially now. Even if it was, they couldn't protect her from those pursuing her, and she'd likely get more people killed or end up with more gruesome incidents like the one earlier. No. It was a no-go as long as everything she touched withered and died. Plus, if her savior lived long enough to call the police, they'd be searching for her once they learned the Jeep in the lake belonged to the old man she dumped by a riverbank sixty miles north from where she now stood.

Mary hopped and climbed down the mountain. When she reached the road, the rain stopped. She looked both ways but her only real choice was to head back into the town. That, or freeze to death.

She moved along the lake as quickly as her legs allowed, but she was too tired to run or warp. At the lake's north end, she saw headlights coming around a bend. She jumped behind pine trees as a truck sped by. Its taillights faded in the distance. She continued and soon she stood in front of an ornately carved city limit sign that read, *Packer City, Colorado, Est. 1876, Elevation 8,765 feet, Population 807.*

Mary followed the two-lane road, hoping to find an empty motel room or rental cabin to break into, dry off, and sleep for a few hours. She planned to rise before the sun, head south, and stay out of sight until she reached desert or found a helpful road sign or found a new map and compass to guide her to Canyon de Chelley. Without gear, a new ride would be nice for at least part of the journey, but someone would have to be dumb enough to leave a spare key over a wheel or one inside an unlocked vehicle like on an old TV show. She wished she knew how to hotwire a car, but that was a skill she didn't have. And before she was abducted, she never would've imagined it was a skill that she would need. She also didn't like the idea of stealing. It brought back bad memories that seemed laughably silly after what she'd endured.

She remembered the look in Peepa's eyes when the police showed up at the house after she got caught shoplifting. She was twelve and it was the new NOFX CD for her snowboarding mix. She had the money but loved the thrill and had since she was five, and had never been caught until then. The incident also caused trust issues since she was dumb enough to believe the store manager wouldn't call the police after she gave him her address. It was a little thing and the manager wasn't in the wrong. It just made her question people's intentions like she did Louis (justifiably so since he was one of her abductors). But that was before he sacrificed his life for her freedom. Like killing to survive, she'd have to get over her aversion to theft. What choice did she have? Contact with anyone was beyond risky. No doubt, her second victim was dead, and she wasn't sure how much more her heart could take. Regardless, she needed supplies to traverse the backcountry since the General would be monitoring the roadways. But she needed to rest first… and maybe something to eat so she could focus. *Good luck with that stomach,* she thought. Then it dawned on her that Louis never told her how to find his shaman once she got to Arizona. *One thing at a time, one thing at a time,* she thought. She would worry about that when she got to Navajo Land. And once she found this Manycows and he cured her… well, she wasn't exactly sure what to do next but she had faith that Louis's medicine man would know.

She neared downtown and stayed clear of the sparse lamplight illuminating the sidewalk-free aspen-lined main street. She glanced at darkened rooms and bungalows without vehicles but saw too many lit ones to attempt a break-in.

She came to a bridge with a sign similar to the city limit that read *Howard Creek*. She heard an engine and saw lights turning onto the street. She scurried down the embankment and under the bridge. She stayed until silence returned, then returned to the road and speed-walked just short of a warp. She was too exhausted to go faster.

At the north end of town, she came to a single-row motel with a bright roadside sign that read *Mount Capitol Suites* in a beveled fancy font. The rooms were dark, except for the red neon vacancy sign in the office window to the left and a single muted light in the room above.

Mary moved in the shadows below the sign, and ran up a steep hill on the far side from the office to a small dirt parking lot. It was sandwiched between the rooms and another steep rise to the better-lit *Northside Lodge* whose sign she could see, but not its parking lot. In contrast, this lot was dark and empty except for a green pickup truck parked by a window with a red neon OFFICE sign.

Mary stood outside room #12, the furthest room from the office. She looked left and right, leaned back to bust open the door, then decided to check the knob. It was unlocked. She laughed and quickly silenced herself. She glanced around and heard nothing.

She entered, locked the door, and went to the draped windows overlooking the town. She peeked outside and saw the scattered lights as far as the bridge where she'd hidden. Above and beyond the town, she admired the shadowy shapes of the tall mountains inset in a backdrop of moonlit blue. Residual clouds lingered from the storm.

She went to the dark bathroom by the door and washed the dried blood and grime from her face. The bleeding had stopped and the gash was already healing. She drank a few handfuls of water and removed her wet clothes. She went to the tall log-framed bed, ascended the wooden steps, and pulled back the sheets. She crawled under the toasty covers and sank into heavenly softness.

Ten

Late night, September 1, 2007, Helix Eternal Laboratories Main Complex, Undisclosed Location.

Mist from the underground waterfall wafted toward the ceiling of the main cavern complex. It almost reached to the platform where General Cornelius Adamson stood savoring a good start. Plan A was going as foreseen and he was delighted, as was his passenger. The passenger was old as homicide and had dwelled within him off and on since Lester Ackerman recruited him for a special project. He was an Army Private, just back to the States from the Korean War and Chosin's frozen hell. Adamson had been overlooked by superiors who seemed to have it in for him. They would send him on the most suicidal missions but somehow he'd return unscathed as if providence had *chosen* him for greatness. Of course it had. The secret of his invulnerability came from the same source as Nathan Miller's. The wily Man in White had revealed himself and what he was when he handed him the contract on this very spot on April 20, 1951. Back then he had stars and bars in his eyes and was now on the brink of receiving all that loyalty to a cause had promised as stipulated in that blood contract.

Adamson breathed deeply. *Mmmm.* There was absolutely nothing like Ethereal infused air with its hint of rose to remind one that the pleasant to horrid smell was what one wished it to be, not the musty, natural odor of cavern and bat guano. To him, it was an acrid mix of blood iron, nitro, and other pleasant aromas of death and destruction. It was just part of the dream created by Lester Ackerman before his planned exit from the mortal stage, name change, and move on to greater things.

He surveyed the main cavern complex and the massive turquoise iron-cross far below that was sandwiched in rock on three sides. It was an impressive structure, composed of a large central dome connected to four enormous arched triangular bandshell-like arrays that extended flush with the cavern's east and west walls. The waterfall behind him plunged through the north section down into the legendary River Styx which exited the south section into an abyss in which no living thing had ever reached bottom. Or at least they never returned to tell about it. In the central dome, the river contained a gateway to a place beyond Adamson's comprehension. While he'd never traveled across, his passenger had many times to spread mayhem and mass murder to many places beyond Adamson's narrow confines within Reality 313. Known as the *Terrarium*, the mind boggling power source and gateway was named by co-creator Ackerman, but Adamson hated the name and said as much during its construction. He preferred a more descriptive epithet and called it the *Dream Machine*.

Adamson's passenger chuckled heartily inside his head. *"If not for me, you would have been among the dead in the abyss of Styx?"*

"That is why I felt comfortable to dare insubordination. Ah, the foolishness of youth," Adamson said inside his head.

"Yes, indeed," the voice said with a distant tone as if reaching back through eons.

Adamson peered left to the horseshoe-shaped lab that surrounded the ridiculously oversized meeting area and its hundred empty chairs that would soon be filled with his next batch of lab rats. His gaze panned as if seeing it all for the first time again. He tried to take it all in but failed.

"Impressive, is it not?" said the voice within Adamson.

He didn't bother to nod as his mentor continued, *"Among my greatest creations if I do say so myself. And Lester was a wonderful shell to work with to complete this part of my father's work. Now your benefactor awaits the harvest which he has left for you to reap."*

"I will not let you down, my friend."

"I have every confidence that you will not. And it is not me you need to worry about. As your contract states, my father rewards those who complete his tasks, but his vengeance is legion for those who fail."

"Yes, indeedy," said a soothing, appealing voice from another mind. It was like morning light after soft rain. *"But like War, I have complete confidence in you, Mr. Fire and Brimstone."*

Adamson snapped to attention, turning about face to the unimpressive, pasty white specimen, Dr. Albert Caine. By his side was the olive-skinned, green-eyed she-devil, Dr. Antonia D'Amato. It was a pairing like French fries smothered in ketchup on a plate next to the finest, most delicately prepared filet mignon that was extra rare with an ice cold center. He wanted to chuckle at the bony research scientist who always worked hard to keep his voice from sounding meek and mild. He normally took pleasure in striking terror into the skinny little dweeb, but he dared not at that moment since it wasn't Caine's mind that had spoken. How the Benefactor could stand possessing such a puny shell was beyond him. Like Adamson, both Caine and D'Amato had signed blood contracts allowing their passengers to dwell within their shells whenever they saw fit. But unlike D'Amato who shared consciousness with the blue-eyed Farseer, Delores Destiny, the Benefactor shared consciousness with no one.

Adamson regarded D'Amato, whose normally green eyes were dark blue, and spoke without speaking, *"Ah, sweet Destiny, where is our Typhoid Mary now?"*

"She is temporarily beyond my sight," said the farseeing Eternal, *"but so is everyone else in the small town where I led her. My last vision was of Ryan Mender. His lips were locked with Mary's as he attempted to revive her after she died. I believe he was successful but I also believe there is more to Mary than I have foreseen."*

"Did Mender survive?" asked Adamson with a wisp of panic as his mind raced. His eyes darted once between Caine and D'Amato's mortal shells.

"I can't answer that," said Destiny. *"I am still recovering from the shock of their meeting that left me blind."*

"Don't worry. This game isn't over yet," said the Benefactor. *"Have faith that what happened in January to the Mender boy was a harbinger of favorable outcomes."*

Adamson didn't bother hiding his apprehension.

"Ahh, Mr. Fire and Brimstone. Come, now. You know my son has your back and has since you inked my contract and swore your soul to me. So chin up, you are among the few in the realities to whom my son, War, has taken a liking. And as always, he will guide you. And when Mender and Mary are fully ripe and successfully harvested, I will see to it that you enjoy a long existence, unknown since the first mortals, to rule this reality as you see fit."

Adamson broke the acne-scarred granite of his face and grinned.

Eleven

9:45 p.m., the Watchtower, ten miles southwest of Packer City, Colorado.

Ryan parked in the garage next to Suzanne's green Land Rover. He dashed to the shower across from the laundry room in the short hall that led to the dining room. He hoped to wash away his night so as not to scare Suzanne.

Once presentable, he'd downplay the injury, tell her what happened, and hope to get through to the Mears County Sheriff's Office. Otherwise, the injured woman would be fending for herself until he spoke to Sheriff Pete or Undersheriff Joe in the morning.

He looked in the mirror. *What the hell are you? And why did you take Mel's jeep?* he thought as the lady's memories replayed, drifting through his mind like a frigid breeze, making him feel slippery again—like he was losing it again—losing everything he'd found since he lost it in Iraq. He had to protect this woman. Why? He had no choice. He had promised the gentleman holding the girl in the pink dress. He gripped his forehead with his good hand to keep his brain from exploding.

Twelve

9:50 p.m., in the Watchtower's Octagon.

Suzanne sat reading a fat book in the old rocking chair in the large octagonal-shaped living room at the base of the tower. She loved that old chair full of history for no other reason than it was Ryan's most treasured heirloom. It had belonged to his Native American grandfather, Edwin, who he still worshipped after he'd left them for the land where spirits dwell. It was also the chair she was sitting in when she broke the news that Alex was on the way when they lived in Fort Collins and attended Colorado State University.

She gently enjoyed the smoky, cedary air, as Soundgarden's *Blackhole Sun* hummed in her headphones. Her lamp's fragile light added coziness to her favorite room. She glanced up and watched flames flicker in the large fireplace that warmed the room. She listened to the crackle and intermittent popping and admired shadows dancing on the walls and over the strange paintings that adorned each. They were left by the previous owner's kids when they sold their father's creation to the son and daughter-in-law of R&B legend, Norine Jasmine Jones.

Suzanne loved the paintings and loved art but wasn't very artistic. The same couldn't be said of the Watchtower's creator, Brigham Norsworthy. The paintings were magnificent and reminded her of work by greats like Edvard Munch, Salvador Dali, Picasso, and Hans Ruedi Giger with bizarre twists that could've escaped from the dark imagination of Howard Phillips Lovecraft. Ryan didn't care for the previous owner's art even though he would say, *"they're interesting,"* whenever asked. Suzanne couldn't understand why. They were just images of heroes, castles, monsters, and other fantastical creatures. Some were a little scary, but no more so than what the mind might create when reading a Harry Potter novel or watching one of the five movies, the latest of which was the scariest of them all. Alex loved the movies and it was the movies that inspired him to want to read. And he also loved the paintings, especially the one on the dining room wall of a cocoa-skinned wizard and white female knight on top his

Hogwarts castle fighting four big scary black birds. He said the lady reminded him of her when she had long hair, if her hair was yellow. He thought it was *"kooky but cool,"* then again, almost everything about the Watchtower was *kooky and cool*, and a little too much. But it was everything she ever wanted. It was the castle she had dreamed of whenever her life fell apart, and the Octagon were she sat was her slice of heaven.

Her eyes returned to the book and soon she lost herself in another chapter of a pre-released, signed copy of Nathan Miller's latest release, *Among the Dead*. It had arrived two days earlier, and she had already devoured a quarter of the eight-hundred-and-forty-six-page tome.

After several more pages, she stopped to turn the chair toward one of the tall northeast windows that overlooked the four switchbacks that ascended Tower Rock. She continued reading, chewing her fingernails, as her eyes drank every word of another riveting, spine-tingling passage. She caught herself not breathing more than once.

She closed the book at the end of the long chapter, took a few breaths, and removed the headphones. She set both on the end table, stood, and gazed out the window, across the cedar deck, into the darkness broken by flood lamps and lights from the Fitzgerald's at the base of Tower Rock.

Where are you, Ryan? she thought as she rubbed her lips. The rain had mostly stopped but there was still a light pattering on the copper awning that covered the porchway and wrapped around to the deck at the tower's base. She saw no headlamps coming up the drive or on the road from Packer City. A crash from the hall to the garage startled her.

She smiled and strolled across the ample front room, through the dining room, past the kitchen, down the hall, and stopped at the bathroom. Ryan was on his knees, picking up bandage material strewn across the floor.

"Are you just trying to wake up Alex?" she asked.

He looked up with weary eyes. His white 2PAC *A River That Flows Forever* t-shirt was wet and tie-dyed crimson.

She gasped. "Oh my God. What hap…"

"Shhh. Let's not wake Alex," Ryan said with his deep buttery voice that had a touch of his mother's Texas drawl. He stood and shot her a harmless smirk, tempting her ire. He held a finger to his lips.

"Me, wake him up?" she asked in a whisper. "You're the one making all the noise. What the heck happened?"

He looked down and smiled at her pink bunny slippers, then ran his fingers through her cropped brown hair. "Your hair looks nice."

"Thanks. Had it done in Grayson this afternoon. Hey, don't change the subject."

"Yeah. Hey, look, I'll tell you everything in a minute. But first, you think you can get me some, uh, dry clothes and help me bandage this hand?"

Suzanne grabbed the covered hand as the sound of shuffling socks slid across the dining room floor. She handed Ryan a towel and motioned for him to cover the wound. She peeked out as Alex approached, rubbing his eyes.

"Hey, Little Clown. What're you doing out of bed?"

"Is Dad home?" he asked as he scratched his tight curls. He yawned and stretched his skinny arms high, his Harry Potter pajama top lifting to reveal his outie. He had outgrown his favorite *jammers* but refused to donate them to the Grayson Goodwill.

"Yeah, but he has a cut and needs a bandage."

"Uhh, let me see. I'll kiss it and make it better."

"Tell you what, squirt—once the booboo's bandaged, me and Dad will be up to tuck you in. You can kiss it then. That sound okay?"

"Yeah, sure, but I want to see it," he said with the budding curiosity of one who might fulfill his mother's former pipedream and be called Dr. Mender.

Ryan shook his head with wide eyes.

"Uhh, no, squirt, you don't need to see it. And, uh, anyway, I think my doctor books say something about magic kisses penetrating band-aids. Plus, your dad's soaking wet and needs to hop into some dry clothes, or he might catch a cold or maybe the flu."

"Oh, man. I don't want Dad to get sick. I heard Gamba James say the flu was going around and Nana Norine says *flu is bad business*. I can wait in my room. But, you better come tuck me in once you're warm and dry," Alex said from the hall.

"Yes, sir, Dr. Mender, sir," said Ryan. "I'll be right up after I clean up. Love you, Little Clown. See you in a few."

"Cool." Satisfied, Alex shuffled back the way he came.

Suzanne released a short chuckle, and then her attention returned to Ryan's hand. She removed the towel, flipped the palm up, and recoiled before medical fascination kicked in. The flapped laceration looked like a seven, a question mark, or maybe a jagged *P*. The wound was seeping, but the belt had adequately slowed the flow.

She put Ryan's hand under the faucet and turned on the cold. He sucked air and gritted his teeth.

She lifted the flap to assess the gouge. He winced as she examined severed tendons, muscles, veins, and visible bone. She released the belt, and veins and capillaries started oozing, but no severed arteries painted the bathroom red. She tightened the belt again.

Ryan removed his shirt.

She gasped again at the sight of a large bruise over at least three ribs on his left side. "What happened? Seriously?" she asked as he took off his pants. "Holy F…"

Ryan pushed a shh-finger to her lips to silence the "… uck" at the sight of more bruising radiating from his swollen crotch. He grimaced as he released a suppressed moan and groaned. "Look, I'll tell you everything when I get out of the shower. Hey, when you head up for a change of clothes, could you grab a bottle of Advil? Couldn't find the one down here. And some ice would be nice, too."

She glanced at her face in the mirror. It was as pale as she felt. She shook her head and ran upstairs. When she returned, Ryan was out and dry. He gulped down four Advil. She applied a chest wrap and pressure bandage to the hand. Once dressed, he sat on the toilet seat and iced his nut sack.

"Did you wreck the truck?" she asked.

"No. Uh, kinda. It's complicated. I'll tell you once my balls stop pulsing and I can think straight."

"We need to get you to Grayson. That wound looks nasty and you need some x-rays."

"Not a chance," said Ryan. "I'm spent, and I'm not keeping Alex up so you can drive me in this weather. My hand and ribs can wait 'til morning. And, hey, give this ice and Advil some time and I'll be walking again like I didn't just get off a horse."

"Whatever. You're so… gahhh!" She pursed her lips and shook her head. Her nostrils flared as she exhaled.

Ryan smiled. "You know you're drop dead gorgeous even when you're pissed off. I just love the way your emerald eyes sparkle."

She felt as if steam might blast from her ears like some angry cartoon character. She snickered at the image, calmed herself, and turned off the ire like her Mormon upbringing and her father, Ira, taught her to do. *Put it on the shelf.* "Well, well, you're a stubborn ass," she stammered. "Look, promise me, you'll go in the morning. We'll just have to close the restaurant for the day."

"I promise. I will," he said as he ran his fingers through her hair again. He kissed her forehead.

"Good. Thank you," she said, nodding, as concern lingered. "Now, tell me what happened."

He sighed. "Truth is, I'm not exactly sure," Ryan said and painted the story.

When he finished, she felt even more unsettled. She worried about the woman. And there was something about Ryan's eyes and the inappropriate pauses when he spoke of his efforts to resuscitate the woman and also when he described her improbable feats of strength and speed. Sure, fear and adrenaline can give some individuals the strength to lift cars and kick a nearly indestructible ex- Ranger's ass, but, Suzanne had been with him long enough to know he wasn't telling her everything. What was he hiding? And why? Then again he might just be as exhausted as he appeared.

She put the rest of her questions and doubts on the shelf and switched on her mommy-face. She followed Ryan as he subtly limped upstairs and tried to hide how much he was hurting. Alex was sitting in bed, his back against his headboard with his night light on. Black round-rimmed lens-less glasses rested halfway down his nose. A hardback copy of *Harry Potter and the Philosopher's Stone* was open in his hands. She smiled.

Alex looked up, snapped the novel shut, and placed it on the nightstand. "Dad—your hand, please."

Ryan chuckled, smiled, and did as commanded.

"That is a really big band-aid," Alex said, his eyes nearly filling the frames.

"Yeah, it is, Clown," said Ryan.

Alex kissed the bandage, and Ryan and Suzanne took turns kissing his forehead.

"Good night, squirt," said Suzanne as she tucked him in. "See you in the morning."

"G'night, Mom. G'night, Dad. I love you guys so much. Y'all are the best."

"Well, you're the bester, and we love you more than much," she said pointing at Alex. She tickled him.

He giggled, then laid back, rolled on his side facing them, and closed his eyes beneath the round spectacles.

She smiled, stepped out, and Ryan shut the door.

They returned to the dining room. Ryan called Grayson dispatch. To her surprise, the call went through. She leaned in to listen.

A raspy female voice answered, "Grayson Dispatch. Rhonda speaking. What is the emergency?"

"This is Ryan Mender. I need to report a stolen car, an accident, and an injured woman…"

The call dropped, and attempts to reconnect failed.

Thirteen

10:15 p.m, Saturday, September 1, 2007, north of downtown Packer City.

Mears County Sheriff Pete Maxwell was at a going away party for Deputy Bob Roberts when he got the call from Grayson dispatch. After ten years of faithful service to the remote Colorado county and its only town, Bob was relocating to Federal Way, Washington, a busy suburb between Seattle and Tacoma. He was moving to fill a detective position for the much larger police force and Sheriff Maxwell (or Pete, as most people called him) wanted Bob to have a proper send off. It was Pete's wife, Patsy, and their grown daughter, Mandy Wicker, who suggested having the entire Sheriff's office and families use their home to say goodbye to a dear friend who was moving up in the world.

The house was crowded, and the party was far from winding down, when Rhonda rained on Bob's farewell parade. Patsy and Mandy would have to entertain since Pete was on duty and would have to brave the storm to visit the Watchtower. He didn't mind. He liked Ryan, adored his wife and son, and loved their restaurant, which had added a few inches to his waistline. The small-town Sheriff did hate that cell service was terrible southwest of Lake Hotchkiss. It would've been nice to know a little more before heading to the tower. All he knew was what Rhonda told him. Something about a stolen car and an injured man, but the call dropped before she could get further details concerning the driver's location and current condition.

Pete grabbed his brown leather jacket and pulled it on over his red flannel long sleeve. He put on his brown cowboy hat with the gold star and walked outside wearing blue jeans and brown hiking boots.

He stopped on the porch. Deputy Don Glickman's red Jeep Wrangler was parked behind his gunmetal 4Runner. He shook his head and stepped back inside.

"Hey, Don, could you move your car?" he asked in a restrained tone.

"Sorry about that. Wasn't much room to park when I got here."

"No problem," said Pete.

Once the way was clear, Sheriff Pete headed down the gravel driveway and turned south onto Grayson Highway. He passed through town, over the Howard Creek Bridge, past Carson's Horse Ranch, and turned toward the lakes. Fortunately, the storm had lifted, but his lids were heavy.

For the next thirty minutes, he kept his mind busy thinking about paranoid old Brigham and his militia group. How glad he was—God rest his soul—that the bastard who built the Watchtower wasn't his headache anymore. How much better that a real war hero lived in his home rather than a McVeigh wannabe who believed the country was out to get him. Before Pete knew it, he was looking up at the lights of the Watchtower, and soon parked in Mender's driveway.

Pete was in his graying late fifties with a couple dozen unwanted pounds and felt every year and every ounce as he ambled toward the front door. He stretched his orbits. He'd slept little the previous night and the itch of the sandman had caught up with him about the time Rhonda called. It didn't help that he'd wolfed down extra helpings of Patsy's good cooking and three too many slices of Jocelyn Turner's drop-dead cherry cheesecake.

It was cold that week—unseasonably cold. And after the thunderstorm, a few extra degrees were shed from thermometers.

Pete blew mist into aching ungloved fingers. He rubbed his hands together as he walked up the steps to the porchway.

All he could think about was getting the call over with, so he could head home and hit the sack. He needed sleep. Precious sleep. It was why he had dreaded Bob's party since that morning. He felt guilty feeling that way, so he'd sucked it up as usual and put on a happy face for his friend. The truth was Pete was mad at Bob for leaving in the first place. Bob was his right-hand man. Without him, he would be one-armed, with Mike, Don, and Undersheriff Joe barely able to fill his shoes. Not making Bob Undersheriff was something he couldn't stop kicking himself over. Also, there was an unshakable feeling that Bob had some unspoken reason for leaving. If there was, his friend's lips were sealed. Maybe it was as it appeared—a good friend jumping at an opportunity to work with a senior detective who helped bring down Gary Ridgway, the monstrous Green River Killer. Whatever the reason, Bob was leaving and there was no stopping him.

Pete panted at the front door, stood straight, and sucked in his gut as best he could. He inhaled deeply and exhaled, then softly knocked instead of ringing in case Alex was asleep.

Ryan answered as if he'd been waiting in the foyer. Suzanne was by his side wearing a green CSU sweatshirt, matching sweatpants, and her funky bunny slippers. She was wearing no make-up—not that she needed any. Even at that hour, Pete thought she looked ready for a photoshoot.

"Pete, come in," said Ryan.

He stepped onto the white marble. "Hey, uh, Rhonda reported a dropped call from you. Mentioned something about a stolen car and an injured man. I tell you—don't mean to be a nag, but you really need to get one of them sat-phones like most people have this side of the lake. I mean, especially after what happened with Alex last year."

Ryan glowered and sighed. "I have—I had one. It's trashed at the bottom of the rock. Alex accidentally dropped it off the front deck while chatting with his nana," he said as he motioned unnecessarily to the deck beyond the three walls of tall windows that created the Octagon's northwest, north, and northeast facets. Pete knew the place. He'd been out more than once before Norsworthy went off the deep-end, his wife divorced him, and he formed his personal militia prior to his stroke and death twelve years later.

"Sorry. Those things aren't cheap."

"Tell me about it. Heading up to Denver to pick up a new one next week."

Pete huffed a chuckle. "So, back to why you called Rhonda. Tell me what happened?"

"Well, first off, Rhonda heard me wrong. It wasn't a guy. It was a girl. A young lady. She almost died, but I brought her back. It was bad, but could've been worse. She has a nasty gash on her forehead, though," Ryan said, pointing at his own with a bandaged hand. "But get this—she was driving Melvin's Jeep."

"Are you sure?"

"Bet my life on it. Look, let's sit. I'll tell you everything."

"I hate to interrupt," said Suzanne, "but can I get you a cup of coffee? You look like you need it."

"That bad, huh?" asked Pete.

She laughed, short and sweet. "Yeah, *that bad*. You look beat."

"Thanks, Suzanne. You're a real sweetheart. A cup of Joe would be nice. Cream and sugar, please."

She smiled with a wink, pointed, and said, "You got it."

Pete sat, placed his hat on the table, and glanced at Brigham's crazy paintings in the dining room. "I see you didn't redecorate."

"Of course not. Why would I? I love these paintings. So does Alex. Kind of kooky but you have to admit Norsworthy was an artist."

"Yeah, he was that," he said, trying not to roll his eyes. He kept his other opinions to himself and turned to Ryan. "So, what about this woman you rescued?"

Ryan repeated the story he'd told Suzanne as Pete scribbled furiously in his notebook. When Ryan paused, Pete asked, "I know it was dark, but could you describe the woman?"

"Well, she was petite. Maybe five-six…" He went on to describe her in unusually vivid detail. Pete etched and shaded as Suzanne kept his cup full. When he was done, he held up the sketch.

Ryan's brown eyes testified disbelief. His lips fell open, exposing a small gap between shiny white teeth.

He shrugged. "I did a *little* work as a sketch artist when I was starting out in law enforcement. That was before I moved to Mears County."

"Wow. That's the girl minus the big gash and blood all over her face."

He shrugged and finished a third cup. He stood and glanced at Ryan's bandaged hand. Important questions percolated in his sleep-deprived mind. Like, *how could you be so sure of the woman's description when you only saw her in dim light?* And, *what happened to your hand?* Before he could ask, Ryan changed the subject.

"Hey, by chance, you know if Melvin made it back into town?"

"No idea. I assume so," he said as he put on his hat and started for the door.

Ryan and Suzanne followed.

He turned. "Tell you what. I'll swing by his house in the morning and check on him. I'm sure he just got in late and went to bed. I doubt he's even aware his Jeep's gone. Of course, I'm the one who'll have to break the news that his baby's at the bottom of the big lake. Oh, and concerning that woman you saved, there's no good shelter around the lake since all the old mines were sealed. Good thing—they're death traps. Only option tonight is to freeze to death or hike back to town and find a shed or a good Sam who'll put her up for the night. If someone does, I'm sure I'll get another call. But if I don't hear anything, I'll issue an APB in the morning and have Undersheriff Joe and the rest of my crew search around the lake. While they're at it, I'll call local lodgings to see if anyone's missing. Well, you two have a good night. You've had a rough one, so get some sleep. I know I'll try, and then we'll talk again tomorrow."

Fourteen

Suzanne's mind continued to race as Ryan wrapped an arm around her. They went upstairs and through the game room past the pool table and Alex's room, and an empty one she hoped to fill soon if Ryan's baby makers still worked after that blow. She followed him down the hall to the large bedroom over the garage.

Neither undressed. She slid under the covers of the king-size bed next to Ryan and stared at the cedar planked ceiling. She thought about the lady from the lake. She sensed Pete had noticed the same issues with Ryan's story which seemed more pronounced the second time through, and slightly different, as if he was trying to remember what he'd told her. And that description of the injured, disheveled woman in the dark... it was vivid enough for Pete to surprise them with a sketch that might look nice in an art gallery. It was as if Ryan had seen the woman before the accident. *No. No way. Not going there,* she thought. Jealousy wasn't her thing and Ryan would never... But still there was something he wasn't saying. But why would he lie to her and Pete? Their relationship had always been an honest one. At least she believed it had always been honest. No secrets. They made that pact in high school shortly after they started going out. But he was hiding something now. Again, why? That made her mind cycle and when it did, it wouldn't stop. She thought it might be time to speak to Dr. Boyd about upping her meds, but she hated the sluggish way they made her feel. *And the weight gain. Ugg!* she thought.

"Ryan, I'm worried about your hand. And Uncle Mel's Jeep. And that woman. Something's bugging me." She paused. "Maybe I'm just being a worry-wart, but something doesn't seem right..." She stopped. Ryan was snoring.

Fifteen

Well before dawn, Sunday, September 2, 2007, the Watchtower.

Suzanne didn't sleep much and Ryan's snoring didn't help. Sometime before sunrise, she rolled to face the windows and door to the deck above the driveway. Outside, innumerable stars dotted the night's last gasp. She started counting, but it didn't help.

She rolled over and stared at Ryan. His eyes were glued shut. A soft whistle escaped his lips with every breath. He smacked his gums and smiled at what must've been pleasant dreams. It seemed an eternity since he'd slept so well. Other sleepless nights came to mind, ones when he woke crying, dripping, and shaking from bloody terrors. Now, she struggled to recall the last time Ryan's sandman was held hostage. It must've been at least a year. Definitely, before his healing hands saved Alex's life.

Suzanne smiled, propped herself on an elbow, and stroked Ryan's cheek. She danced her fingers down and twirled them on his chest above the wrap, leaned in, and kissed his lips. He didn't stir. She sighed, sat up, faced the windows again, stretched her arms toward the ceiling, and dropped them like wings.

She stepped softly onto the heated cedar floor and put on wool socks, green Nikes, a matching beanie, and a headlamp. She went out to the cedar deck, gently closed the door, and continued to the stairs and down to the driveway. She stretched, then warmed into a ten-minute-mile pace by the time she reached the base of Tower Rock. She continued through Watch Tower Private Drive's wooded area, past the Fitzgerald's place, and across the Hotchkiss Lake Road to the trail that led around the smaller Crown Lake. She picked up her pace and continued to where the trail split into two. One path continued northwest to the Mount Capitol summit and the other, northeast to Gold Mountain. She followed the former as her legs screamed and the grade increased and endorphins made her mind sing. Her lungs burned in the progressively thinner air as she dodged mud puddles, sometimes not, occasionally slipping, but never falling. She thought about Ryan's story. About the injured woman dashing up Gold Mountain. And those blows to the man who just saved her dang life. *Adrenaline? Really?* What was she? A female Bruce Lee? Okay, maybe she wasn't somebody Suzanne wanted to meet in a dark alley, but Gold Mountain? No freakin' way. The trail Suzanne was on was murder for most, but the face of that mountain was a challenge to climb much less scurry up in a sprint like running on flat land at sea level. Something didn't add up but she pushed the thought back down as her head lamp bobbed its light back and forth.

She saw the outcrop up ahead with the view she loved and pushed harder, ignoring her body's cries for mercy. The final push to the finish was steep and she bounced and pivoted like a deer over and around the rough spots and rocks until she stood overlooking the moonlit lake and the lights of the cedar and red rock rook-shaped Watchtower in the distance set against the shadow of Greenly Mountain and dark blue night. The light of the dining room and kitchen were enough to illuminate the twenty seven, tall, triple-rowed, triple-stacked, weatherized windows that created the tower's three northern facets. From the viewpoint it looked like a fairy tale castle set in a Thomas Kincaide painting.

Suzanne sat on a rock facing east with a mind clear of worries as predawn began to mute the harsher blues with purples, pinks, and layers of yellow upon orange. She thought about her father-in-law. How he got up every morning to sing his dawn prayer. She remembered the first time she watched in fascination as he did his yellow pollen ceremony at the Hacienda in Grand Junction while Alex was sick. She could almost feel the peace it brought his troubled spirit when guilt must've been eating him alive. It was contagious and carried her through when Ryan failed her for the first time before he resurrected Alex from the dead.

Oh, James. She thought about the man he used to be and how he once abused her and his grandson. Not physically. Worse. Bruises and cuts healed, but words from a bitter man left wounds that festered and broke open when least expected. She still wanted to hate him and forgiveness was a virtue she wrestled with every day. The medication had helped, but it would've worked better had Ryan taken his father's advice when he returned from Hell and visited that distant Navajo cousin. The medicine man had helped his granddad, Edwin, tame the ghosts of war and walk away from the demon alcohol. He'd also been instrumental in James's metamorphosis into a magnificent human being who now adored his mixed race grandson whom he had since nicknamed Little Clown. Before then, she couldn't fathom how her legendary mother-in-law—the one and only Norine Jasmine Jones, Mrs. *so-full-of-faith-hope-and-love* with every reason to hate from the moment of birth—saw in the man for whom she wrote her iconic classic, "Hey Baby, I Love You," about true love with rough edges.

Yeah, things were better now, much *better*, just like before Alex got sick last year. *Better* like before 9/11 when Ryan decided to follow in his granddad's footsteps and became an Army Ranger… and before Nathan Miller came into their lives. *Better* like before she married Ryan. It hurt to admit, but it was true, though she loved him with all her heart because there would be no Alex without him. And materially, she had a life most people would kill for, but living it with the Menders had nearly made her lose her ever loving mind. Yup, life was just *peachy* like before her daddy, Ira, died. *Better* than before her egg donor left them when she was thirteen for an elder in their LDS ward and moved out of her life. Was last night more of the same? A harbinger of life's next shitstorm? It was bad enough that Uncle Mel's Jeep was stolen, but what if… She bit her lip. She didn't want to think about how Ryan would take it if anything happened to that gracious man. She rubbed her lips. She'd feel better once Pete spoke with Melvin. Until then, her Neuroxitine would do nothing to stop her worry wheel from spinning.

The last thought sapped her remaining runner's high as the sun cracked the horizon. She sighed and looked back at Crown Lake and the Watchtower. In dawn's light, the parapeted red rock and cedar tower appeared almost crimson. Multifaceted reflections off the front windows made her think of a mechanical insect eye watching the valley, but the sparkling tall conical ironwork skylight in the center of the tower's top deck fractured the illusion. Normally the view made her heart skip, but not that morning. Yup. On Monday, she would definitely be talking to Dr. Boyd about upping her meds.

Sixteen

Early morning, September 2, 2007, Mount Capitol Suites, Packer City, Colorado.

Mary's eyes shot open and her body up to a sitting position as a Hindi accent boomed, "Who are you? And why are you in my motel room?"

She scrambled and wrapped the blankets around her naked body. "I'm, I'm sorry. So sorry. Please, pleeease, don't call the cops," she pleaded. "I just needed a place to sleep. It was so cold, and I, uh, didn't have any money. Just, just let me... let me put my clothes on, and, uh, and, uh, I'll leave," she finished almost in tears.

The man flipped on the light. Before her stood a dark brown complected someone, about her height, but rounder in the middle. She guessed he was in his late thirties or early forties and he looked *really* pissed. She suspected he was the owner and that she wasn't the first traveler to steal a night at his motel.

The man looked at the damp clothes tangled on the floor, then into her eyes. His expression softened. He stood silently for several seconds as if in a trance. It creeped Mary out, and she worried she might have to kill again if this perv tried anything.

Seventeen

Sunday, September 2, 2007, Mount Capitol Suites, Packer City, Colorado.

Raj Batra did not know what was happening to him as he lost himself in the young lady's pools of blue. Little did she know that he was peeking through windows to her soul and a kind heart twisted by torrents of tragedy, joy, heartache, and terror—glimpses of memories of a life that should not have been.

Raj, your head is being tricksy with you, he thought. But the images seemed so real. He had seen the eyes of the older white gentleman who held the little girl in the pink dress. Now he was duty bound to keep this woman safe, who looked no older than his oldest daughter, Anaya. *Oh, how I miss you, Anaya, Kyra, and Krish.*

He smiled softly, sighed, and said, "Sorry, I was thinking about my children." He sighed again. "You may stay as long as you need. Do you need something to eat?"

The young woman started crying. "Yes. Very. Thank you. Thank you for helping me. But I gotta warn you, if certain people find out I'm here, they'll... they'll kill you."

"That is okay. Karma will repay in kind. No one will ever know you were here, and I will not betray you. Do you have a name?"

She paused as her eyes narrowed with distrust. She answered, "Julie Springfield."

He knew that was a lie but played along. "Nice to meet you, Julie. I am Raj Batra, the owner of this motel. Is there anyone I can contact to let them know you are safe?"

"I don't have anyone in this world who knows I'm gone. That's why... that's why they took me."

"Who took you?" asked Raj, his eyes narrowing, his voice one of a protective father ready to kill. He couldn't shake the images but had no names and only blurry faces.

"I'm sorry. I can't tell you more. I'm not putting you in any more danger than I already have. Thank you so much for letting me stay here. But I'll be gone before the sun comes up tomorrow. And I promise I'll pay you as soon as I can."

Raj stepped toward the woman.

"Don't come any closer!" she said as she pulled the sheets tighter around her body. "And don't ever, under any circumstance, touch me. Your life depends on it."

"I was not going to..." He gasped. "I am not like that! What did these people do to you?"

She paused.

"Look, you are safe here. I promise. Again—tell me. What—did—these—people do to you?"

The woman looked down. Her lips trembled before she found words. "After I was taken... things were done to me, experiments, and now... and now everything I touch dies. I don't want to tell you this, but you'll hear about it soon enough."

"What?"

"There was an old man who died north of here. And there's probably one more. I swear... I swear to God, I didn't mean to kill either one of them. It was an accident. They were both accidents." Her voice broke as she continued. "They were only… only trying to help me like you're doing now."

Raj stepped back. "I believe you. And like I said, I will never betray you. Now let me get you something to eat and find you some warm clothes for your journey ahead. And tell me—what is your real name?"

"Can we just stick with Julie for now? The less you know the better."

"Okay, then Julie you are."

Eighteen

9:11 a.m., Sunday, September 2, 2007, The Watchtower.
Ryan awoke to find ruffled sheets and a half-empty bed. He sat up, yawned, stretched, and slid onto the warm floor. He opened the door and stepped onto the cold, cedar walkway over the garage. Suzanne's running shoes by the door were dark brown from her morning run. He leaned on the black steel railing and looked to the horizon and the midmorning sun. The air was brisk. He felt great. Really great. Strangely great. After what happened last night, he was surprised considering how drained he'd felt following contact with the lady from the lake.

The feeling was familiar, but he'd only experienced it once before, eight months earlier when he brought Alex back from the otherside. Grandpa Edwin had told Ryan about his Ute great-granddad who had the power to heal with a simple touch and could raise the dead. But reanimation led to the *deep sleep* which Ryan had experienced after

Alex's resurrection. His oncologist had called it a brief coma. Thankfully, no such *coma* had occurred when he revived the woman. And that bizarre stinging sensation? That was something new. But the manic elation he currently felt this September morning wasn't. On January 10, he chalked it up to the thrill of knowing Alex was still alive. But after last night, he knew it had everything to do with the blood that ran through his veins. And that lady… she was something else. He wasn't sure if that *something else* was entirely human, because while he felt phenomenal, the image of the gentleman holding the girl in the pink dress lurked in the shadows, reminding him of his promise to protect his granddaughter from the hell that was coming for her.

Ryan breathed deep, then exhaled and frowned. He pulled up his shirt and felt his broken ribs. They didn't hurt like they should under the wrap. He stepped inside, went to the bathroom, and removed his shirt and the chest wrap. He lifted his left arm and examined the large area that had been a massive reddish-black blotch on cocoa skin. It looked normal now. He jabbed his thumb into the fracture patch and felt only pressure. *Surely the Advil… Nahhh.* He checked his junk. He had iced his jewels for some time, but there was no evidence of sub-q hemorrhage. He shook his head. *Well, if that ain't the damnedest. Huh.* He stared in the mirror and rubbed stubble with his right hand as he flexed and extended his bandaged left. The injured hand didn't hurt and it wasn't numb.

He headed downstairs to the kitchen and was welcomed with a whiff of bacon, eggs, and waffles. At the bottom by the fireplace, he saw Suzanne looking gorgeous as usual at the stove in her white and cherry blossom silk robe. She was singing Blondie's *Heart of Glass* out of tune with her headphones on as she danced in place and cooked bacon and eggs. A stack of waffles was on a plate to her right. A fresh pot of coffee was brewing. The blend made his stomach growl. And the sight of Suzanne… well, they had an empty room that needed filling.

He wrapped his arms around her waist and kissed her neck.

She removed her headphones.

"You think you can help me with my hand?" asked Ryan. "I need to check that gash."

"Can't it wait until after breakfast?" she asked as her hand stroked his cheek.

"It'll only take a minute. It don't feel right. I think the bandage is on too tight… or somethin'."

She turned off the stove and followed him to the bathroom. She retrieved the bandage kit as he sat on the fluffy pink toilet seat. She knelt, unwrapped the bandage, and flipped the hand over. Her jaw dropped.

He stared, stunned to see that the deep gouge of gore now looked like an old P-shaped scar.

She looked at him.

His eyes said, *don't ask me.*

She shook her head and began to speak.

The doorbell rang. "I'll get it," she said.

She left him sitting dumbfounded, tracing a finger over the scar for no particular reason. He thought, *P for what?* The night before, he skipped the part about the strange sensation and the violent jolt he received when he touched the woman or the omniscient memories that followed. Ryan couldn't explain any of it and didn't want Suzanne and Pete to *know* he'd gone stark raving mad. Or that he'd made a promise to a figment of his imagination. Or that he owed anything to this woman who'd stolen Uncle Mel's jeep. Now this? His head suddenly throbbed. He rubbed his temples.

"Hey, Ryan. It's Pete," she yelled from the foyer. "Says he needs to talk to you again."

"Tell him it'll be a minute."

Ryan ran upstairs and threw on a faded Norine Jasmine Jones t-shirt, navy blue shorts, but remained barefoot. He hopped down the steps two at a time. Pete was in the foyer dressed in his usual brown with hat in hand. The skin around his eyes was a few shades lighter than a raccoon's.

He met Pete in the dining room.

"Would you like some coffee?" asked Suzanne. "Just started a fresh pot."

"That would be amazing," Pete said as he set his hat on the table and himself in a chair.

"Cream and sugar?"

"Always. I'm struggling, so keep it coming, please," he said with a half-smile.

She brought out two cups for the boys and the extras for Pete.

"Thank you so much, Suzanne," he said. He dumped three heaping teaspoons into the black, topped it with cream, and stirred, spilling a sip.

"You staying for breakfast?" she asked.

"I wish I could, but this'll be a short visit. I need to get back to the office and make some calls. I got a busy day coming up."

"So, you get a chance to chat with Mel?" Ryan asked as he sipped.

"No, I haven't. That's why I'm here. Last night when I got back to the office, Melvin's son, Joseph, called from Breckenridge. Said he was worried about his dad. He told me Melvin left yesterday after his son and daughter-in-law headed to Denver with Henry. Joseph didn't start worrying until evening when his dad didn't call to let him know he got home safe. By then the Weather Channel was issuing travel advisories for that freak storm that came through. That's when he called his dad, but Melvin didn't answer. After that, he started calling every police department between here and Breckenridge. When I hung up, a Grayson police officer called me about a badly decomposed body found at Walton's Landing, a few miles west of Grayson. You know the place."

Ryan nodded and took another sip.

"Anyway, a woman passing through found the old gentleman among the driftwood. She'd stopped to take a few shots of the small canyon there—beautiful place. Well, on the shoulder across the highway there was a broken-down Land Rover. Now, I don't usually give this much information to civs this early in an investigation, but since this has to do with your uncle from another family, I'll make an exception. Well, the officers at the scene ran the plates, but the registered driver's age didn't fit the body found on the riverbank. So, I asked the officer what the unlucky man was wearing, and he described pretty much what Joseph said his father had on when he left his place. Well, when I asked about the man's ID, the officer said that he and his partner were waiting for the coroner before touching a thing since they'd never seen anything like it before. While it's possible the man was murdered several weeks earlier and dumped there, it seems an unlikely coincidence. While I can't explain the body's condition, my gut tells me it's Melvin. Before I hung up, I shared my suspicion with the officer, as well as your information about the young lady you claim drove Melvin's car into the lake. That said, if that was his Jeep and the body turns out to be Melvin's, your girl may be responsible for his death. And even if she's not, she'll be a person of interest. Anyway, once the deceased gentleman's identification is confirmed, I'll head back out to let you know. Like I said, I don't typically share information this early. So, do me a favor and keep this between us."

"I... I don't..." Ryan sucked in a trembling breath and pushed out a shaky exhalation. "... I don't know what to say." His chest tightened. He looked to Suzanne for a life preserver to stop him from sinking into the growing darkness as the room dimmed and the walls breathed around him. She looked beyond worried, like she needed one herself. He'd seen that look in her eyes many times before whenever life was about to take a shit on her. More than once it'd been his fault or his family's. Still, she laid a comforting hand on his shoulder.

"I... I've never known life without Uncle Mel," said Ryan. "But this woman..." He shook his head. "She's running from something. Somethin' bad. I saw it in her eyes before she ran up Gold Mountain. She was terrified."

"Or maybe she killed somebody to steal their vehicle after hers, or the first one she stole broke down. The guilt might've been eating her alive," Pete said with a crass lack of sympathy. Prematurely judging was completely out of character for him.

Ryan curled his hands under the table. He felt his blood pressure rise and the back of his skull burn as a murderous urge screamed for him to pop up and crush Pete's throat. *What the fuck?* He shook his head and rubbed his forehead with the scarred hand.

"You okay?" Pete asked with a raised eyebrow.

"Yeah. Jus', just a migraine. I get them sometimes. Look, I don't think she's a killer. Or if she did kill Uncle Mel, it had to have been an accident. I can't explain why I feel this way. Just… just if you find her, don't hurt her."

"Well, we haven't even confirmed that was Melvin's Jeep, have we?"

"Yeah, whatever. I saw the license plate. It was his."

"Okay, then—we go through the formality of verifying what you're telling me. When we do, and if that was Melvin's body found at Walton's Landing, and if we or the Grayson police find the suspect, she has nothing to worry about as long as she doesn't resist." Pete finished his coffee, stood, and donned his hat. "Thanks for the coffee, Suzanne. I was planning on another, but I think I should go." He put his hat on and headed toward the foyer, stopped, and looked back. He glanced at Ryan's unbandaged hand. "How's your hand?"

Ryan narrowed his eyes and regarded Pete quizzically. *What fuckin' business is it of yours?* he thought to say but said, "It's… it's fine. It was just a little cut."

Pete scoffed. "A little cut? That was quite a bandage you had on last night. I never asked what happened."

"I scratched my hand on a rock by the lake. Like I said, it was nothing. Feel kinda silly about the bandage now. But you know Suzanne—she's the best. Always taking good care of me. Don't you worry about it. Hand's fine now." He extended his left hand, palm up. "See. It was nothin'."

Pete glanced at Suzanne. She returned a less than convincing grin. "Weird, don't see a scratch on your hand. Only an old scar. I swear it looks like a P. Where'd you get that?"

Ryan frowned at his overzealous curiosity and said, "Almawt Lilkifaar."

Pete blushed. "I'm... I'm sorry. I'm sorry for being nosy. My curiosity sometimes gets the best of me—all these years with a badge, you know. Glad your hand's okay. Well, gotta go. I apologize if I'm a little cranky. I haven't slept much the past few nights. Well, thanks again for the caffeine. It's hasta la vista for now. And, like I said, I'll let you know as soon as there's an ID on the body. Don't lose hope. There's a chance I'm wrong."

His words failed to reassure.

Ryan and Suzanne followed him to the driveway steps. They waved as he turned his 4Runner around. He returned the formality and headed down the driveway.

"BOOOO!" boomed a ferocious minion making Ryan jump.

Alex giggled like a junior mad scientist. "Gotcha!"

Ryan picked him up, turned him upside down, and started tickling.

Suzanne smiled wide and toothy. "Yeah, you got us, and now we're gonna get you!"

Alex giggled and screamed.

Nineteen

Noon, September 2, 2007, Grayson County Morgue, Grayson, Colorado.

Grayson County Coroner Francis T. Pickens was flummoxed as he examined the rapidly rotting corpse on the table. Since the stiff's delivery from Walton's Landing, it had decayed at an exponential rate and was now little more than bones and cavities filled with a sticky, gelatinous concoction of skin, muscle, and internal organs. Based on the Colorado Driver's License found on the body, what lay before him were the remains of Melvin Anderson, age eighty-three, of Packer City, Colorado. He knew Melvin. Everybody knew Melvin and loved him (or at least he'd never met anyone who didn't). Regardless, his death was most likely due to foul play since his body was moved and his Jeep was stolen. But why leave his wallet with two credit cards, a debit card, and one-hundred-sixty-two dollars? Maybe it was some kind of an accident.

He scratched his head then looked at the gummy gore-covered glove. "No siree, Bob—Melvin, you were murdered," he said to the corpse in front of him. He pushed his glasses further up his Mentholatum-greased nose. "Hmmm. Whether you were or not—what did your killer use to leave you in such a state twenty-four hours after you were reported missing? Hmmm."

He thought about his examination at the scene. It'd only been slightly more enlightening. He had quickly ruled out hit-and-run since Melvin had no injuries consistent with trauma. There were also no punctures or bullet holes to suggest his killer used a weapon, but even that was hard to determine by the time he arrived. He felt downright silly going through the motions of considering anything but what was blatantly obvious to this county's only coroner and coffin salesman.

He removed his gloves, went to his office, and sat at his desk. He shuffled through his drawer for a peppermint then composed an email marked urgent to the director of Centers for Disease Control in Fort Collins. He closed the email with, "*the elderly male almost certainly died from exposure to a fast-acting biological, toxic, or radiological agent.*" He followed with a call to make sure she got it.

Twenty

Noon, September 2, 2007, Helix Eternal Laboratories Annex, Fort Collins, Colorado.

Dr. Antonia D'Amato smiled as she hung up with the CDC director down the street. Mender was indeed still alive, but she already knew that. She'd seen it through Destiny's far-seeing eyes which had cleared since the previous day. Still, there was a shadow—more like a fog—over Packer City that limited her passenger's sight. The Eternal believed this meant that Mary was still in the small town. But why hadn't she kept running? That was what her previous vision had revealed before Mary's contact with Mender. Now escape would be far more precarious for one who despised killing after the county Sheriff alerted the residents of the presence of a killer. *My sweet Mary and your precious little heart. It will be your undoing,* thought Antonia in a subtle German accent.

"*No doubt she found a willing thrall,*" said Delores Destiny in sultry tones inside D'Amato's head.

"*Of course she has,*" she thought.

"*Yes, the connection has begun. Mary can't run. It's not in her ancient blood to leave once the symbiosis has begun, though she hasn't a clue what she is yet. That's why we wait for the coming opportunity in the sands of your reality.*"

"*Yes, we wait. Great Destiny—I am so hungry,*" thought D'Amato. She licked her lips as something south of her stomach growled.

"*Huh? Oh. Dr. Caine will be back with lunch soon,*" said the Eternal.

"*That is not what I hunger for.*"

Destiny's laughter echoed through her mind. *"Oh, I know. I have the same cravings. If only Dr. Caine was a more substantial table with which to satisfy then we wouldn't have to wait to be fed. But there are limitations on the Benefactor's movement that I, my brothers, and sister do not have. There are guidelines in the Afterworld that inhibit his movement within the realities—certain limits that will be done away with when the greater game is won. But don't despair, we'll be done here soon enough and then we can return to Ackerman's world of wonder. The Benefactor will be waiting there for you.*

Twenty-One

Early afternoon, September 2, 2007, Mears County Sheriff's Office, Packer City, Colorado.

Pete's office manager was out with the flu and he was asleep at his desk. Only soon-to-be Federal Way Detective Bob Roberts was in the office. Everyone else was out searching for the missing woman.

Bob's boots were on his desk as he sat engrossed in the final installment of Stephen King's *Dark Tower*. A dog-eared well-read copy of King's first novel, *Carrie*, was under an adjustable lamp where a silver crucifix with a downcast Jesus on a silver chain and rosary beads hung.

Screaming, tortured, mechanical whistling broke his trance as an incoming fax plunged him back into reality. He finished the page while the message printed.

He shut the book and laid *Dark Tower* next to *Carrie*. He stood, stretched, yawned, and rubbed his hungover temples on his way to the fax machine. He picked up two warm pages and started reading.

The first one was Coroner Pickens's preliminary report concerning Melvin Anderson's possible cause of death. The other contained the CDC's instructions for the containment of a potential biological threat. When he finished, Bob woke Pete and handed him the bad news.

"Ahh, Francis. You gotta be shitting me," he said as he rubbed stubble. Pete wiggled up, put on his coat and hat, and trotted out of the office with belly bouncing and keys jingling.

Twenty-Two

Pete struggled to stay awake on his third trip to the Watchtower in less than twenty-four hours. When he got to Watchtower Private Drive, he could see Ryan sitting at a table on the front deck with Suzanne and Alex. Pete lost sight of the Menders in the aspens at the base of Tower Rock. He exited the woods and ascended the switchbacks.

Pete parked and saw Ryan starting down the front steps. Before he made it to the second step, he flung open his door and raised an emphatic stop sign hand. "I'll have to ask you to stay where you are."

Ryan stopped and frowned. "W-Why? What's wrong, Pete?" he asked as Suzanne and Alex came up behind him.

"Suzanne, it might be best if you take Alex inside. I need to speak with Ryan alone. He can fill you in after I leave."

"What's going on, Pete?" she asked, sounding alarmed and a little peeved.

"Suzanne, trust me. I don't think this is something you want Alex to hear—not like this."

"Okay, then. I'll go inside and let you *boys* talk," she said. She grabbed Alex's hand and went inside.

Pete walked to the front of the SUV, keeping a healthy distance from Ryan as he delivered the grim update.

"I'm sorry to tell you this, but the Grayson County Coroner positively identified the body as Melvin Anderson. We still don't know if the abandoned Land Rover is connected, but Grayson police suspect whoever killed Melvin stole that vehicle as well. When it broke down at Walton's Landing, they suspect Melvin stopped to help the woman before she killed him and took his Jeep. Tomorrow morning, we'll be dragging that Jeep from the lake to verify that it's Melvin's to confirm what you told me. As of now, his death is being treated as a homicide, and our prime suspect is that woman you rescued and seemed so worried about this morning. And there's more. Due to the bizarre condition of Melvin's body, the CDC suspects the woman killed him with some kind of weaponized biological agent. The Colorado and Federal Bureaus of Investigation and Homeland Security are even involved and are probably fighting over jurisdiction as we speak. They're worried this might be a forerunner to a major terrorist attack. That said, everyone exposed to Melvin's body, including the coroner, the officers at the scene, and the woman who found him, have been placed under temporary quarantine pending autopsy results and screens for toxins and infectious agents. Unfortunately, even if that woman didn't murder Melvin, she's a carrier or she's been exposed to whatever killed him. She may even already be dead. Look, until the CDC confirms that no biological agents were used, your family can't leave the Watchtower."

"What? Nah. What the… Come on, Pete."

"I'm sorry. You know I hate doing this, but the CDC's being cautious, that's all. And since so few people were exposed and our suspect is still at large, I've decided to keep this on a need-to-know basis. Currently, only Undersheriff Joe and the rest of my office know about the bioterrorism concern since they'll have to take necessary precautions if and when they apprehend the woman or find her body."

Ryan stood, shaking his head, with a disbelieving scowl.

"Come on, Ryan, I need your cooperation. I mean, there's no need to alarm everyone. We'll just warn them that the woman is armed and dangerous so they don't try to capture her themselves after we post wanted flyers."

Ryan added a raised eyebrow to the scowl.

"Okay, maybe that is alarming, but we have to keep people away from her until we know what kind of threat she poses. And hey, thanks to that photographic memory of yours, that suspect sketch is really gonna help. Look… I'm sorry for the inconvenience, but you know it's for everyone's safety."

"This is some major bullshit, Pete. That woman isn't a killer and she surely isn't a terrorist. Like I said, there's something happening here that neither of us understands."

"Maybe you're right. But I… I don't get it," he said, shaking his head, his tired words growing testy as he continued. "How can you be so sure about this woman when she's at least guilty—according to you—of grand theft auto, possibly twice, and destruction of Melvin's property? You act as if you've peeked inside her and discovered she's pure as the driven snow. Kind of makes me think you aren't telling me everything that happened last night."

"I told you what happened," Ryan spat.

"Then I'll take your word because I like you and respect you for more than just your service and who your mother is. And for the woman from the lake's sake, I hope you're right. Again, I'm sorry about all this, and I appreciate your cooperation." Pete's tone softened. "Look, I'm in the same boat and I'm quarantining myself voluntarily to be extra safe since I was exposed to you." His eyes locked with Ryan's. Neither spoke for several seconds.

Ryan sighed. "Okay. It's cool. I guess if you're playing it safe, I will too. Think you can have somebody bring me some good masks to limit Suzanne and Alex's exposure in case I haven't already exposed them to whatever Francis and the CDC is worried about?"

"Can do, and I'll have Joe or one of our deputies come check on you guys daily to make sure everything's okay. And don't worry—moment the quarantine's up, we'll let you know."

"Thanks," Ryan said, shaking his head. "Ya think you can do something else for me?"

"What?"

"Our dish is out, and WORLD Net isn't sending a tech to our boondocks until the fourteenth. Can't even send an email. We *were* relying on the landline at the restaurant after Alex dropped the satphone off the rock. Think you can call Alex's school and let my employees know the restaurant will be closed until we're *well*?"

"Consider it done and done. Just need your employees' numbers."

"Oh, and call my mom. She's liable to worry herself sick if she don't get a call from us. It's Alex's birthday Friday and we were supposed to have a big shindig at the restaurant. I need to let her know it's postponed."

"Consider it done."

Ryan nodded and said, "Alright. Let me get my address book."

Twenty-Three

Suzanne watched through the peephole. She had heard everything and her heart was sinking.

Ryan turned.

She ran for the old rocking chair before the door opened. She grabbed Miller's book, sat, and pretended to read.

Ryan rustled through drawers and papers in the office by the front door. "Hey, babe," he said in a croaky voice, "you know where the employee numbers are? They're not where I put 'em."

"They're in the kitchen in the drawer left of the coffee maker. Meant to put the black book back in the office."

"No biggie," he said with heavy eyes that made her want to cry. He went to the kitchen, and then back outside.

She closed the book and looked out at the viewpoint where she watched the sunrise that morning. She was spiraling and wondered what life would be like when she stopped. She was right about the woman that Ryan rescued. He hadn't told her everything and it was time he came clean.

She looked to the game room and listened to Alex play Harry Potter as imaginary friends stood in for Ron Weasley and Hermoine Granger. She wished he had someone to play with but from what she overheard, he'd be having a lonely birthday with just his mom and dad.

Ryan approached. He wasn't crying, but he looked like he might. He kept his distance as she stood. "Let's go up top and talk," he said.

"Hey, Alex, me and Dad will be right back."

"I'm not Alex—I'm Harry Potter," he said, peering between balcony slats from his lens-less round frames.

"Okay, Harry—have fun being a wizard. We'll be back in a bit."

"I will be waiting, Professor McGonagall."

Suzanne snickered through her nose and found a grin in her grimness. Even when he was dying of leukemia, Alex could always make her smile. But unlike her, Ryan's face was too heavy for his lips to budge. She nodded and Ryan exited the sliding glass door onto the mountainside deck. She followed him up the cut-rock steps that wound around to the tower's top deck. They crossed the deck and skirted the portly cone-shaped skylight, and stopped at the northeast red-rock parapet that was a head shorter than her and taller than Alex. A gentle breeze chilled as her gaze joined Ryan's as he stared toward the big lake, half of which could be seen over a substantial hill.

"How much did you hear?" he asked.

"Most of it."

"I figured." He rubbed his lips.

"Ryan, what aren't you telling me and Pete? You know I can read right through you. You're a horrible omitter and worse liar, so don't try."

"I know, but…"

"But, what?"

"But you'll think I'm crazy."

"You're not the one on meds, but you should be. They do help, but what you're not saying is making me crazy. Making me think things that I don't wanna think."

A corner of his lips rose to create a sad smirk. "Okay, I'll tell ya. You remember how I said I felt right after Alex died in my arms last January?"

"Yeah, you said you felt tingly, right before you passed out."

"Dr. Carter said it was a coma and my granddad told me his mother called it the *deep sleep*."

"Yes, I know."

"Well, when I was resuscitating the lady from the lake, same thing happened but the tingling was more like stinging and hurt like hell. And I didn't go to sleep this time. Instead, I felt a jolt that did a hard reset on my brain. Everything went black for a few seconds, then I saw the light, so to speak." He told her about the gray-block cell, the student, the funeral, the gentlemen in Seattle, the girl in a pink dress, the overdosed dead woman and man, and the unspoken promise.

Suzanne didn't know what to say and didn't want to say the first thing that came to mind, namely that her high school sweetheart had lost his marbles.

"I know it sounds crazy—maybe I am. People that are insane don't realize it. And everything I told you—it was real… or least that's what my head tells me. You see why I didn't say anything to Pete?"

Suzanne didn't nod or shake her head as she tried to take it all in, but she was failing and falling.

"Well, when I came back to my senses, that's when she woke up. I tell you, I think she was dead like Alex. Like I told you last night, she wasn't breathing and I didn't feel a pulse. And I think she did something to me, too. That's how I healed overnight. Must've been. Now, that old man and that girl in the pink dress are stuck in my head… always there… lurking in the shadows."

Suzanne looked over the parapet and saw Sarah Fitzgerald coming up the third switchback with her son, Zeke, and daughter, Blossom. Each was holding a kitchen container. A bug-sized Jeremiah Fitzgerald waved from their front door in the distance.

Ryan sighed and shot Suzanne a glance. He closed his eyes and a tear trickled out.

"Sarah," yelled Suzanne.

She looked skyward and hollered, "Hey, Suzanne. I whipped you guys up some chicken and dumplings and Death-by-Brownies and some other goodies."

"Thanks, but you'll have to leave it at the front door. We all caught that bug that's been going around."

"Sorry to hear that. We're just getting over it ourselves. Hope you guys feel better soon. Need us to go into town or call anybody?"

"No, but thanks. Pete's got us covered."

"Alrighty then. When you guys feel better, why don't you come down to the house for dinner when you're not busy with the restaurant?"

"Will do and you're welcome up here anytime."

Sarah smiled and the three Fitzgeralds continued trudging up the drive.

"I found you, Lord Voldemort."

Suzanne wheeled around to find an aspen wand pointed at Ryan.

"Expelliarmus!" Alex boomed like Harry Potter.

Ryan tried to smile. His lips trembled and he began weeping.

"Dad, why are you crying?" asked Alex.

"Little Clown, Uncle Mel is in Heaven now," he said, his voice cracking twice before finishing the sentence.

Alex lowered his wand and wrapped his arms around his dad's waist. "Don't cry—Heaven is a good place. The old man in the black clothes told me so, you know, after I died. But that was before you pulled me out of the funny yellow room where he lives. Dad, there's nothing to be afraid of. You'll see Uncle Mel again."

Twenty-Four

Sunday Evening, September 2, 2007, Mount Capitol Suites.

Raj Batra was sitting at the check-in desk when Undersheriff Joe Turner walked through the glass door. The television was tuned to an episode of Hogan's Heroes. Actor John Banner as Sargeant Schultz was delivering his signature line, "*I know nothing. I know nothing.*"

Joe chuckled. "Love that show."

"Me, too. And very nice to see you, Joe. How is Jocelyn?" he asked.

"Uhh, she's good," said the tall, manly white man of the mountains. "Got well just in time for Bob's going away party. She had it bad though. Don't think I told you—we're having a baby boy. Her with that flu so early was a big scare."

"I can imagine," said Raj.

"Now Pete's got the bug. Just a matter of time before it catches me. But niceties aside, I really need your help."

"What can I do for you?"

"Um, did any of your guests come up missing this morning?"

"No, unfortunately business has not been good enough to miss any. So I sit here praying to Ganesha that he will clear away obstacles and bring me fortune and success," Raj said, reverently regarding an icon on the wall of the elephant-headed son of Shiva and Parvati.

"Uh, yeah. Okay. Um, well, look, here's a copy of a sketch Pete drew last night from Ryan Mender's description of a missing woman. She was in a car accident. She has a head injury and a large gash on her forehead—that's not in the sketch."

"Wow. Pete is quite an artist," he said as he tried not to give himself away. It was the perfect likeness of the only guest currently staying at his humble motel.

"Well, if you could ask around and keep your eyes open for any stranger in town, that would be appreciated. You're the last lodging I've checked and no one recognizes the woman. My office fears the worst, especially if she didn't find someplace to stay last night."

Raj studied the sketch and headline below. *If you see this woman, please call the Mears County Sheriff's Office at 970-967-5309.* He looked up at Joe.

"Yeah... if you could post that on your board over there in case anyone comes through, I'd greatly appreciate it."

"I would be happy to and I pray that this woman is warm and well somewhere."

"Yeah, me too. I guess I'll call it a long day and short evening," Joe said with a melancholy smirk. "Catch you later, Raj."

"Would you like some tea before you go?"

"No, I'm good, thanks." Joe tipped his hat and stepped out.

Raj waited for Joe's engine to sing, then jumped up and placed the sketch on the bulletin board with *Julie Springfield's* face hidden under an advertisement for a yard sale next Saturday.

Undersheriff Joe had failed to mention the mutilated body found outside Grayson earlier that day. There was no need. Raj had already heard about the suspected homicide of the local veteran on the news. He was sure the victim was the same whose death, whether accidental or intentional, this woman, who calls herself Julie, already claimed responsibility. He knew from her eyes that she was innocent, or at worst, not responsible for her actions.

After nightfall, he went to *Julie's* room to let her know the police were looking for her.

Twenty-Five

Mary sat in darkness, and quietly cursed herself for stealing a night at this kind man's motel, regardless of how exhausted she might've been. Her enhancements would've allowed her to endure much more suffering. Suffering far beyond what she and Peepa had faced before they took the final steps to Everest's summit to enjoy the view from the top of the world before the devilish decent into the storm and one more night in Camp 4's death zone. There was no excuse for staying any longer, but as insane as it sounded her legs refused to let her walk out the door. But she had to go. She approached the door again after she was sure Raj was gone. Her feet felt like cement blocks. She reached for the knob, turned it, and heard voices from the Northside Lodge in the parking lot above. Her lips quivered and her hand shook. She ran to the bathroom, vomited, and sobbed as quietly as she could.

She couldn't risk touching anyone else. Raj knew that she was a killer but he'd proven his loyalty. She would make sure he took all necessary precautions to prevent any more *accidents*. No one else would understand the danger she posed if they foolishly tried to detain her.

Hours earlier, she had watched the news and learned that the old man she'd killed was a World War II veteran. It was only a matter of time before that Sheriff's sketch was everywhere. And for the love of God, the man she killed—of all people. At the time of their fateful meeting, Mr. Anderson was headed home after visiting his first great-grandchild in Breckenridge. He had told her as much and now she had listened to his son's tearful interview. *What the actual fuck*. She never knew her biological father. The only father figure was her grandfather, who raised her after her mother died of a heroin overdose.

She curled up in the ceramic shower and barely slept as she grieved for the Anderson family. She cursed Dr. Caine, Dr. D'Amato, and the mad General for abducting and making her into a monster. Only the desire to see them die horribly kept her from ending her pointless existence.

The next morning, she watched a repeat of the Anderson story and waited for reports of another strange death, followed by more heartbreaking interviews. There were no reports.

"Could he have survived?" she whispered hopefully. "But how?" She pondered this further as she sat close to the TV and caught up with the world outside as a state wide womanhunt got under way and a vehement public demanded her capture.

Over the next week, she went to the door often, but crippling fear made it progressively easier to hide in the safety and comfort of Raj's motel. And still, there was no word about the man who saved her life.

Twenty-Six

September 3-10, 2007, Mears County Colorado.
The fog of Mary persisted, seen by one and revealed to another, but an Eye greater than Destiny's saw all during this uneventful week in this fateful fall in Reality 313.

At the Maxwell House, Pete had settled into his man cave where he slept alone. His wife, Patsy, understood the necessary precautions especially after hearing the gory details of Melvin Anderson's demise. As such, Undersheriff Joseph Yukon Turner was carrying the weight of the office and was there at the lake when a wrecker retrieved Melvin's Jeep. Word of the Anderson murder spread like a gas fire as did wild rumors. Joe only added fuel to fears by refusing to give details while plastering updated wanted posters around town that read: *Suspect considered armed and dangerous. If seen, do not approach. Call 911 or the Sheriff's Office at 970-967-5309. Again, DO NOT under any circumstance approach or attempt to apprehend the suspect.*

The wording could've been better, but how else was he to mention the health hazards the suspect posed without raising suspicion about the hush-hush quarantine. Plus in a town filled with hunters and those whose favorite pastime was popping off rounds at the firing range, he knew several citizens who were unlikely to heed his warning. He especially worried about members of BNM—the late Brigham

Norsworthy's Minutemen who refused to disband after their leader's death.

By that evening, Joe and the rest of the office had distributed posters to every police department and sheriff's office across the state. And over the coming days, the woman's likeness was shown on newscasts all over Colorado. Numerous calls came in, but most led to dead ends. The two that didn't led to the arrests of two parolees on charges unrelated to the Anderson murder.

With the assistance of the larger Silver City and Grayson Police Departments, roadblocks were set up around Packer City as he, along with two fulltime deputies, two part-time deputies, the Alpine Ranger, and additional officers from surrounding counties searched the wilderness southwest of town and the rest of Mears County. No traces of the woman were found.

By the following Monday, Joe assumed the suspect was dead, but needed a body. The greater worry shared by Pete was that the suspect had wandered out of the county or, worse, had left Colorado and was spreading whatever killed Melvin Anderson to surrounding states. Joe couldn't understand why the Centers for Disease Control, the Bureaus of Investigation, and Homeland Security Investigations hadn't considered it. If they had, he couldn't understand why the Feds weren't involved in a nationwide womanhunt. On top of that, there'd been no mention of the case on the national news. Joe Turner knew Francis Pickens, and while he thought he was a bit of an oddball, he was a great coroner and wouldn't have expressed his concerns as he had unless he suspected the unidentified woman from the lake carried something very nasty.

At Mount Capitol Suites, Rajesh Batra began each morning like every other since he purchased the motel five years earlier, with a few *minor* changes for his *wanted* guest. Mary (or Julie as Rajesh still knew her) might as well have been a mouse because she was neither seen nor heard. Still Rajesh felt her presence and the prodding of the gentleman's eyes for the promise he made to protect the girl in the pink dress.

Following his morning cup of Earl Grey, he would don a fully buttoned long sleeve flannel, double glove, then push his laundry cart along the sidewalk to Mary's room as he hummed, whistled, or sang his favorite upbeat Bollywood tune beneath his N95 mask. Even though he couldn't come within six feet of the magical lady with the touch of death, she filled his heart with joy, something he hadn't experienced since before his wife, Riya, left him and received full custody of their children.

After tidying magical Mary's room, he left fresh towels, wash rags, motel sundries, and feminine items. Every two or three days, he would leave two paper sacks on the kitchen counter filled with groceries for her voracious appetite. He would then double-bag her trash, wrap it in a sheet, and place the sheet-ball in the cart. He left a few makeshift biohazard bags for the next delivery/trash day and locked her door. He then tidied the other rooms and locked each, something he hadn't done before Mary stole her first night at his motel. When he was done, he would park the full cart in the laundry room by the office, make another cup of tea, and return to the check-in desk where he would sit beneath icons of Ganesha and Krishna, read or watch TV, and wait for the next guest to arrive, who rarely did.

A few hours before dusk, he would close the office and head out to a small cabin north of town which was outside the Fog of Mary and burn her biohazard in a large metal barrel. Destiny never noticed and her eyes failed to see Rajesh's secret since her focus was elsewhere.

After disposing of evidence, Rajesh would return to the check-in desk as the sun tucked itself behind Mount Capitol. He would watch more TV or read when he wasn't pining over photos of his three children. Around 10 p.m., he would close the office, then ascend to his apartment, burn incense at a shrine, and pray over photos of his children as melancholy Bollywood classics played at low volume. He would end his prayers with one for the woman he knew wasn't named Julie, to guide her to wherever she needed to be, though he never wanted her to leave.

Like Rajesh Batra's cabin, Mary's amorphous fog didn't extend to the Watchtower where the Farseer's eyes remained glued. Destiny and D'Amato were a bit bored but observed with baited anticipation for what would come next... or at least what they *believed* would come next now that magical Mary had cast a shadow of doubt.

Twenty-Seven

4:40 p.m., Monday, September 10, 2007, *the Maxwell House.*

"Thank you, sweet Jesus," Pete said with a big grin as he held the warm fax in his hands, a fax that Joe was undoubtedly holding and thanking the sweet Lord for himself.

"What is it?" asked Patsy.

"It's the final report on the Anderson homicide. CDC says no biological, toxic, or radiologic agents were found to explain Melvin's death. Quarantine's over, baby," he said and kissed his long suffering wife for the first time since he *barricaded* himself in his man cave. "Hey, I'm heading up to the Watchtower to let the Menders know they can re-open Mama Maria's tomorrow. I'm just dying for some tamales. Ah, crap," he said and smacked his forehead.

"What?"

"I forgot to call Norine Mender. No doubt, she's worried sick about her grandson."

"I wouldn't worry about it. Ryan or Suzanne can call her," she said waving him off. "Norine's a sweetheart. She'll understand. And anyway, you shouldn't have to go out there. Send Joe or Deputy Don." She scoffed. "God, I don't understand some people. Why haven't the Menders gotten a sat-phone? I mean, especially after Alex's cancer scare. Almost everyone past the big lake has one. They're a bit spendy, but it's not like they can't afford it."

"Patsy—they had one until Alex broke it before the quarantine."

"Oh. Sorry. What about an email?"

"Their World NET's down."

"Well, shoot. That's poopy."

"Yup, sure is," he said through a sigh. "Well, see you in a bit."

"Okay, love you." She kissed him again and he was off to the Watchtower.

Twenty-Eight

Monday Evening, September 10, 2007, The Watchtower.

Suzanne closed the door and leaned against the wall. Pete had removed a massive load off her shoulders though she'd have to deal with a worried sick mother-in-law (who she adored) in the morning…

or Ryan would. Pete did offer to call Norine that evening, but it was getting late. She could wait until life was back to normal in the morning... or as normal as it could be without Uncle Mel. At least, she cared a little less after increasing her meds—something she didn't mention to Ryan and she sure as heck wasn't mentioning it to Dr. Boyd and risk a lecture. She wasn't too worried (obviously). She'd checked her dusty formulary to make sure she'd only slightly exceeded upper dosing range for Neuroxitine, and she was still well below the Lethal Dose 50.

Still, the meds and her daily runs (limited to running up the tower steps and the mountain in their backyard) were barely cutting through castle fever after a week that had started as pleasant as could be expected given the circumstances.

Sarah Fitzgerald. What a doll, she thought as she headed to the garage where Ryan was working on the truck. Each afternoon, Sarah and the kids would slog up the rock to leave feasts at their door, providing leftovers for days. As much as Suzanne loved to cook, the break was nice. It was something she did almost every day all day and her break would end when she dropped Alex off at school in the morning. Suzanne pondered what to do for Sarah to repay the support she'd shown after learning of their family's loss.

That was the extent of her homebound thrills. Ryan had kept his distance from her and Alex and had slept on the sectional for fear of giving them whatever he might've contracted. He also wore a N95 mask (provided by Undersheriff Joe) and rubber gloves to be safe. It was hard watching him battle grief and being unable to hold him. And like almost always, he soldiered through doing tasks around the property and unpleasant chores like removing the Ford's ruined grill and washing and picking away caked excrement, blood, and remnants of the elk he hit on September 1.

Suzanne popped her head into the garage. He wasn't there, so she headed outside and up to where they'd spent nice evenings watching the sunset above the tower, roasting sausages and making s'mores at the fire pit by the solar panels. Like Sarah's cooking, it was nice, but sadly, the worst part of the week should've been the best.

Alex was devastated when he learned that his birthday party at the restaurant had to wait until the quarantine was lifted. Even so, she was able to entertain him and his imaginary friends with board games and movies. He also played his Xbox when he wasn't playing Hogwarts Castle with Ron and Hermoine or reading in the Octagon next to his mother while she took a break from Miller's newest and darkest for something more cheerful. By Friday, Alex and his invisible buddies were tired of playing Harry Potter. He'd even lost interest in Harry's books. After starting first grade the week before, he just wanted to go to school and play with his real friends. And, he let it be known during several uncharacteristic outbursts.

"Ryan," yelled Suzanne.

She heard the snapping of twigs as he emerged from the densely wooded trail up Greenly Mountain with an arm load of firewood.

"What?"

"Quarantine's over. You're not infectious, but CDC doesn't know what killed Melvin."

Ryan nodded and dropped the split logs by the firepit. "Little Clown will be happy this shit's over, that's for sure," he said in a blank tone.

Suzanne broke the good news to Alex in the gameroom. He hugged and kissed her and Ryan and apologized for being such a brat. That evening, they sat close together at the firepit, laughed, and when Alex wasn't looking, shared a tear or two.

After sunset, they descended to the Octagon. Ryan started a cozy fire as Alex sat in Grandpa Edwin's rocking chair and opened his hardcover of *Harry Potter and the Chambers of Secrets*. Suzanne sank into the recliner on the other side of the end table and continued her disturbing journey into Miller's mind as Ryan stared at the rising flames.

Twenty-Nine

Shortly after dawn, Tuesday, September 11, 2007.
A déjà vu terror woke Suzanne, and for several shakes, she believed it was just a rerun of last year's hellish roller coaster ride.

"I don't feel good. I don't wanna go to school today," Alex moaned as he tugged her arm.

"What's wrong, Little Clown?"

"My tummy hurts, and I feel all achy."

Ryan sat up and rubbed his eyes. "Wh-what's wrong?"

"Alex doesn't feel good. Says he doesn't want to go to school."

"Sorry, little guy. Hope you don't have the flu now."

Ryan's probably right, but flu could be bad, especially for Alex. But it wouldn't kill him... she hoped... and prayed.

Before the quarantine, several kids at Alex's school were out sick, but none were in class the first week. Also, it'd been eleven days since he'd been around anyone except her, Ryan, and Pete. Of course, it's possible he could've picked up something from the Fitzgeralds, but she doubted it because Sarah was an ultra-clean freak. Still, they'd recently been sick and flu incubation time varied with strain. What terrified her most was that his leukemia had returned, but according to the last battery of tests in August, he was still in remission and had a strong immune system after Ryan's healing hands. But was his mystical cure permanent?

She checked Alex's temperature. *98.6 F.* She breathed easier.

Ryan picked him up and followed her to Alex's room. He tucked him in and kissed him. He went downstairs to start breakfast while Suzanne took a shower. When she got out, she checked on Little Clown. He was sleeping. She joined Ryan at the dining room table.

She nibbled quietly and occasionally caught Ryan's eyes as he worked on a mask but failed. She didn't bother. And then she thought of the woman from the lake. The Neuroxitine wasn't working. Her mind did not feel well.

Ryan finished eating and rinsed his dishes. "I'm gonna shower and head to the restaurant. I'll check on you guys at lunch."

Suzanne nodded.

He ran upstairs as she picked at her omelet. She stabbed it a few more times, then got up and scraped the eggs and potatoes into the trash. She went to the old rocking chair and stared out a window.

Her face rose slightly when Ryan returned downstairs.

He smiled sickly.

She returned what might pass as a nod and mumbled something that came out as a high pitch moan. Her eyes drifted back to the mountain view.

She watched Ryan drive away, then opened her book and continued reading *Among the Dead*. She wasn't quite finished, but dozed off before finishing a chapter.

Thirty

9:00 a.m., Tuesday, September 11, 2007, Grand Junction, Colorado.

Norine fumed as the call connected. She'd been waiting and worrying since Friday to hear from Ryan and Suzanne. Friday had been Little Clown's seventh birthday. She and James had wanted to wish Alex a happy one after learning his party at *Mama Maria's* had been postponed on account of the whole bunch of them being home with the flu. She only knew that from the restaurant message. Flu was serious business, especially for Little Clown, but no matter how sick Ryan or Suzanne might be, she expected a call A-S-A-P to let her know how her grandboy was doing. And as Sunday became Monday, anxiety had turned to dread and a sleepless night followed.

She listened to the third ring. She didn't want to listen to the message again for the umpteenth time. She was about to hang up when her boy said, "Mama Maria's Southwestern Bar and Grill, Ryan speaking. How may I help you?"

"Ryan Bear Mender, why haven't you called us? We been sick with worry. Is everything okay with Alex?"

"Dang, sorry I didn't call. Alex is fine. He's just feeling under the weather this morning so he stayed home from school. He's with Suzanne."

"What? He, he's still sick?"

"It's a long story. None of us were sick until Alex started feeling bad this morning. Pete was supposed to call you but he didn't. Mom, you guys heard about Mel?"

"Yes, yes we have, dear. It's… it's terrible. Just heartbreakin'. Melvin was one of the kindest souls I ever knew. Such a generous man. His murder really hit your daddy hard. But you know James, he don't show it except to me. When he learned it was Uncle Mel they found outside Grayson, he called his son, Joseph. Regardless what he's doing, James plans to be in Breckenridge for the funeral this Friday. Sadly, there won't be a body since the CDC wouldn't release his remains. Public health concerns, they say. It's just so sad. I saw a sketch of that woman they think done killed him. She don't look like a killer, but you never know these days. If she's guilty, I hope she gets what…"

"Mom, I gotta tell you something. And you have to promise it stays between us. I mean, you can tell Dad, but the same goes for him."

"Okay. I promise, dear. What is it?"

"Well, when Coroner Pickens finished with Melvin's body, he called the CDC. They contacted the Colorado Bureau, the FBI, and Homeland Security. The Feds suspect Uncle Mel was exposed to some kinda biological agent that the woman was carrying and everyone who came in contact with his body was placed in home quarantine."

"The news didn't mention any of that," she said.

"I'm sure they didn't. But that's not all. By some strange coincidence, I saved that lady from drowning after she drove Uncle Mel's Jeep into Lake Hotchkiss. So, I got sucked into that quarantine business while Pickens and the CDC did their thing with Melvin's body. Sheriff Pete asked us to keep it on the downlow to prevent panic until they found the lady, but they still ain't found her. Yesterday, the CDC released a statement saying they couldn't determine what killed Uncle Mel. They also said they didn't find anything else that posed a threat, so they lifted the quarantine. I'm sure you'll hear about it soon."

"Well, bless the Lord above. I'm just so glad y'all are okay, but I hate to hear that Alex is feeling puny. So, how is Suzanne getting along?"

"Uhh, she's okay. Like I said she's at home with Alex right now. I'm gonna check on 'em after the lunch rush. Staff can carry the afternoon until I get back. And if she needs to get to Doc Boyd before that, she's got the Land Rover. Hey, Mom, I wish I could talk more, but I got a load to do before we reopen. I promise I'll call you tomorrow and let you know how Alex is getting along or later this afternoon if anything changes."

"I'll be waitin'. Give Suzanne our love and Little Clown a big hug from Nana and Gamba. And you wish him a better-late-than-never happy birthday from the both of us."

"Of course. Of course, I will. Love you, Mom. Bye now."

"Love ya, too, sweetie. Alright, you take care now."

Thirty-One

11:13 a.m., September 11, 2007, The Watchtower.

Suzanne awoke and looked at the clock. "Damn." She shook away the fog, ran upstairs, and peeked in Alex's room. He was still snoozing.

She smiled, entered, and sat. She felt his forehead, and her smile melted. "Oh my God. Not again," she said and shook Alex until his eyes sluggishly opened. "Sweetie. Sweetie, I gotta get you to Dr. Boyd."

"No, I don't want to go," said Alex in a whimper. He retched once, twice. Suzanne pulled him into a sitting position as he spewed blood onto the wood floor, barely missing her shoes.

Thirty-Two

11:45 a.m., September 11, 2007, Mama Maria's Southwestern Bar and Grill.
"Excellent as always, Ryan. Almost as good as Suzanne," said Pete.

"A good word is always appreciated."

"And sorry again for not calling your mom."

"Don't worry, I didn't spit in your food. Thought about it though," he said as he handed the Sheriff his take out order of tamales for Patsy and later.

Pete raised an eyebrow.

Ryan slapped his shoulder and cracked a gap tooth smile, "I'm just giving you a hard time. It's all good. See you next time, Pete."

"Yes, you will. Again and again."

"Table three, order up," hollered the new cook that was rocking it.

Ryan grabbed the tray. His cell phone rang on the way to the table. The restaurant was packed as usual and there'd been a line outside a half hour before *Mama Maria's* reopened. He set the tray down, reached into his back pocket, and flipped open his phone. He read the ID. "Sorry. Gotta take this. Sick kid," he said to the middle-aged man and woman visiting from Montrose.

"No problem. Totally understand. Hope Alex is okay," said the woman.

"Thanks," Ryan said with an appreciative smile, and pressed *talk*.

He started to speak but Suzanne cut him off, her words shattering as she spoke. "Alex is *really* sick. I don't know what's wrong with him. He vomited up blood. I'm freaking out. I'm freaking out. Oh God, I'm freaking out. I'm almost at the clinic. Meet me there." She hung up.

Ryan closed the phone, shoved it in his pocket, tore off his apron, and threw it behind the bar. He flew out the back door, hopped in his truck, and sped the few blocks to the medical center. He arrived as Suzanne pulled into the parking lot.

He ran to the Land Rover and opened the back door. Alex was unconscious in the car seat. He unbuckled his straps and ran with him into the waiting room with Suzanne close behind.

"We need help! We need help, now!" he yelled.

P.A. Lei Tran stopped what he was doing and led him to the treatment area.

Thirty-Three

11:50 a.m., September 11, 2007, Packer City Area Medical Center.

"Eugene, I'll be right back," said Dr. Raymond Boyd. "I need to see what's going on."

"Seriously! God dammit, I got stuff I gotta get done today," said Eugene Lee.

Dr. Boyd ignored him and jog-stepped to treatment. His heart sank when he saw Suzanne and Ryan. Alex was unconscious in his father's arms and looked much worse than the year before. "What happened?" he asked.

"I-I don't know," she said as her hands shook as much as her voice. "Alex was fine last night, then woke up feeling sick, but it didn't seem that bad. He didn't have a fever like last year. So, I stayed home and had Ryan go to work. I fell asleep and when I got up and checked on him, he was burning up. Then, then… he started spitting up blood. I came straight here."

Dr. Boyd put on his game face. "It'll be okay, Suzanne. I know you two want to stay with Alex, but would you mind waiting up front while Lei and I stabilize him for transport? I don't want to take any chances and you know how limited we are here."

Suzanne fast-nodded with machine gunning breaths as tears streamed.

Ryan's eyes were fixed, his face stern, halfway to tragic. Tran took Alex from his father and laid him on a treatment table. Ryan stepped backwards, mouth half-open, unable to take his eyes off his boy. Dr. Boyd turned his attention to Alex and he and Tran went to work.

Thirty-Four

Ryan turned and walked away, weeping. He put an arm around Suzanne. She was sobbing, snorting, and struggling to catch her breath.

He sat in the waiting room, his face cupped like Suzanne's. After an eternity of minutes, Dr. Boyd entered the waiting room. His face was ashen and grave, but he maintained some composure as he struggled for words that shook with every syllable. "Suzanne, Ryan… Alex didn't make it. We did everything we could…"

"Noo. Noo," whimpered Suzanne.

"... I am so sorry we couldn't save him," Dr. Boyd said with thready breathes as his eyes glistened.

"No. No-no-no-no-no. NO, NO, NOOOOO! It can't be. It can't be. Not my baby. Not my baby. Not my Alex!" She tried to catch her breath again.

Ryan put an arm around her.

She slapped it away.

"What happened?" growled Ryan.

"I... I don't know. I don't know what killed Alex. But I don't think it was leukemia this time. And what my gut's telling me... well, it's too unlikely to consider. Still, I contacted Fort Collins with my suspicions. The person I spoke with said a few infectious diseases can present this way—and they kill fast," he said as he shook his head with no attempt to hide the fear of something he might've seen before. "They asked me to lock down the clinic while we wait for specialists to get here to examine Alex's body and run some tests. As of right now, no one can leave this building, and that includes me and Lei. And to prevent panic, the folks at the CDC insisted there be no communication with anyone outside until we know what killed Alex—you know, to keep people from skipping town."

Eugene's head popped up. His eyes narrowed, adding canyons to his forehead's wrinkles.

Before Dr. Boyd's return, Ryan had to listen to the piece of shit mutter profanities as he impatiently waited while Alex was dying.

Eugene sneered as his eyes tore into Dr. Boyd. "I will call anyone I Goddamn well please any time I want! This is a free country last time I checked." He took out his phone and started punching numbers.

Tran snatched it from his hand before Eugene pushed *call*.

"You little gook bastard," he said. "If I'er younger, I'd kick your yellow ass like I did your gook cousins back in 'Nam."

Tran inhaled deeply through his nose, exhaled, and kept his cool. "I hate to do this, but thanks to Eugene, I have to collect everyone's cell phones. Marcy, can you hand me a plastic bag?"

Marcy Green, the clinic office manager, met her boyfriend's eyes with slight panic as she handed Tran a clear vinyl pouch from behind the desk. Tran returned a reassuring nod and dropped Eugene's phone inside as the old vet grumbled under his breath. Ryan, Suzanne, Dr. Boyd, and two elderly women gave up their phones without protest. Tran added his and returned the bag to Marcy, who added hers. She placed the pouch in the safe behind the desk while Tran locked the front doors and left to lock the back. When he returned, Eugene fired another expletive salvo that made the two grandmas blush.

Ryan bludgeoned Eugene with tear-swollen eyes. *If you weren't an old man, I would fuckin' end you now*, he thought. He needed his phone to call his parents to let them know Alex was gone. He regretted not doing it when Dr. Boyd sent them to the waiting room. A few hours earlier, he had told her everything was okay—that Alex only had a touch of the flu. All kids got sick, but Alex dying… again?

After Tran took Alex, Ryan was afraid to alarm Norine until he had a better idea of what was wrong. Now, his parents would have to wait until the specialists arrived to learn that Little Clown would never make them laugh again. Then it hit him—what the fuck was he waiting for? If he'd done it once, he could resurrect him again.

"Dr. Boyd, Dr. Boyd, I have to see Alex's body. I have to see him now."

Dr. Boyd's face twisted like he'd been punched in the gut and was trying not to let on. "I... I can't. The CDC instructed me to seal his body to prevent further spread of whatever he died from. Maybe, the specialists will let you see him when they get here."

"Goddamnit, Raymond. Let me see my son NOW!" he roared.

Dr. Boyd recoiled. He stepped back, visibly shaken. With eyes moist, voice quivering, and lips trembling, he said, "Ryan, I'm sorry. I can't. I just can't." He left the room and Tran followed. Marcy and the two grandmas sniffled and sobbed. Eugene folded his arms and glowered at a wall, his face contorted in a permanent scowl.

Ryan's sorrow burned to fury. He opened and closed fists as hot needles tickled his skull. He looked at Suzanne. She was rocking back and forth as waves of grief crashed over her. He leaned to comfort her.

She elbowed him away and spat, "Don't fuckin' touch me! Just don't. Why did you let them take our boy? Why didn't you save him like you did the last time?"

"I, I..." He bit his lip and made it bleed. He looked away. He wanted to die.

Thirty-Five

3:13 p.m., September 11, 2007, Above the open lot southwest of Packer City Area Medical Center.

Dr. Albert Caine gazed from the chopper's window at the medical center where the Benefactor's prize was likely grieving for the loss of a child. He remembered his children and the wife and tried to feel something for the man, but couldn't. Like Mary, the famous Ranger was a lab experiment and he had trained himself long ago not to get attached to lab rats.

Dr. Antonia D'Amato sat across from him in her finest white hazmat, her green eyes were closed and likely blue as her passenger did her thing. Two guards in matching hazmats sat to her left across from two more of General Adamson's likewise dressed Black Berets. All four were armed with standard issue M4 Carbine rifles that could be set to automatic if needed.

The white helicopter, emblazoned with the company's H.E.L. logo, touched down, rustling the colorful fall leaves of surrounding aspens and sent many spinning.

Caine and D'Amato stepped from the chopper and followed the four guards led to the front door where an Asian man held the doors open. The front two guards brushed past him and took up positions on each side of the double doors. The Asian went inside as the other two took up similar positions outside.

Albert followed the Asian and stopped in front of the town doctor. He addressed the M.D. and his assistant in his sterile academic voice. "Dr. Raymond Boyd, I presume, and you must be Lei Tran. My name is Dr. Albert Caine, and this is my associate, Dr. Antonia D'Amato. We're here to examine patient zero."

"Right this way," said Dr. Boyd with a hand directed toward treatment.

"His name is Alex," the child's famous father bitterly corrected.

Caine stopped and regarded the black man with as much pity as he did insects before squashing them. The visual helped with objectivity. He looked to his assistant and caught D'Amato's barely concealed smirk below her bottle-green eyes.

"Show our boy some respect," said the Benefactor's prize. "And, when do I get my phone back? I gotta call my mom and dad to let them know their grandson's dead."

Caine glanced at the grieving mother whose eyes revealed murderous intent. She reminded him of a research chimpanzee who threw a pile of dung in his face. *Just try it,* he thought. He grinned, remembering how much he enjoyed putting that ape bitch down. He pulled his flip phone from his pocket as D'Amato did the same. No bars. He regarded his associate. Her lips held the hint of a grin. His gaze returned to the famous son of the Queen of R&B, then around the room at sad, fearful, and angry expressions. He flicked his hand. "Let them have their phones back."

A young, plump white woman retrieved them and the Asian man returned them to their owners.

Dr. Caine followed the doctor and his P.A. to the makeshift morgue. Inside on a table sat a small black body bag with a tag attached.

"I must ask that you wait outside," said D'Amato with her sharp German-tinged accent. "No need exposing yourself any more than you already have."

"May I ask... is this what I think it is?"

"Yes, it likely is, Dr. Boyd. But our snap tests will determine if the Mender child died from a strain of the Ebola virus."

"But how would he have gotten it?" asked the town doctor as his P.A. looked on gravely. "I mean, I've seen it before while I was in the Peace Corps. I've seen what it can do. I'm lucky to be alive. I was even called for a consult when that strain showed up in Reston, Virginia, back in '89. But all those cases came from non-human primates. But the Mender boy hasn't even been to a zoo since his leukemia went into remission last January."

"Well, that is for the CDC and our lab to determine. And if we are right, I truly hope you survive your second exposure," said D'Amato.

The P.A. swallowed hard.

Caine almost slipped in a chuckle as he asked, "Any more questions before we get to work?"

"No," said Dr. Boyd.

"Okay, then," said Caine and slammed the door in their faces.

He held his breath, unzipped the bag, and regarded the rapidly decaying remains of Alex Mender. He regarded D'Amato whose lips were curled in a rare smile. It made him smile, too, but unlike her, he was afraid to breathe. She seemed to savor the stench while he was doing his best not to eject the breakfast they ate together at that nice restaurant a block from the lab annex. He was sensitive to death's aromas, but had to admit this was the fragrance of freedom. Well, at least one step closer to freedom to return to the research for which his company was founded before it was stolen from him. Unfettered freedom to return to what General Adamson had derailed for the Benefactor's purposes. While the General's purpose was blatantly clear, the Benefactor's was enigmatic and one he refused to expound upon when occupying Caine's consciousness.

Thirty-Six

5:13 p.m. EST, September 11, 2007, The Pentagon, Washington, D.C.

General Cornelius Adamson was in his office when Caine and D'Amato landed outside the Packer City Area Medical Center. Before him were two hovering paper-thin monitors. Known as Reality Windows, they were virtual and created by Ethereal powered ocular implants with touch screen capabilities and direct feeds to each of his Black Berets, all of whom had similar required enhancements, as stipulated in their blood contracts. The implants allowed visual and one- or two-way audio. Standard communication devices were used as backups, but they were archaic in comparison.

Adamson spread all ten fingers in the air to enlarge his Reality Windows to clearly see the POV of ten fireteam leaders in four Black Hawks loaded with ten security contractors each. He watched as each chopper landed outside Packer City to secure the county. One landed at the Mears/Grayson county line to lock down Grayson Highway north of town. Another landed south at Bullion Pass. The remaining two landed east to secure the difficult and less traveled Nutmeg and Alpine Passes. *Can never be too cautious,* he thought. War agreed. These extra roadblocks would remove access to several ghost towns, Bakersville, and Quenche near Telluride. Of the ten contractors exiting each helicopter, two would set up and guard the roadblocks while the others would break into groups of four to secure Packer City.

The exiting contractors were good soldiers—his best. He watched them move in tight formation like one would a beach bimbo's bouncing boobies, but he was not gay. Heaven forbid no. He just appreciated a finely dressed soldier with the power to kill with a word from his lips or from an obedient subordinate. And these good soldiers in their black and white camo and backpacks with their solid black berets, their M4 carbines with scope, and a hip holstered air pistol… Yes—this was why he loved command. It was the power over life and death… but mostly death… and mass destruction. He thought of the orange mushroom over Almawt Lilkifaar. *Better than sex.*

He picked up his phone and made a call. The subordinate answered as if they were waiting for his call, which he damned well better be.

"It is time. Initiate Operation Comm-Black," he said to the subordinate. Adamson hung up before he could reply, "Yes, sir, General, sir."

His phone buzzed. He push the intercom. "Yes."

"General, sir," said Sergeant Major Skip Fossum. "The President wishes you to speak at 1700 concerning the troop surge in Iraq. I have your talking points ready. Shall I bring them into you now?"

"No. I already know what I need to say. I do not need Cranston's namby-pamby speech writers to speak for me."

"Yes, sir, General, sir. Can I get you coffee or anything?"

"That will not be necessary, but you are welcome to leave and get yourself something."

"Thank you, General, sir."

Fossum was a good soldier, but had not yet been approached by the Man in White to sign a contract. Fossum still had not earned his trust unlike his old secretary. But Lance Corporal Maynard Coltrane never signed one either. It would have been best to do before he was nearly killed during the arranged ambush in Almawt Lilkifaar. He was somewhat sore over that and left the military the next year. Adamson regretted not keeping him in the loop that one time but the ruse would not have been convincing to all parties involved. And if not for that damn Navy Seal, Captain Marty Rice, no one but Nathan Miller within his tight circle would have known. He grinned thinking about his confrontation with Miller. He chuckled. Oh, how that sniveling mouse had backed down and remained comfortably mum on the issue while basking in fortune and fame. Yes. Miller was a project that was moving along on schedule, but Adamson knew Mender would not be so easy. Unlike Miller, Mender was a good man, the kind the Benefactor took great pleasure in destroying. And as for Martin's loose tongue, the only repercussions Adamson suffered were blackened eyes, a Picasso nose, and four missing teeth from Mender's fists of fury.

Adamson regarded himself in his desk mirror. Everything had healed good as newborn and the teeth had regrown since that notorious Fourth of July ceremony. "Better than any plastic surgeon." True, his acne-pocked cheeks were anything but pretty, but he was pleased that Caine's formula, for whatever reason, had failed to remove them. They added grit and steel to his menacing countenance. After all, he was Mr. Fire and Brimstone.

His gaze returned to the Reality Windows. He watched as his Black Berets set up the four roadblocks to contain the Benefactor's prize. He still did not understand why Mender and Mary had to be captured together. It was one of the few things that War-Inside-His-Head and the Benefactor had not divulged. But Adamson was a good soldier and knew how to take orders and when not to ask questions. This was a need-to-be-known by the one who controlled his fate. And the only thing he needed to know anyway was that failure was not an option.

Adamson watched the southern roadblock to Bullion Pass as the first driver was caught in the snare attempting to leave town. He listened to the audio in his mind.

"What's going on?" the woman asked as the audio cut out. Adamson tapped his temple. Static followed and returned with clear fidelity as a black Jeep Raptor pulled up behind the woman's car.

"Packer City and the surrounding area are locked down by order of the CDC."

"What? Why?" she asked, her voice raised in alarm.

"That's all I can tell you. You'll have to turn around and head back into town and stay put until I have orders to let you do otherwise."

"This is ridiculous. I don't even live here. I was just passing through for a drive to enjoy the scenery."

He lifted his rifle as his tone changed to one that did not give a fuck. "Look, I told you. Turn your car around, now."

"Okay, okay," she said in a pleading whimper.

The team leader peered down the growing vehicle chain that now included four links. He saw the last link pull into the opposite flow lane and approach the barrier. The good soldier raised his hand to halt the vehicle but the car accelerated and skirted the first barrier. The fool ignored a second hand warning, nearly hit one soldier, and was about to skirt the second barrier. A less than stellar soldier who was zipping up his pants after leaving his post without permission raised his rifle. Without a word of warning, he fired several shots into the unoccupied passenger side before taking out two tires, redeeming himself in Adamson's eyes. *Would have hated to use him as an object lesson,* he thought. War agreed.

When the car stopped, the redeemed soldier yelled, "Get the fuck out of the car—NOW!" The team leader and the other two soldiers closed in with rifles raised as the man tried to comply. Before he could, the team leader opened his door. Another soldier yanked the man from his seat and dragged him back into the quarantine zone by his white collar and gray suit coat. The team leader looked at the woman who had halted her U-turn back to town. Her phone was up, capturing the incident with one of those new camera phones. Others snapped photos. *Not good,* thought Adamson, *but no matter.*

On other RW picture-in-pictures, other fireteams were entering town. Four teams were already searching the first homes and businesses they came across. The other two that were dropped at the northern county line were already at the courthouse for their *meeting* with Sheriff Peter Maxwell, his staff, the Alpine Ranger, and the Divisional Wildlife officer, who just happened to be in town. The proposed purpose of the meeting was for Dr. Antonia D'Amato to discuss security measures for the lockdown. Sadly, D'Amato had business elsewhere and could not attend.

Adamson made prayer hands and grinned as the meager police force was hustled into the only working jail cell in the one or more horse town. His good soldiers said nothing as curses were hurled their way. They locked the door to the jail museum, left, and immediately began searching the neighboring businesses. A few local residents were less than cooperative but the black eye of a Carbine shut the mouths of the most recalcitrant.

Thirty-Seven

3:45 p.m MST, September 11, 2007, Packer City Area Medical Center.
Dr. Boyd entered the waiting room. He rubbed his lips then said, "Can I... can I have everyone's attention? Ryan, Suzanne... I hate to tell you like this... I hate to tell you all this... but this affects us all."

He sighed. "We've, uh… we've all been exposed to the first case of Ebola ever reported in Colorado."

Gasps and expletives interrupted.

"I know. I know. It's hard to believe, and how little Alex contracted the virus is currently a mystery. No matter, the town will be locked down for the next three weeks while the CDC solves it. Due to our direct exposure to Alex, the CDC will be housing each of us for testing and observation in separate units to prevent spread of the virus between us if it hasn't already happened."

The two elderly women moved to separate sides of the waiting room. Dr. Boyd watched as Eugene's eyes shifted back and forth in horror but at least his mouth was shut. But Boyd could see that his worst patient had no intention of remaining around others who might soon be coughing up copious amounts of blood and dying horrific deaths.

Dr. Boyd glanced at the guards in hazmat suits. One had stepped away to use the john. Eugene stood then sat again as the guard reentered the waiting room. As the guard approached the door, his partner stepped away from the entrance and faced him. They exchanged hushed words and failed to notice Eugene as he rose as fast as his arthritic joints allowed and shuffle faster than Dr. Boyd had ever seen him move. He passed the guards and was out the door before either noticed his empty seat. Dr. Boyd watched with surprise as he ambled in a trot toward his red truck parked across the small lot. Eugene made it about twenty feet when he heard a loud CRACK.

Eugene screamed as he crashed to the pavement, crying curses as his faded jeans turned crimson. The two waiting room guards ran and dragged him back inside. A widening crimson streak followed. They dropped him and blood pooled beneath him.

When Dr. Boyd's shock faded, he ran to Eugene and squeezed the wound with both hands. "Lei, get a tourniquet and a gurney!" He turned to the guards. "What's wrong with you people? You didn't have to shoot him."

The two men ignored him and resumed their places. They looked on nervously, like Buckingham Palace guards caught slacking.

Thirty-Eight

Dr. Caine heard the gunshot, an old man cursing, and the town doctor yelling. He looked at Dr. D'Amato. She sipped her tea, grinned, and set the cup on the treatment counter and casually strolled past him with no sense of urgency. He followed. The Asian P.A. squeezed around them. Seconds later he returned with a wheeled gurney. Dr. Caine moved to allow him to pass but Dr. D'Amato made no effort. The P.A. huffed and squeezed around her.

"I don't wanna die! I don't wanna die! I don't wanna die!" the old man hollered through sobs as the Asian man applied a tourniquet and helped the town doctor lift the profusely bleeding man onto the gurney. Caine observed the chaos in the room as the man was wheeled out. The bleeding man continued ranting until he went quiet halfway to treatment.

"ACHTUNG AN ALLE!" shouted D'Amato, startling even the guards. No translation was needed since she had the attention of everyone in the room.

Caine strangled a chuckle.

The famous ex-Ranger flashed him a lethal glare as D'Amato cleared her throat and spoke with her usual heartlessness, no doubt to incite fear and rage, potent catalysts observed in earlier test subjects. "As representatives of the Centers for Disease Control, we apologize for your current inconvenience. As Dr. Boyd informed you, Alex Mender died from a novel strain of Ebola. You have all been exposed and there is nothing you can do about that now. We are here to prevent further exposure to those outside this medical facility. Since it is unknown how the child contracted the virus, we have instituted a lockdown of Packer City and the surrounding area. No one leaves, and no one comes into the area for the next twenty-one days. This is a high-level quarantine. We hope there are no further challenges to our authority since we are authorized to shoot to kill to keep this virus contained. Make no mistake—we will use all means necessary to protect the public. Please, do not test our resolve again. As before, we apologize for this inconvenience." She punctuated her CDC service announcement with an insincere smile then made for the exit, ignoring murmurs and questions. Caine followed.

They strode toward the waiting helicopter. He glanced back as outside guards chained the front door, locking their fellow contractors inside.

Blade-wind buffeted his hazmat suit until he stepped into the chopper. As the chariot rose, D'Amato removed her hood. Her auburn ponytail was tucked into her suit. Her eyes were their usual unnatural radiating bottle-green, a gift from her grandfather to whom Caine owed everything. While he questioned the ethics of experimenting on one's children or grandchildren (he would never do such a thing), he was astounded with those hurricane irises. And oh, how they complemented her perfect olive skin, small, narrow nose, and thin lips. He wanted to taste them again, among other things. He missed what they had before Farseer took control and he signed the contract and left his wife and kids for the pipedream the Benefactor had offered.

He sighed, removed his hood, and slid a hand through his hair. He nervously tapped his leg as he looked out the window at the shrinking medical center, the Grayson River, and the mesas and mountains surrounding the remote town. "Are you sure Mary is still here?" he asked.

"Without a doubt. True, the Farseer has been partially blind since Mender and Mary crossed paths. This Fog of Mary was unexpected and not what was foreseen. But my dear Albert, you must understand, while Mender and Mary's psychic connection shields them, that connection requires proximity. Mary's fog did not hide Mender from the Farseer during our test quarantine. Therefore, Mary's absence from Farseer's eyes can only mean that she is somewhere in town and found a willing thrall like Louis Suerte. One that will hide her and protect her with his or her or their very life if need be. Wherever she is, the Farseer will know if Mary leaves without Mender. Yet, within the Fog of Mary, General Adamson's men have only two days to find her before they lose control and Mr. Fire and Brimstone has no choice but to initiate Plan B. I would like to avoid that if possible. Potential paths for failure multiply, and you know how unhappy the Benefactor will be if we fail to harvest Mary and Mender together. In any event, if Plan A fails, we will have Mender under our thumb while Adamson prepares."

Caine stroked his bald chin. His face was tense. He felt a migraine coming on as he tapped his thigh. He exhaled when he realized he was holding his breath. "Then we'll have to let this charade play out and observe Mender's development and monitor the others for evidence of exposure. The Benefactor's guinea pig is evolving faster than the others. If my calculations are correct, his powers will soon be cataclysmic if not controlled. It's fortunate that Mender is unaware that he killed his son. If he knew this he might end his life prematurely before he is ready for whatever the Benefactor has planned. I don't want to think of what the Benefactor—much less the General—will do to us if we ruin what they hired us to create. We must find Mary—she is the key to everything."

Thirty-Nine

4:00 p.m., September 11, 2007, Packer City Area Medical Center.

Ryan glowered at the hazmat guards as they escorted the two grandmas into separate exam rooms, who were still shaking from what they witnessed. He studied the ruby pool, smears, and polka dot trail that Eugene left behind. His attention turned to Suzanne. She sat motionless, her mouth ajar with her lower lip curled out, but she hadn't started drooling yet. He imagined she would soon if she kept staring at the crimson jelly. He checked his phone for the... well, he lost track of how many times. Still no bars. He wanted to throw it across the room but instead slipped it into his back pocket. He'd thought about sending an email to break the news to his mom and dad (as sickening as it sounded) but that wasn't an option either. Marcy had tried to send one to her brother after those CDC piece-of-shits left, but complained that the internet was down.

But inability to reach his parents was the least of his frustrations. He was beyond pissed at how that cold-ass queen bitch and bean pole motherfucker and their goons handled the situation. *Don't make no sense. What the fuck is wrong with these people?* he thought. If Ebola killed

Alex, the lockdown made sense, but not the heavy-handedness. And while he was guilty of harmful thoughts for that sonuvabitch Eugene, seeing fellow Army go out like that made him feel sorry for him again. *Why, oh why? Son of a saint, I am. No matter. He's a goner after that shot.*

The guards returned. One escorted Marcy from the room, while the other stormed up to Suzanne and barked, "Stand up!" as if she were a prison inmate, not a woman who'd just lost her only child.

She ignored him as Ryan glared at the guard.

The guard matched his stare as he undid his holster clasp, and tapped the pistol stock. It looked like an air pistol. The guard turned and grabbed Suzanne's arm.

"You're making a big mistake, buddy," said Ryan. He lifted the guard's gloved hand off Suzanne. "Now, keep your fuckin' hands off my wife."

The guard went for the pistol, and the world moved in slow motion—not figuratively—literally. And there was no sound. It was quiet as Gold Mountain's summit on a windless summer day.

Before the guard could turn his head or pull the pistol, Ryan stood and delivered an upward hook through his jaw. He followed with a lightning jab through the man's flexible face shield and nose beneath. The guard left his feet and learned to fly, his arms flailing as if swimming in something much thicker than air. He landed several feet away on a chair, spun, and fell on his face. His rifle, pistol, and the wooden chair followed hitting the laminate floor with the force of feathers. Or so it seemed before the odd slomo caught up with real time.

The guard struggled to his knees and moaned as blood streamed and bubbled from his misshapened nose that was painting the shield red.

Ryan turned as the other guard left Marcy in the hallway and ran into the waiting room. He looked at Ryan and the guard on the floor. He flipped the safety and raised his rifle.

Well, Alex, I'll see you soon, Squirt, he thought as he met Suzanne's gaze. Her face was blank as if she didn't grasp what was happening. Like she was watching TV and he was an actor in the box.

"Sthop! Down'th thewt him! We haf... we haf orderths not ta kell hem," said Broken Nose.

Ryan turned to the first guard on his knees, grabbed the front of his suit, and picked him up with one hand. "What orders?" he asked as an air pistol discharged and a bee stung his shoulder.

He dropped the guard.

"MUDTHER FUCKER!" cried Broken Nose as he hit the floor.

Ryan saw the dart and pulled it from his shoulder. He panted and staggered as he studied the blurred projectile in his scarred palm. He dropped it and growled. The air around him shimmered blue and crackled. His eyes drooped. He shook his head, snarled, and charged like a rhino toward the second guard.

The guard pleaded for backup and shot another dart into Ryan's chest. The man managed a weak, high-pitched "help" before Ryan slammed him into the wall, cracking wood and snapping bone.

Forty

Mender fell limply to the floor. Ex-Army Lieutenant Wayne Stiner stood in the wall imprint, groaned, and collapsed onto Mender.

The outside guards unchained the door and rushed in with rifles up and safeties off.

Stiner lifted his head and groaned as ex-Army Sergeant David Eubanks staggered to his feet across the room, gurgling as he sucked air through his mouth with its broken jaw. He coughed, spat up blood, and almost doubled over.

The outside guards helped Stiner up. His ribs crackled with every shallow breath. "Fuck, fuck, fuck," he said as he expanded his chest for something deeper. He looked at Mender. He was snoozing with a faint whistle between breaths. How he wished his hood was off. He really wanted to spit on that sonuvabitch. He gingerly turned to the wall. As bad as it looked, he was surprised he'd only broken ribs. Then again, he might have internal bleeding.

Stiner watched as the uninjured guard held his breath and felt Mender's neck. He could see Mender's chest rise and fall. The guard exhaled and gave a thumbs up as if it were needed. He rolled Mender over and handcuffed him behind his back as the other unbroken guard escorted Stiner and Eubanks to treatment.

Forty-One

8:00 p.m. EST, September 11, 2007, The Pentagon, Washington, D.C.
Secretary Fossum went home after the new conference and Adamson was again alone watching the Packer City show unfold.

Adamson had hoped to catch the first glorious glimpse of Mary's face when the darts hit her. He also hoped for minimal gore that she could produce with her hands, teeth, and anything handy before she went down. Blood contracted soldiers were hard to replace and he worried that forty was far too conservative for this undertaking after seeing what Mary and her fellow lab rats had done to the orderlies and each other in the Terrarium finale.

Instead of Mary's capture, he witnessed a re-run of the Benefactor's prize in its embryonic state. He saw the blue aura as anger welled around Mender. Soon similar displays might make him go blue nova. That was something he wished to avoid. *Keep the pot simmering, but don't let it boil over*, he thought. While Mender was maturing faster than anticipated, he had not achieved that level of volatility.

As Ryan slept off the sedative tranquilizer, he watched five white RVs, one tanker, and three unmarked eighteen-wheelers with flatbed trailers enter Mears County from the north. Each RV had Helix Eternal Laboratories emblazoned on their sides. One RV parked at the county line while three others continued to the other barricades. The rest of the convoy parked by the open lot southwest of the medical center and unloaded flatbeds of what looked to be storage pods. Each was a containment unit but one was subtly more substantial than the rest. It was made of unique alloy forged from something special from the Afterworld.

The units were nothing special when it came to comfort, but nicer than the ones in the Hole under the mountain. Each had a single reinforced entrance, a skylight, a small bed, a table, a sink, a toilet, and a corner shower. Each was equipped with heating, plumbing, and LED lighting. Once set up, the nine-unit facility would be attached to the waste collection tanker. The entrance to each unit would be connected to a wide, seven-foot-tall tunnel with mock decontamination rooms separating their doors from the main corridor. This would feed into the back of the RV that would serve as the lab.

Once the containment facility was ready, armed hazmat-suited guards escorted two old biddies, a plus size brunette, the Physician's Assistant, and the town doctor to their *suites*. As ordered, the Benefactor's doctors would care for the old fool who attempted to escape. Miraculously, the town doctor and his Asian sidekick had saved the fool's life. It was a mild relief since unnecessary civilian casualties complicated things, though, if Plan A failed, it would no longer be a concern.

His attention returned to the waiting room. The good soldier who shot the old fool grabbed Suzanne Mender's wrist. She did not resist. She appeared catatonic, looking nearly zombified. She said nothing as the good soldier escorted her across the street. They entered the tube and continued to the last unit which was about twenty feet from the attached RV. A female and male doctor wearing masks and gloves stood with clipboards jotting down observations. The other two research assistants were in the RV.

The good soldier opened the heavy door of Unit 1.

Suddenly Suzanne Mender broke from her catatonic state and turned hysterical. "Where's Ryan? Where's Ryan? Is he okay? Is he okay?"

The good soldier said nothing, nudged her inside, and slammed the door. Adamson grinned as he watched her scream. She fell to her knees, wailed, and beat her fists against the door. Her knuckles were soon bloody but still she continued. *She sure does have spunk, I'll give her that*, he thought. War agreed and they enjoyed the show without popcorn until she stopped, slumped her head against the door, slid down, curled up, and sobbed.

Adamson's attention turned to the tube's entrance as Stiner and Eubanks entered with Mender. Stiner's nose was taped but the marooning had already extended around his eyes, cheeks, and upper lip. His face was distorted, grotesque—a dark-purplish mess under a clean face shield. Eubanks had fared slightly better and was now breathing easier, thanks to the chest wrap under his suit. Like Stiner, he limped like a decrepit old man and frequently winced as the two wheeled Mender toward Unit 9 which had been treated with Black Ethereal. It was furthest from the lab and placed for easy access in case Mary attempted to warn the man who saved her life about the special *touch* she gave him.

The Benefactor's prize was face down, handcuffed behind the back, and securely strapped to the gurney. He was unconscious, but for how long? Adamson did not know. If Mary's transfer was complete, Mender's awakened DNA would already be incorporating Caine's tranquilizer to add to the nasty things she'd already given him.

Eubanks grimaced as he attempted to pull open the heavy door that would hopefully contain the monster Mender was becoming. Stiner assisted. Once open, they pushed the gurney inside. Both soldiers were on Adamson's shitlist and he swore that neither would survive his dressing down when the mission was complete. But he was pleased with the beating Mender had dealt them after they failed to take the danger he posed seriously. Granted, they were new and had not been under the mountain to witness the final cull. Nevertheless, they would have to redeem themselves somehow if they hoped to enjoy their rewards this side of Afterworld.

Stiner removed the straps and handcuffs. He looked at the bed, then at Eubanks. He chuckled. Eubanks tried, but gritted his teeth instead as Stiner rolled Mender off the gurney. Adamson glared at the Reality Window as the Benefactor's prize hit the floor face down with a *THUMP*. Stiner and Eubanks looked at each other again, then at Mender. Their lips drew into wide grins. Adamson shook his head.

Don't do it. Don't do it, he thought. The bad soldiers nodded and started kicking and stomping Mender, ignoring shared aches and pains as their desire for revenge clouded their life-preserving judgment lest the beating kill the Benefactor's prize. The abuse continued until those aches and pains made them stop. The bad soldiers left the unit, panting, sweating, and groaning.

Forty-Two

Ryan was running through a Texas hailstorm. Each icy rock was the size of a softball and hurt as they pelted every inch of his body. He continued running on a high mountain trail. The pummeling hail followed and he saw no shelter. He attempted to dodge the onslaught without success. He saw a cliff, and ran for it at a dead sprint, anything to stop the beating. He jumped and fell and fell. He felt like he'd never stop falling, then, SPLASH.

He tread water. The hail stopped but rain fell in sheets. He started swimming and saw Uncle Mel's orange Jeep under the water even though it was full dark night. It was glowing, fluorescing. The lady was in the driver's seat, her head against the steering wheel as crimson eddies swirled from her head.

He dove and swam for the jeep, ignoring the hand he remembered was sliced open. He broke the window like it was a thin sheet of ice and pulled the woman free as the Jeep crept into the deeper blue. He held her tight and kicked and kicked for the surface which seemed impossibly far away. Air became precious as their blood swirled, embracing them in a shimmering crimson aura. Ryan gasped. Water filled his lungs and he coughed as he broke the surface. He coughed again then kicked harder and harder as every muscle burned and every bone and joint ached. He continued without progress, as if caught in a riptide.

He rested and tread water and saw that the woman's chest wasn't moving. He could sense she was dead. He started kicking again and bumped into a log. He turned. A milky-eyed face greeted him. Ryan's eyes darted around and went wide with horror. The lake was filled with bloated, putrid corpses. The shoreline was a fiery hellscape. Suddenly, he could see the world around him. What were once cities now lay in smoldering ruins. Mountains of bodies whispered, "You did this." He gasped, refilled his lungs, and coughed.

Before he caught his breath, black tendrils erupted from the surface, sending spray high into the air. The razor-tipped tendrils paused, undulating for pregnant seconds, then arched down and sped toward Ryan like wiggling snakes. They found their prey and slid in and out of his skin and flesh and then in and out of the woman's, lacing them together. Thousands of micro-tendrils sprouted from the larger ones, anchoring them in place.

The woman's eyes opened. She screamed as micro-tendrils slithered under her skin while the fiery glow rippled and danced over bobbing floaters. He felt worm-like projections needle their way through his and her spine and brain, fusing every pathway. The woman's agony and terror became his, amplified many fold. Tendrils slid into his and her mouths, silencing shared shrieks. Others tightened and bluntly cut to bone as the new creation was dragged beneath the dark water.

Ryan woke face down, firing breaths in and out. He was sticky with sweat. He rolled over and slowed his breathing as he tried to focus in the muted light pouring in from above. *Am I still dreaming?* he thought.

He realized he wasn't and tried to think where he might be. He suspected he was in the containment unit the green-eyed bitch said would be his home for the next three weeks. He pushed himself to his knees and winced. He felt sore all over, but that was expected a day or two after a big workout, like the mind-clearing one he had two nights ago before Pete came out to the Watchtower with his *good* news. Before...

He sighed and moved to the small bed as bitter reality sank in. It couldn't have been more dreadful. Alex was gone, and Suzanne was alone somewhere else. And her last words, *"Why didn't you save him like you did the last time?"* Fuck. They cut deep.

Suzanne was hurting. Later, she'd apologize but she'd have to live with those words until the quarantine was up. Like everything else, he couldn't understand why the CDC had been so cruel, separating them like this, among too many other things. Yeah, their asses would be facing a major lawsuit. *Again—what the fuck is wrong with these people?* he thought. Nothing made sense. Uncle Melvin had died of some strange shit after contact with that lady from the lake. Ryan had come in contact with her but he was still alive and the CDC said there was nothing to worry about. And even before that, he took every precaution to keep Suzanne and Alex safe until the CDC said he was clear. Then out of the blue Alex dies of Ebola? It smelled like bullshit. Even if it wasn't, what was the point of separating them now? If either he or Suzanne died, the other would have little to live for... Well, at least, it was still true for him. But Suzanne was right, and that's what hurt the most. If he was such a great healer like his G3 grandad, why didn't his love protect Alex like it did last January?

Ryan sat on the bed or paced until night through the skylight began to have color. He laid down and tried to sleep. He drifted between tortured thoughts and ones about the specialists, their guards, and the cosmic joker who cursed his life. He wanted them all dead. When he finally dozed, the sandman delivered repetitive nightmares about the lady from the lake and the death and destruction their meeting would bring. He couldn't stop dreaming about her, worrying about her. Every time he opened his eyes, he never knew if he was still dreaming because the old gentleman and the girl in the pink dress were always standing on the other side of the unit, staring with their haunting blue eyes, reminding him of the promise he never really made. He'd blink and they'd be gone but the obsession kept him from spending time with Alex, even if it was subconscious fantasy.

Strangely, he sensed Alex nearby and thoughts like that and those about the woman made him think he was going insane. Really insane this time. Straight-jacket Lithium nutty buddy crazy. *If you think you're going crazy, you might not be insane,* he thought or said. He wasn't sure. He began laughing. He couldn't stop. His side hurt like he'd been punched and kicked but he still couldn't stop. He panted hard and rubbed his side and felt a tender spot.

Who was he kidding? His sanity had been slipping since Almawt Lilkifaar. Alex was the linchpin keeping his worn wheels from flying off. And those wheels were spinning, spinning, spinning away. He rocked back and forth. "Keep it together. Keep it together. Keep it together for Suzanne. Gotta keep it... gotta keep it together for Suzanne," he said loud enough to hear over the mocking laughter in his head.

"But how?" he whispered, almost in a whimper. The loss of Alex, Uncle Mel, and his brothers in Iraq. Suzanne grieving alone. Nagging thoughts of the lady from the lake. It was too much. And those guard's words, *"We have orders."*

"What the fuck?" Ryan rubbed his forehead and tried to think straight. *Why threaten to kill, shoot an old man, and have orders not to kill me? Makes no fuckin' sense unless something bigger's going on. But what?* Whatever it was, he knew the woman he pulled from the lake was responsible for everything happening to him and his family.

Forty-Three

8:00 a.m., Wednesday, September 12, 2007, Mount Capitol Suites.
　Raj wasn't smiling when he entered Mary's room earlier than usual. She was still Julie Springfield to him. The less he knew the better.

　"Packer City was locked down yesterday," he whispered.

　"Why?" asked Mary.

　"I do not know and no one I asked knows why. But there is more. This morning when I went out for my morning Frespresso, I saw a large temporary facility across from the medical center that looked like something out of a movie. The movie was about a quarantine where many people died. The facility must have been put up overnight because it was not there yesterday. Outside were four guards in white hazmat suits holding military rifles. I did not make eye contact and kept walking until I arrived at Charlotte's Espresso, but it was closed. I must say—this is quite unusual for Charlotte Lee. She knows how important her Frespressos are to everyone in town. I will bring you one when she is open again. They are most enlightening. But as I said—when I got there, another disappointed customer was waiting. She told me the entire police force was being held in the courthouse and that those in charge had declared martial law and threatened to shoot anyone who goes out after dark. She said four of these thugs forced their way into her home after midnight, searched it, and broke a lot of things. They also spent the night and left her place a mess. But she was not the only one. She said they were searching every home and building. No one knows what they are looking for, and they threaten anyone who asks questions or tries to stop them."

Mary shook her head and asked, "Did she say what they were wearing?"

"Yes. Yes, she did. She said the men wore black and white army uniforms—camouflage—like you would wear in the snow. Oh, and they also wore black army caps."

Mary held a hand to her mouth. "Shit—they're from the lab, and I'm what they're looking for. If they find me, they'll kill you... and then ask questions," she said, pointing a finger gun at her head. She released the thumb hammer.

Raj smiled and comically pushed out his chest and straightened his back to look taller. "Well then, I will have to make sure they do not find you. It may be some time before I can check on you again. I brought you extra food. Keep it hidden and do not turn on the lights or the television, even during the day. If anyone comes to your door, including me, hide under the bed. In fact, it would be best if you stayed under there as much as possible."

He met Mary's gaze. She nodded. He closed and locked the door.

Mary quickly gobbled some Nutter Butters and wedged the rest, along with the other snacks, under the mattress. She used the restroom, drank water, then hid under the bed.

To pass the time, she tried meditating like Peepa had taught her. Thurston DeMure had been a Zen Buddhist and frequented the Three Pillars Temple in downtown Seattle before he died from a stroke. She often went to the temple with him and had spent hours in full lotus following breaths and seeking the peace of pure nothingness. But zazen was hard to do without sitting properly to breathe from the tanden (a point below the navel). So she tried koans, her favorite being, "*What did your face look like before your parents were born?*" She pondered and pondered but still couldn't clear her mind. And so, she escaped (as she often did) into daydreams about lives she wished were hers. Sometimes, she forgot she was dreaming and would tumble, disoriented, back into her perpetual suffering. Eventually, deep sleep found her, and the nightmare ended.

Forty-Four

10:00 a.m., September 12, 2007, Grand Junction, Colorado.

Norine Jasmine Jones-Mender slept like a stone but awoke with a premonition that something bad had happened. It was irrational but understandable. Alex was under the weather and she wouldn't be able to relax until she was sure Little Clown was right as rain. And that story Ryan told her about him rescuing that lady after Melvin died mysteriously and, to top that off, that quarantine that was kept all hush-hush... well, that didn't help. She felt silly. *Worries jus' getting' the best of you, Norine. That boy will be calling any minute,* she thought.

An hour later, she wasn't so sure as those worries went in and out of control. She had to know how her grandboy was doing and she had to know now.

She called the restaurant but got the message, *"All circuits are busy now. Please try your call again later."* She tried several more times but got the same recording. Frustrated, she called the Mears County Sheriff's Office, Alex's school, and several friends in town but still got the same message. Finally, she called Donner Telecomm which served Mears County to find out when service would be restored. As it turned out, she was the first to report the outage. The woman she spoke with promised to check into it and asked her to call back if service wasn't restored in a few hours. By early afternoon, she was still getting the same message. Paranoia turned to panic, so she decided not to waste any more time with the phone company and called James instead.

"James, sweetie, I've been tryin' to call Ryan all morning, but service is down in Mears County. I called the phone company, but they didn't know anything about it. If you ain't too busy, you think you could make some calls and look into it?"

Forty-Five

Mid-afternoon, September 12, 2007, Mender and Associates, Attorneys at Law, Downtown Grand Junction.

"Sure, I'm not busy at all," James said as he pushed aside a stack of files. "I'll get right on it, dear. I'll call you when I know something."

He looked at a framed photo by the phone. It was of Ryan and Suzanne holding Alex. *That smile,* he thought. He shook his head at Little Clown and remembered the first time that boy melted his heart, looking like Bozo the Clown in his best loafers as he held a red ball to his little nose. James chuckled at the memory. His smile fell.

He was worried about Little Clown, but couldn't shake the guilt over the man he'd been for the first few years of his life. Or how he'd let his prejudice sour his earlier relationship with his daughter-in-law who'd loved Ryan through his darkest days, like his mother Maria had his father, Edwin, when he went through a similar hell after World War II. But that James was the past—nothing he could do to change who he once was. He could only control how he behaved in present as he continued to work on being a better man in the future.

He owed so much to his grandson who helped him see the light and his Diné cousin who guided him there.

He looked at the stack of files. He had so much to do before trial. He nodded, sighed, and started making calls.

James called Jasmine a half hour later. "Turns out the cell tower over Lake Hotchkiss is down. The man I spoke with said there was a power surge yesterday. For whatever reason, no one reported the problem until you called. A crew's already gone out to check on it but they were turned back at a roadblock at the northern county line. The guards said they'd have to access the tower from Bullion Pass. But the second crew was stopped at another roadblock a few miles southeast of the access road and guards gave no ET as to when they'd be allowed up. Seems the whole area is locked down, and the guards at the roadblocks won't give any details as to why. Something's not right. Look, I know you're worried about Alex, and so am I after what you told me last night. I'm due in court next week and have to head to Breckenridge for Melvin's funeral Friday. My interns will just have to handle things for the rest of the week. We need to head south to find out what's going on."

"Oh, thank you, sweetie. I'll be ready to leave when you get here."

Forty-Six

Two hours later, James turned south toward Packer City at Grayson Highway. Norine had spoken little since leaving Grand Junction, and her eyes remained fixed on familiar fields, mesas, canyons, and rivers.

As he left the Grayson Reservoir Bridge behind, he glanced over and smiled. Jasmine was chewing a manicured fingernail, a habit she had broken years ago for her stage image. He was also worried but had to keep it to himself. He had to be strong, and it was taking every ounce of will to keep from breaking down after two of the worst weeks of his life. When things settled down, he planned to head south to see his cousin. The respected Hataalii would know the right ceremony and after that, everything would be okay again.

"I'm sure Alex is okay," he said. "And I wouldn't worry too much about that quarantine last week. I can't see the CDC lifting it unless they were sure it was safe to do so."

Norine ignored him and continued staring out the window.

They arrived at the roadblock at Bridger Ravine an hour before dusk. A white RV was parked on the ravine side. Two guards stood behind the barricade dressed in black and white fatigues and black berets. They were armed with automatic rifles and embroiled in a tense conversation. One of the guards (a late-twenty-something African-American male) broke from the chat and jogged to James's rolled down window.

"So, what's going on in Packer City?" James asked while mentally recording the guard's face and name tag. *Joshua Stone, H.E.L. Security Contractors.*

Stone replied in a thick, German accent. "I am very sorry, but I am not at liberty to say. You will have to turn around and go back the vay you came."

Norine leaned over, looked up with her man-melting eyes, and said, "Joshua, why haven't we heard anything about this on the news?"

"Again, as I said, I am not authorized to give details."

"Then, can you at least get a message to our son, Ryan Mender? He's the owner of Mama Maria's Southwestern Bar and Grill. Tell him his mama and daddy are stuck at the roadblock up north of town and need to know how their grandboy is doing. Our poor little Alex is at home with our daughter-in-law. He isn't feeling well, and we're just, we're just worried sick about him. Joshua, you gotta understand we had a real scare last year. We almost lost him to cancer. So, would you be a dear and do us this little favor?"

Stone peered into Norine's hazel eyes. He sighed, then returned to the RV. He spoke to two guards who'd stepped outside. They laughed. Stone didn't. The guards went back inside as Stone spoke into his headset. He nodded and returned to the BMW.

"My commanding officer will not allow messages in or out of Packer City under any circumstance at this time. Again, I am very sorry."

James lost it and tore into Stone. "That's bullshit," he shouted, pointing a finger in the guard's face before shaking it to the rhythm of his speech. "You have no idea who you're dealing with. Everyone in this town has the right to communicate with the outside world, regardless of the reason for this lockdown. I demand to know how my son, my daughter-in-law, and my grandson are doing. So, you go back and talk to your commanding officer and convince him to be a reasonable human being, or I'll be contacting the State Attorney General and then the press. By morning, there'll be a swarm of media here to wake you guys up bright and early."

"Alright, alright, let me see what I can do."

Stone left earshot and spoke into his headset again. After moving his lips for a few words, he swallowed hard. He nodded in resignation and returned to James's window. "My commanding officer refuses to speak with you and repeated my orders. I wish I could help, but my hands are tied."

James glared and said, "You really don't know who I am... do you? Well, you and your commanding officer will know soon enough, as will whoever authorized this lockdown."

He rolled up the window. He shifted into reverse, spun around, and threw the SUV into drive. He shot Stone one last glower in the rearview and floored the accelerator. The tires screeched and kicked up dust and pebbles as the vehicle sped north.

He handed Norine his phone and said, "Call Nate Murphy. If you don't get through, just keep trying until you do. He'll get the word to the Associated Press that something big is going down in Mears County."

Forty-Seven

It was a quiet drive as James fumed and Norine worried as she dialed non-stop for the next forty minutes. She finally connected with Nate Murphy, the WNN's National News Director, as they passed the Grayson River Reservoir near Walton's Landing.

"How's it going, J.R.?"

"Sorry, Nate. This is Norine. James is driving," she said as calmly as she could.

"Well, It's nice to hear from you, Norine."

"Good to hear your voice, too, but it isn't a social call. James wanted me to call and let you know what's happening in Packer City."

"Alright, let me grab a pen. Okay, go on."

"Well, the whole area is locked down for some God-awful reason."

"Uh-huh."

"There's a roadblock north of town with at least four guards dressed in black and white camo carrying military rifles. We asked one what was going on, but he had strict orders not to release any information. He couldn't even tell us how the folks in town were doing, including Alex. He's home sick right now. That's the whole reason we came down this afternoon."

"Yes, got it. Go on."

"Well, yesterday, I called Ryan only to learn our little Alex was under the weather. The strange thing is Ryan told me that he, Suzanne, and Alex had just been released from a home quarantine the day before. Now, Nate, what I'm gonna tell you next hasn't been released, but this quarantine business was related to the Melvin Anderson murder and the woman everybody's been looking for in connection with his death. After that woman up in Grayson found Melvin's body, the coroner believed our son was exposed to some kinda biological weapon. But Ryan told me the CDC ruled that out on Monday and lifted the quarantine. I feel bad telling you this. I mean, I promised Ryan I'd keep this on the hush-hush."

"Norine, don't feel bad. The public needs to know. Anything else?"

"Yeah, there is. When my son didn't call this morning, I tried but couldn't get through. So, James looked into it. Come to find out, all communication to Packer City was knocked out by a huge power surge this morning or yesterday. The phone company wasn't sure since nobody but me reported the problem."

"Got a question," said Nate.

"Yes."

"How is your son involved with Melvin's murder investigation? I know Melvin was a close family friend going back to when J.R.'s father was a commando in World War II, but I'm not getting the connection here."

"Yes, Melvin was a very dear friend. So close, we called him Uncle Mel. Well, by some freaky coincidence, my son was exposed to the suspect when he saved her after she drove Mel's Jeep into Lake Hotchkiss."

"That was Ryan? You gotta be kidding me. What are the odds? So, let me get this—they won't release information about what's going on in town after all communication mysteriously goes down right when Packer City is locked down by military contractors. Obviously, the communication blackout was intentional. I suspect higher-ups are trying to cover their butts before this situation blows up. I'll contact the AP and head your way as soon as my crew is ready."

"Thanks, Nate. You're a dear. I gotta tell ya—the not knowing is just killing me."

"I can imagine. And don't you worry. In the next twenty-four hours, whoever's responsible for this will have no choice but to restore communication and let the public know what's going on in Packer City because this is going worldwide. I'll see you soon."

"Yes, you will. And thank you, Nate."

Norine hung up as James pulled into a gas station next to an all-night diner in Grayson.

James got out, pumped gas, and looked west toward Walton's Landing. He looked tragic, as if he might cry. He inhaled deeply, exhaled, and replaced the nozzle. He got in the BMW and parked. "Norine, let's get a bite."

She nodded and said nothing as they headed into the quiet diner, ordered burgers and fries, and ate. When they finished, Norine waited in the Beamer while James went to the mini-mart and picked up supplies to last through Friday's trip to Breckenridge.

He got in and handed Norine two plastic bags.

"Should we get a motel for the night?" she asked.

"No. I say we head south so we can be there when the circus comes to town."

"Alright. Let's do it. I doubt I'll sleep a wink tonight anyhow."

On the drive south, the highway was a dark, lonely tunnel. The silence deafened until they reached the roadblock. There, they slept little and when they did, uncomfortably, until dawn.

Forty-Eight

The sun beat down on Mary as she sat on a towel and looked through dark sunglasses, across the bay, at the cityscape she loved. Just another summer day at Alki Beach. It was good to be alive.

Seagulls dotted the West Seattle shoreline and sky. Sailboats, cruise ships, and ferries floated by on the gentle Sound as water burst from a whale who'd wandered into human traffic. Her eyes returned to the skyline and the Space Needle. She could almost see her old apartment in Queen Anne where she lived before her family moved to their north end beach condo.

Her mother lay beside her, sleeping on a SpongeBob SquarePants towel. Her brunette hair was tucked beneath her head as her eyes hid behind two mirrors. She wore a powder blue one-piece that fit snuggly around her perfect figure. Mary wished she'd wear sunscreen. Cancer scared her, and losing her mother was unimaginable in this perfect life.

Mary watched her father play in the water with her brother, Alex, and sister, Blossom. Like the locals around them, they were taking advantage of the short summer that would give way to a cool and rainy fall.

A car pulled up and parked. She twisted to the two-lane road that divided the beach from Alki's restaurants and shops. Peepa Thurston and Meema Agnes exited their creamy Cadillac. She smiled as upside down rainbows filled her heart.

Peepa and Meema strolled her way. Her grandfather held a white plastic bag with a take-out order from her favorite fish and chips place down the street. They looked so cute together—a gentleman and his fair lady. Proud smiles bloomed as they approached. They had much to be proud of (in Mary's not-so-humble opinion). After all, their oldest granddaughter would be returning to Boston for her final year at Harvard, and job offers were piling up.

"I got your favorite," said Peepa as he sheltered her in shadow. He pulled a Styrofoam container from the bag.

"Thanks, Peepa. I love you."

She took the container, opened it quickly, and screamed at the sight of two rotting rats. She dropped the box like a hot rock and looked up.

Peepa and Meema were gone. In their place stood Dr. Caine and Dr. D'Amato, laughing, cackling, bent over guffawing. Above her, the sky was now cloudy and gray. Around her, the seagulls and everyone on the beach, including her grandfather, grandmother, father, mother, brother, and sister, lay dead or were floating in the water. Everyone's skin was darkened, mottled purple, with areas of exposed flesh melting off their bones. Across the bay, black and gray smoke billowed from the burning Emerald City. Dark blue soot fell like snow. She felt cold, so cold. She shivered. Her teeth chattered. This was her fault. Everything was always her fault.

Mary looked up as four black winged guards descended from the sky. They landed softly behind Dr. D'Amato and her laughter ceased while Caine's continued with vaudevillian flare. Her unnatural, piercing green eyes turned as serious as the Wicked Witch of the West. She waved her hand, and directed the General's monkeys to grab her little pretty. Mary crab crawled backward. She tried to stand but tripped over her mother and fell into the sand. The Black Berets picked up their pace with pistols drawn.

Forty-Nine

Ryan gazed into a snow globe like a sorcerer holding a crystal ball. But the snow had melted into rain. Inside was the scene of his encounter with the woman of his nightmares—the lady from the lake. Four contractors clad in black-and-white camo wearing black berets stood between his wounded truck and the ruined elk. Each carried a carbine.

The men walked in lock step to the road's edge. They gazed down the steep embankment to the dark water. The orange Jeep was sinking slowly. The fireteam descended the steep cliff with deliberate grace and stepped into the water. They treaded slowly, ominously, sinking no deeper than their knees, toward the Jeep which took on water but refused to sink further.

The bloody-faced woman in the driver's seat was conscious, and increasingly panicked as the fireteam drew closer. She struggled to undo her belt, but it only tightened the more she fought. Her efforts turned frantic, erratic, as she banged windows that wouldn't break and worked door handles that wouldn't open. A loud Nokia ringtone made the fireteam look up to the sorcerer outside the globe. Ryan looked up as well and saw a shadowy silhouette with a dark hand. The hand held a black cross with dangling white strings. He looked at his hands and elbows and saw that the strings were attached to him. The ring tone repeated once more.

Ryan's eyes opened as he tumbled onto the floor. He scrambled toward the sound until he saw his phone under the small table. Until the ringtone, he thought the guards had taken it. He flipped it open.

Fifty

Well after dawn, September 13, 2007, Mount Capitol Suites.

Mary's eyes opened. She heard yelling and sadistic laughter. She shook off the fog, squeezed out from under the bed, and moved quickly and quietly to the small kitchen window by the door. She peeked out a curtain corner. Near the office, Raj was surrounded by four Black Berets. One had a rifle pointed at his chest.

"Shit," she spat in a whisper. She bit her lip and stepped from the window. There was nothing she could do if the Black Beret fired. She wasn't that fast—at least not yet. She listened.

"You cannot search my motel without a warrant," Raj protested.

"Seriously?" a Black Beret asked through a chuckle. "Unless you want some of this, you best stay the fuck out of our way and let us do what we need to do."

Silent seconds followed, then Raj said, "Okay. Okay. Proceed with your search, but please do not mess up my rooms. I have been working all morning on them. Here, let me get you the keys."

"No need," the same Black Beret said through a derisive chuckle. "I've got my own."

Mary peeked out as the Black Beret kicked in the door closest to the office. *Well, that was mean... and pointless. Fuckers.*

Two from the fireteam rushed inside as the one who spoke covered the fourth who had a pistol ready to deliver the sleepy-time darts that she knew too well.

Raj looked defeated but there was nothing he could do now except get himself killed, but he was already dead. When General Adamson's goons found her, he would get a bullet in the head like anyone else who knew they were searching for her.

Two... The Black Berets ransacked each room while she counted each kicked in door. *Three... Four...* As the din of destruction neared, she crawled under the bed and fought the urge to reveal herself and kill them while they were distracted. *Five...* But if she used the Touch or any of her other abilities, she would have more to worry about than just Dr. Caine, Dr. D'Amato, and the Chairman of the Joint Chiefs of Staff. *Six...* Plus, Raj would still disappear without a trace when Adamson learned who harbored his prototype.

Seven... Still, it was the only chance she had. *Eight...* Once they reached her room, she'd be cornered and unable to take them all out before one or two hit her with enough tranquilizer to kill an elephant. *Nine...* If she survived that, she'd wake up inside the lab complex and Adamson would either find a new use for her or dispose of her like he was trying to do before she escaped. *Ten...* Soon, she wouldn't have a choice but to fight since hiding under the bed wouldn't conceal her once that door was busted open.

Eleven... The door next to hers exploded. She jumped, bumped her head, and bit her tongue. She tasted blood and hoped no one heard.

Twelve... She breathed deep as her door smashed open and two sets of black boots stormed in. They checked the bathroom.

"Stop! We gotta move out now," said the Black Beret who spoke first. "National Guard's on its way. We gotta be outta here before they get here. General says he has what he needs for now. We'll get the girl later. Let's go!"

Two sets of boots filed out.

Mary held her breath until she could no longer hear them. She exhaled and a sweat drop splashed on the wood.

Fifty-One

Well after dawn, September 13, 2007, Ebola-Colorado Containment Facility.
Ryan raised the phone to his ear. "Hey, Mom," he said shakily.

"Oh my God, are you okay?" she asked.

His lips quivered as his eyes welled. "Don't worry about me. I have… I have some real bad news… the worst. Alex… He's, he's gone. He passed on Tuesday, not long after we spoke. I am so sorry," he said in a whimper.

Stunned silence was followed by hysterical screaming. When his mom could speak, she spat, "Goddamnit. Goddamnit. Goddamnit. Those bastards! They knew. They knew. They knew, and they wouldn't tell me and James our Alex was gone."

His mother rarely cursed and, if she slipped, it was never her Lord's name in vain. "Mom, Mom, I'm sorry. I am so sorry. I am soo, soo sorry. I tried to call you, but the CDC told Dr. Boyd to take up our phones before I could. And when I got it back, there was no service."

"So, the CDC did this?" she asked bitterly.

"I assume so. But I don't know. I did get the names of the two in charge. Dr. Albert Caine and this bitch—sorry 'bout the language. Her name was Antonia D'Amato."

His mom seethed through the receiver. "Don't you be sorry. And I'll remember those names. You better believe it, dear." She gathered herself enough to continue. "Last... last night, your daddy and I learned the cell tower above Lake Hotchkiss was tampered with. Nate Murphy—you remember Nate... don't you? WNN national news director?"

"Yeah, sure, I do."

"Well, he confirmed that an EMP device was used to knock out the tower. There's even suspicion that a satellite serving your area was taken off line. That's being investigated as we speak. I still don't understand why the CDC didn't want information getting out. But Ryan Bear, I gotta know what happened to Alex. Did it have anything to do with that quarantine?"

"I don't know. And I don't know why they wanted to keep this from the public unless it goes a whole lot higher than disease control. According to Dr. D'Amato, Alex died from a new strain of Ebola, but she wouldn't say how he got it. I mean, there's never been a case in Colorado or in the U.S. other than Reston. This is so messed up. It don't make any sense."

"You think that woman you saved has anything to do with Alex's death?" she asked.

"I can't see how, and if so, why did the CDC lift the quarantine if they thought Melvin died of Ebola, I mean, of all things, especially if they thought we were incubating the virus? To be honest, nothing makes sense anymore. Mom, I can't think straight." Ryan's voice faltered. "I'm tired and irreparably broken. Alex is gone, and all I have left is Suzanne and you guys. And these…" He pursed trembling lips and chose words he'd feel comfortable uttering in church. "… these *people* only made it worse by keeping Suzanne and me apart. I'm sure it was out of spite for what I did to those guards."

"What happened?"

"Well, when they tried to take Suzanne, I… I lost it, and beat the crap out of two of them. They shot me with tranq darts. Can you believe it? The police and military don't even use those on people. And before that, they *really* shot Eugene Lee when he tried to escape after they told us not to leave. He lost a lot of blood. I don't even know if he's still alive. I doubt it. I know he's a terrible person, but whether he deserved it or not, they didn't have to shoot him when they coulda restrained him or tranqued him like me."

"Oh, my Lord Jesus, this is beyond the pale. Just crazy. Don't you worry. Your father will make those responsible pay for what they done to you, Suzanne… and our family… and everyone else in Packer Cit…"

"Mom? Mom, you there?" He looked at his phone. It was dead.

He tossed it across the unit and let his face fall into his hands. His mind began cycling. *Why didn't you save him? The lady from the lake. What happened to her? Is she safe? Why didn't you save him? The lady from the lake. What happened to her? Is she safe? Why didn't you save him? The lady at the lake. What happened…* "GET OUT OF MY FUCKIN' HEAD!" he screamed.

Fifty-Two

9:00 a.m. EST, Thursday, September 14, 2007, The Pentagon, Washington, D.C.

General Adamson nervously doodled on the pad in front of him. It calmed him. He *had* to remain calm since War was out of *his* mind at the moment. He really needed his old friend, but the Benefactor's son did not say when he would return. So, Adamson doodled. Always the same thing—a double crossed ankh in various sizes, but always ornate and reverent and always in red. It was the symbol of his Benefactor for whom he had not pleased.

Plan A had failed and Destiny had been unable to change what she had foreseen, namely, that Mender's mother would force him to move on to messier Plan B. One would think that finding Mary in her fog would be simple. Go to the eye of her storm, but according to Farseer's eyes, the fog was amorphous, constantly changing, making it impossible to pinpoint her location. Still, Destiny and D'Amato suspected Mary was somewhere around town, hiding for fear of killing more innocents while on the run.

Adamson doodled harder as he pondered why the hell the Benefactor insisted on snatching Mender and Mary together. Why the silly game? It made little sense, and while Adamson was a *good soldier*, he craved better understanding.

"Put your questions on the shelf. Have faith..." said War inside his head.

War's abrupt return jarred Adamson and made his pen stray and ruin a near-perfect double-crossed ankh.

"... My father has a greater plan than your mortal mind can possibly understand."

Adamson quickly cleared other disparaging thoughts. "Ah, you're back. Praise be Marduk. And yes, I know. I just wish..." he blurted, then awkwardly pursed his lips, somewhat embarrassed, hoping Fossum had not heard him talking to himself. He continued, "... I mean, I wish he would confide in me like you do."

"Maybe he will in the aging of Timethy, but even I, his most favored son, am not privy to all his machinations."

"Yes, of course. I will remain his loyal servant and not ask questions I do not need to know."

"Good, good," said War inside his head.

Adamson relaxed and put down the blood-red pen. He leaned back and he and War thought about the previous day's disappointments together.

The National Guard (who Adamson was compelled to deploy) had entered Packer City from the north. When they arrived, his mostly good soldiers were nowhere to be found. The lab's RVs had left the area headed south an hour before. Witnesses had reported seeing them driving through Silver City, but he was the only mortal who knew where and *how* they went from there.

Once the town was secured, National Guard members released the town sheriff and his staff. Since the lockdown began, they had been held—not so nice and very cozy—inside the historic courthouse made famous by the trial of Dr. Morgan Bell (a fine soul he'd gotten to know and who they *both* respected).

Before War's return, Adamson had watched Sheriff Peter Maxwell's statement concerning the ordeal. It was a bit rude that his good soldiers left them crammed like sardines without food and water and, as Sheriff Maxwell was quoted after his release, *"those *bleep* *bleep* didn't even leave us a bucket."* He and War chuckled at the memory.

Once Sheriff Maxwell and his staff were freed, they resumed their normal duties within the quarantine perimeter and, as such, Adamson lost his implant's audio and visuals. Now, he had to rely solely on news reports and words from subordinates. Since then, all but four National Guard members had returned to Fort Carson. The four who remained guarded the roadblocks at the north and south sides of town. The other two barricades were dismantled.

The previous evening, the curfew was rescinded. But it was unnecessary. No one much felt like getting out, especially after residents and visitors learned the area had been sealed due to an Ebola outbreak.

"That was a good choice," said War inside his head.

"Why, thank you," thought Adamson. "Coming from you that means a lot to me. I thought about a hemorrhagic flu to explain the Mender boy's bizarre demise, but that is so last century."

That made War laugh. "Yes, yes, the public needs something more exotic to sink their fears into. And from the media buzz, my father will have his three weeks to make sure Mender is fully ripe for the reaping."

Fifty-Three

10 a.m. MST, September 14, 2007, Mount Capitol Suites, Packer City, Colorado.

knock… knock-knock.

Mary was yanked from one nightmare and thrown into another.

knock… knock- knock.

The quiet rapping paused and repeated once more with the same pattern.

She was too shaken to answer and she remained stone still under the bed.

"Julie, it is safe now," whispered Raj. "The Black Berets are gone. I am coming in."

The broken door squealed open. Raj's white New Balance high-tops stepped inside and went to the kitchen. He set at least two plastic bags on the counter, returned to his laundry cart, and set a tool kit on the floor. He began work on the door and didn't attempt to engage in whispering small talk.

When the door closed again, Mary got out from under the bed, went to the bathroom, and peed. She stripped, stepped into the ceramic-tiled walk-in shower, turned on the hot water, and simmered.

She exited the steam cloud wrapped in a towel. She wiped the mirror and regarded her forehead and traced the barely visible scar with a finger. She thought about the man who'd fished her out of the lake. She still wondered what had happened to him. She looked at her hands and sighed.

Mary went to see what was in the bags. From one, she removed a pair of men's Fruit-of-the-Looms underwear, a medium-sized men's Mountain Dew t-shirt, a pair of oversized cargo shorts, and a belt to keep them from falling to her knees. She dressed, then grabbed a two-liter bottle of Coke from the other bag and a club sandwich. She spun the cap off and emptied half the bottle before taking a breath. She belched, set the bottle on the counter, unwrapped the sandwich, and took several bites before breathing again.

She grabbed a plate from the cupboard for the sandwich, picked up the half-drunk bottle, and walked to the TV stand. She set the plate and bottle on the stand, picked up the remote, and turned to WNN News. She kept the volume low and leaned close as she took another bite and a big gulp. Reporter Julie Florid appeared on the screen outside Packer City. A ravine and a mesa were in the background. The lead story was the lockdown of the remote mountain town.

"This is WNN's Julie Florid here outside Packer City where the lockdown is in its third day. Already Ebola-Colorado has claimed one life—seven-year-old Alex Mender, son of ex-Army Ranger Ryan Mender of Berets fame and grandson of the legendary Norine Jasmine Jones. Only eight people, including Mender and his wife Suzanne, were exposed to the famous grandson. They are currently being held in containment for public safety to monitor for symptoms which can take up to twenty-one days to manifest."

A family photo popped up on the screen and her jaw dropped. On the left was a tall, handsome, and deeply-tanned Native American attorney named James Ryan Mender. Next to him was a face that one would've had to live under a rock on a deserted island their whole life not to recognize. It was the face of music royalty—the face of the elegant, legendary Queen of R&B, Norine Jasmine Jones. By her side was her white, modelesque, green-eyed daughter-in-law, Suzanne Collette. And next to her was Jones's son, a close-trimmed, tall, buff, gorgeous hunk of chocolate, named Ryan Bear who held his giggling, curly-headed son—the boy who died. She recognized Ryan. He was the man who saved her life.

"What the... He's alive? *He's alive!*" she said too loud for an unoccupied motel room. Her thrill turned to nausea. "Did I kill his boy?" she asked in a sickened whisper with a hand over her mouth. She kept the hand there as Florid spoke about Ebola to the listening laymen and women as only Florid could.

Mary knew it was bullshit. No doubt, Adamson, Caine, and D'Amato had orchestrated the quarantine to lock down the town once they suspected she was trapped. As far as she knew, her deadly touch extended no further than the person that came in contact with her skin or bodily fluids. If it did, the effect dissipated rapidly, leaving no trace of what killed the victim, usually before rigor mortis set in. The precautions Raj took were in case she was wrong.

To kill without detection was Adamson's goal when he decided to use Caine's formula to turn her and the others into his unwilling assassins. A victim touched by those with average ability, might survive for several minutes to a few hours, but she was anything but average. Mr. Anderson died in less than a minute and was probably nothing more than bones when he reached the morgue. She shivered at the thought of that kind man's painful horror. "How did *you* survive, Ryan Mender?" she asked in a whisper.

Had she infected Mender and made him a carrier? If so, she was guilty of taking another life. Mender needed to know what she'd done to him before he killed someone else, like his wife. To Mary's relief, Florid reported that Suzanne Mender was being held in a separate containment unit. She was safe for now. Mary would have to wait until the elaborate charade was over, then move as fast as her special gifts allowed to warn Mender before he infected his wife. Or, she would have to risk killing more innocents, to warn him at the containment facility. Nineteen more days was a long time to wait, and maybe, just maybe, she could sneak inside using her slow warp... *No, too risky.* She didn't even know the set up beyond Raj's rough description. Even if she stopped time to find him, she'd have to convince Mender to listen and believe her and not try to kill her when he learned that she was the reason his son was dead.

She laid back and stared at the ceiling. Sleep was a pipedream as unanswered questions gnawed away. Then a plausible but remote explanation for Mender's survival crept into her head.

Louis had told her that Manycows was more than a medicine man. He claimed the shaman absorbed illness and cancer from the sick, consumed the maladies, and grew stronger afterward. These mystical healers were extremely rare among the general population. Almost everyone who claimed to be one was a charlatan. The real ones, while rare, were found among the Navajo, Apache, and related tribes in Canada and eastern Alaska. Scattered reports placed a few among Siberian tribes and the Northern European Sami. Yet, the odds of randomly finding one of these healers to save her life and remove a curse were at least equal to winning several big lotteries in a lifetime or being struck by lightning multiple times and surviving without a scratch. While it was a long shot, she needed to know if she was still infected before getting anywhere near the Menders, or ever again contemplating the desperate foolishness of breaking into the containment facility.

Fifty-Four

Late morning, Friday, September 15, 2007, Mount Capitol Suites.

Mary was still in bed for a change when Raj entered her room. The fear of the previous day had subsided, but she hadn't slept.

He opened his mouth to speak, but before he could, she asked, "What do you know about Ryan Mender?"

His eyebrows rose, and his chin dropped at an angle. He asked his own question. "How long ago were you abducted?"

"Last October. Why?"

"And before that, did you ever watch the show called *Berets*? Or have you ever heard of Nathan Miller? And Ryan's mother... You must know who Norine Jasmine Jones is?"

"No. Yes... and, um, yes. Who hasn't heard at least one song by Norine Jones a hundred times? I mean, she's a legend like Aretha Franklin. And Nathan Miller... Of course, I know who he is. Everyone knows who he is. *The Indestructible Nathan Miller*. He's like a modern-day Ernest Hemingway, just not as big of an asshole as I've read the original was. But I, um, didn't start getting into Miller until after my grandfather died. That's when I saw an interview with Miller about the series' tragic end on a TV at Walmart where I worked. It was, uh... it was hard to watch, but I couldn't look away. They showed a picture of Miller and... Yeah, now I remember. Ryan Mender was in it, standing with his Ranger buddies in Iraq the day before everything went to shit and Adamson dropped the bomb. After that, I went to my high school library and checked out Miller's first book, *Ghosts of Bosnia*. I've read several of his since. Can't put 'em down. Real midnight oil burners. I wanted to watch the series, but between food, utilities, saving for tuition... well, um, satellite TV wasn't in the budget. I mean, after my Peepa died, I couldn't even afford a phone or internet service. Wouldn't have mattered anyway. I never had time to sit down and watch anything. I was always working. And, uh, when I wasn't, I was sleeping or studying or taking night classes at a college near my place. Even so, I still found time for a good book. It was about the only thing I could afford to do."

"Okay then, have you read *The Menders: A First American Story*?"

"No, but it's funny that you ask. The day before I was taken, I checked it out, but I never got the chance to crack it. Probably still sitting on my nightstand." She chuckled ironically. "I guess I don't have to worry about late fees?" She grinned. "Uhh, you wouldn't happen to have a copy, would you?"

He smiled wide, showing shiny white teeth. "Do I have a copy? *Do I have a copy?* Of course, I have a copy. I will bring it to you tomorrow. Same time, same place?"

Mary nodded, matched his smile, and chuckled. It felt good to smile and even better to laugh.

Fifty-Five

Late morning, Saturday, September 16, 2007, Mount Capitol Suites.
Halfway through Raj's daily duties, Mary awoke but pretended to be sleeping until the door opened, closed, and locked again. She sat up, saw the book on the nightstand, and bounded off the bed. It was a fancy special edition. She picked it up and returned to the fluffy mattress.

She admired the cover's sparkling southwestern colors as she caressed the embossed lettering. She set the book on the bed, positioned the pillows for a long, comfortable read, then climbed the steps. She slid under the covers, grabbed the book, and leaned against the headboard. She opened the best-seller, smelled the intoxicating pages, and began searching for clues to suggest that Ryan Mender was one of Louis's healers. She needed to look no further than the introduction.

The novel opened with a prologue about a legendary Ute Indian medicine man who happened to be Ryan Mender's great-great-great-grandfather. The medicine man was born sometime in the 1810s or 20s. While his original name faded with the sands of what is now the

Four Corner States, he was known as Healing Hands because of his amazing gift that required no chanting, singing, ceremonies, or anything else. He needed only to lay his hands on the sick to cure whatever ailed them. Witnesses reported that wasted and dying patients were restored to health overnight and rose stronger than before their illnesses.

Mary read on about Uto-Aztec origins and their conflicts with the Spanish Conquistadors. She learned that the Utes stole Spanish horses and shared them with their cousins, the Comanches. Together, they became two of the most powerful tribes and later enemies in what is now Utah, Colorado, Texas, and the Southern Great Plains.

In chapter two, Miller spoke of the enmity between the Great Ute Nation and the Navajo tribes (or Diné as they preferred to be called), who lived to the south in Diné Bikéyah (the land of the Diné). The bitterness and cycles of revenge began when Utes used their horses to raid Diné villages. They took sheep and other livestock and kidnapped and enslaved Diné women and children. Their Ute captors would either incorporate them into the tribe or sell them to other tribes or the Spanish, and when the Spanish were gone, the Mexicans and the English white man. Mender's direct ancestor, Chief Big Mountain, was guilty of the former. He fell in love and married a Diné slave six generations before the coming of the great healer.

In chapter three, Miller came to the legend of Healing Hands. What captivated Mary most was the story of a nine-year-old Diné girl who wandered into the healer's camp pleading for help early in the summer of 1857 in what is now Quenche, Colorado.

Long before that fateful day, the healer's reputation spread far and wide. Afflicted from surrounding tribes, whether friend or foe, and even some Whites and Mexicans, traveled long distances to find him. Many died on the way with hope in their eyes, but for those who survived the journey, the medicine man cured whatever ailed them. The Diné girl hoped Healing Hands could do the same for her father, who was dying of consumption.

The girl entered the camp alone, crying for help, but no one understood her words since she didn't speak the Numic tongue. Two Ute warriors saw the distressed girl and led her to Healing Hands' teepee. According to legend, the medicine man had another gift—he understood and spoke the languages of all who sought help.

The girl entered the teepee and told Healing Hands that she and her father had traveled many moons from Canyon de Chelly in the land of the Diné. She went on to say that the healing ceremonies of her clan's Hataalii had failed to restore harmony to her father's health. When all hope was lost, her mother persuaded him to travel to the land of the enemy to find the great healer.

Against his beliefs, her father agreed to go out of love for his wife and daughters. They left on one horse, but the animal died on the trail a few moons back. The young girl's father walked as far as he could but was now lying in the grass by a river that cut between the red rocks, not far from the healing springs. She said the wind of life was about to leave him if it had not already gone. Hearing this, Healing Hands dispatched the two warriors to find a good horse for the girl and told them to follow the girl to where her father was and bring him back to his teepee, dead or alive.

On three horses, they galloped along the trail until they reached the girl's father, who was lying on two of the finest Chief blankets either warrior had ever seen. As it turned out, the man was the son of a master weaver, who some swore descended from the Spider Woman herself. The blanket was one of two he brought to pay the medicine man. The man was told before he left for the land of the enemy that the great healer never asked for payment. He brought the blankets anyway because he refused to believe any Ute could be so gracious.

One warrior helped the frail man to his feet, and the other draped the blankets over the back of his daughter's horse. Together, they lifted the dying man onto the steed and walked and trotted the three horses back to camp.

The man struggled to stay upright and used what strength remained in his fragile arms to wrap them around his daughter's waist. Once outside Healing Hands' teepee, the man let go, fell sideways off the horse, and hit the ground with a snap of bones.

The girl slid off the horse, knelt, and shook her father, but his eyes were fixed on the sky. She held him and cried as the warriors laid the Chief blankets on the ground inside the teepee. She wailed when the warriors returned and tried to take her father's lifeless body. She wouldn't allow it and wrapped herself around him, ignoring all she knew about corpse sickness. Healing Hands stood at the teepee's entrance and tenderly convinced the girl that everything would be okay and for her to let the warriors bring her father inside. She nodded and released her grip.

The warriors carried the man's body inside and laid him on one of the blankets. The girl stood in the opening as Healing Hands kneeled at the head of her father's wasted, broken body. He waved a hand over the man's face, closed his eyes, and placed both palms on the man's cheeks. The warriors stood on either side of the healer. No one spoke. The only sounds were distant bird song, water trickling in the nearby river, and the wind rustling through the aspens. The girl's eyes were red and puffy, but she was no longer crying, her face now full of hope and wonder.

Healing Hands closed his eyes, swayed, and went limp. The warriors grabbed his arms before he fell forward onto the man. The great healer had entered what was called the *deep sleep*, which often happened during difficult healing rituals. As the warriors carried Healing Hands to his bed, the dead man coughed and opened his eyes.

The great healer awoke well after the dawn. The resurrected man and his daughter were standing over him with wide smiles. He sat up, and the Diné man offered him water and roast mutton from a freshly slaughtered lamb. Healing Hands asked them to sit and eat with him. The man and his daughter did as requested. It was then that the man offered Healing Hands his mother's blankets.

Known as Chief blankets to the Utes, they would've been the envy of anyone in the tribe. Healing Hands grinned and studied the well-fleshed man who had been skin and bones a moon before. He told the man he didn't need or want the blankets. He said his restored health was payment enough. He did ask one thing, though, that the man allow his daughter to return and marry his only son when the two came of age.

The man sat speechless for several minutes. Healing Hands respected the long pause.

The man had watched the two children play the evening before and that morning while the healer slept. Neither could understand the other's words but communicated in other ways. He sensed a deep connection as if destiny had brought them together.

The Diné man finally replied. *"I would be honored for my little lamb to marry the son of Healing Hands who gave me back the wind of life and more seasons with my family. Among the Diné, your kindness will be remembered, and your descendants will always be welcome among my clan and my people."*

Mary read on. She learned what became of that little lamb, Dibé Yázhí, and the boy who would soon be named Fighting Bear (whom James Mender would honor with his son's middle name). She also shed tears over Healing Hands' tragic murder by a Ute of another clan on Utah's Nuche/Quenche reservation. The tale of tears continued through more heartbreaking history up to the birth of Ryan Mender's grandfather, Edwin James, in 1924.

When Mary turned the page, she saw the edge of a newspaper clipping poking from the back of the book. She removed the clipping and unfolded it. It was from the *Denver Post*, dated January 10, 2007. The headline read, *"Norine Jasmine Jones' grandson revived after death from Acute Myeloid Leukemia."*

She devoured the sensational article that started with the line, *"Miracles do happen."* She had chills and goosebumps when she finished. Without a doubt, she'd randomly found one of Louis's healers, and her carelessness had corrupted Mender's gift and turned it into a touch of pestilence. Any intense emotion—hate, rage, fear, even love—the passions that made Mender human and allowed him to resurrect his son—had now killed Alex Mender and put everyone else around him at risk. Only two possible outcomes existed for him if he couldn't control his dueling powers. Either the dark energy would grow until he was as malignant as her, or it would destroy him in one big bang as it had several of her fellow lab rats.

There was another problem. If she knew Mender was infected, the lab knew it, too, and was keeping him separated from the others to observe his development. It must've been a surprise since every attempt she'd witnessed or participated in to create carriers without the lab's miracle drug had ended with a rapidly decaying mass of flesh. Or maybe it wasn't a surprise once the lab knew the carrier was the miraculous Ryan Mender, who accidentally raised his son from the dead before killing him nine months later. Her head pounded.

The lab wasn't going to let Mender walk out of quarantine and back to his normal life. When this ended, the General and his Black Berets would be coming for them both. After what she'd taken from the man, she was determined, whatever the risk, to find and convince Mender to go with her to Arizona to find Louis's medicine man.

Fifty-Six

Sunday Morning, September 17, 2007, Mount Capitol Suites.
Raj entered Mary's room, beaming. "Well, did you like the book?"

"Yeah. Finished it last night. It was, uh, awesome. Really depressing in parts, but... great... and inspiring to see how the Mender family turned out. And guess what?"

"What?"

"I... I don't think I'm contagious anymore."

"That... that is good."

"Well, sort of. Bad news is, the only way to know for sure is to risk killing someone or something. But other than the ones who made me into a monster, there isn't anyone and anything I want to test my theory on. I don't know what to do. What do *you* think I should do, Raj?"

He peered into her eyes, creepy like, but kind of sweet, as he did the morning they met. He lowered his mask, removed a glove, and extended a hand.

"Oh, hell no! Nah. Unh-uh. You're my friend—my only friend now. You protected me when I... when I don't think anyone else would've. You fed me and clothed me. You risked your life by letting me stay here. Damn, you nearly took a bullet for me. I've only known you for like two weeks, but I... I really care about you. You're like a father I never had."

Raj dropped his hand, chewed his lip, and looked though Mary and the window blinds across the room. He closed his eyes for a few seconds, opened them, and met her gaze with sorrow, but no tears.

"Since I met you, I have found purpose in life that I have been missing since my wife left me and took away my children. There is something about you, Julie, that I do not think you understand. I know I do not. I only know that when you leave here, I will be in your thoughts, and you will be in mine if I survive your touch. Either way, I will live on until we both die." He extended his hand once more.

She swallowed as a tear ran down her cheek. She gazed at Raj, his eyes filled with the faith of a child. She stepped forward and took his hand, held it for a few seconds, then brought it to her cheek to catch another tear. Then she sobbed.

He pulled her close, wrapped his other arm around her, and hugged her like a father. If the darkness remained, he would be dead soon. Until then, he wouldn't know he was infected.

They embraced a little longer, then sat knee-to-knee in two chairs by the small table. He removed the other glove and held Mary's hands. His gaze never faltered as he waited to die looking into her eyes without a hint of fear. The minutes passed, and nothing happened. Raj finally smiled.

She grinned back and said, "Oh, and I guess you can stop calling me Julie. My name's Mary, Mary DeMure."

Raj chuckled, "Well, it is very nice to finally meet you, Mary, Mary DeMure."

Fifty-Seven

Monday, September 18, 2007, Charlotte's Espresso: Home of the World Famous Frespresso, Packer City, Colorado.

The day after Mary learned that she no longer had a touch of pestilence, she asked Raj to do some reconnaissance on his morning Frespresso run. *Charlotte's Espresso* was the only business open and several residents had overcame their fears for their daily fix of the mind-enhancing concoction. Sheriff Pete Maxwell, Undersheriff Joe Turner, and Joe's pregnant wife, Jocelyn, were two customers in front of him. The rest of the police force, which included three deputies and a Hispanic replacement for Bob Roberts, were behind him talking about donuts.

Raj danced inside his mind while tapping his foot to a rhythm only he could hear. He joyfully endured the long wait as each happy customer sipped on by and he neared the promised counter where Charlotte Lee was bubbly and bouncing with southern charm at the sound of her cash register ringing again.

With frosty Frespresso in hand, he headed outside, sat in the sun, and put on his shades. He paced himself and sipped slowly to prevent a brain freeze as his synapses sang and giggled with delight as Charlotte's secret ingredient made everything seem alright. He thought of a movie about a secret agent man and fixed his hidden eyes on the comings and goings across the two-lane highway at the Ebola-Colorado containment facility.

He counted nine large storage units connected to the white RV by a large tube-like tunnel. The unit closest to him seemed more substantial than the others but not enough to catch the eye of someone not looking for something amiss. On the right near the RV was a power generator and septic tank. Flood lamps surrounded the facility as far as he could see that would turn the field to daytime at night. Outside the tube's entrance were three gentlemen and one gentlewoman dressed as rent-a-cops, armed with pistols. The woman and one of the male security guards entered the tube as his Frespresso hit the half-full mark. Moments later another woman and man exited wearing white lab coats. The man lit up a cigarette, and offered one to the female doctor. She accepted. He lit her cancer stick and then the two stared off in Raj's direction or magnificent Mount Capitol as they polluted the pure, mountain air.

He watched a little longer until the doctors re-entered the tube and his drink hit slurping-empty. He went back inside and got back in line for another Frespresso to enlighten Mary.

Fifty-Eight

Monday afternoon, September 18, 2007, Mount Capitol Suites.
Raj delivered Mary's Frespresso and revealed what he observed. Mary sipped. There was something familiar about the drink. It reminded her of a Starbucks Frappuccino with a little something extra, but unlike Raj, she didn't see what the big deal was.

"Is it as good as I promised?"

"Yes. Absolutely. So much better than Starbucks."

"I think so, too. So what are you going to do?"

"I don't know. I suspect Mender's unit is the first one. Figures. The lab is baiting me. They know me and know what kind of person I am. They know I won't leave without warning him about the monster he's becoming—the one I accidentally created. Fuckin' bastards."

"Are you going to try?"

"Yeah—I have to."

"Please do not. I could not survive it if anything happened to you."

"Raj, I am a whole lot more than I look. I may not have the touch but I still feel what the lab did to me. It's coursing through my veins."

"Okay. Just be careful."

"I will," she said and squeezed his hand. "Can you get me something black to wear?"

Raj returned with a black ski balaclava and matching turtle-neck long sleeve dryride with thumb holes, long thermal underwear, thick wool socks, glove liners, and hiking boots.

She grinned.

"The underwear should fit you. I accidentally got the wrong size. But I am sorry, I did not have any black pants. Will this do?" he asked.

"Yeah. It'll do. Thanks. You ski?"

Raj furrowed his brows and said, "I may be a lot of things, but I am not a skier. I like to snowboard," he finished jestfully with a grin adding a little levity to the potential gravity of her night's activities.

She laughed. "Really? Me, too. You and I are gonna have to talk."

"I hope that we will. Be safe," he said as the jest left his sails.

That's when she realized she had no plan for after he contacted Mender and that she might not be able to return to the motel without bringing attention to Raj. She sighed and said, "I will."

He nodded and left.

She got dressed. When she got to the boots she stopped, picked them up, and examined the tread. The sole had a very unique pattern of grippy shapes. Possibly unique enough to leave evidence that might be useful if things went south and body bags were needed. She peeked outside. The dirt parking lot looked bone dry. The boots would stay. *Well, socks are quieter anyway,* she thought.

It turned cloudy that evening and by the night it was full dark. It was cold, but luckily, no rain or snow was falling. Raj flipped off the motel sign making it even darker. Mary pulled the balaclava over her head, tucked her blonde locks away, and stepped out of #12 for the first time since September 1. She snuck across the road to the Packer City Cemetery and continued to the river and down to the bank. She worked her way south, went under a bridge, and followed the water upstream to the medical center, then slinked up again to a clump of bushes kitty-corner across the street from the well-lit containment facility. She ground her teeth when she saw H.E.L.'s logo on the RV connected to the long tunnel Raj described from the coffee shop opposite where she crouched. A feral thought crossed her mind to kill the doctors inside, but the rent-a-cops were likely innocents hired after the National Guard forced the General's assholes out of town. No doubt, the Black Berets were hiding somewhere close enough to swoop in if she fucked up.

She studied the floodlights. She thought about knocking out a few to create a diversion then slow time to slip into Mender's unit. But would that give her enough time to warn him and get him out before the General was alerted or there were innocent casualties? Who was she kidding? Innocent casualties? Oh hell, yeah, there would be innocent casualties. But if Mender was allowed to wander out of containment without knowing what he was, there'd be far more. She had to act.

She picked up a stone, weighed it in her hand, and hurled it toward the lamp. The light went out. She waited. No one came out to check on the light. She huffed and pursed her lips pensively. She thought about hitting another light but changed her mind.

She listened to the humming generator on the other side of the RV. She skirted the perimeter in the shadows and came to an old monument with a cannon facing the river. Next to it was a four-high pyramid of cannon balls. She looked back at the generator then again at the pyramid. She reached for the point ball. It was welded to the others. She thought about all the boards and cinder blocks she'd broken on the way to her black belt. She remembered how honored Peepa had been when her picture was put up in the Seattle dojo next to Sensei Kimura's with his teacher, Bruce Lee. She looked at the cannon ball. She looked through the cannon ball. Her palm exploded forward. A metallic crack followed, and the ball flew five feet, landed with a loud thump, and rolled ten more. Porch lights came on in a few nearby houses. She ducked out of sight as one resident stepped onto his porch with a shotgun. When he didn't see anything, he went back inside.

She exhaled and waited until the lights went back out, then slinked to the cannon ball. She picked it up. It was at least as heavy as a standard male shot put. When she was in high school track, she could barely send a woman's shot ten meters, but since Dr. Caine's experiments she would have no problem embarrassing the male world record holder.

She crept to the edge of shadow, lifted the cannon ball between her shoulder and neck, crouched, breathed deep, and fired. A loud BOOM followed along with all the lights, leaving the field dark. Four silhouettes ran out of the tube to investigate. Two more quickly followed.

She blinked and silhouettes began moving slower until they almost stopped. She sprinted for the tube, passing them. The door to the tube was open. She slipped in and looked down the darkened hall. She could make out the first two or three vinyl doors. Each led to the decontamination room with a shower before the main door to the containment units. She compared the first and second containment units. The first was heavier than the second. She hoped its door lock disengaged with the power outage, but she knew that was wishful thinking.

She unzipped the vinyl door and stepped inside the first decontamination room. There was a slit in the main door large enough for an arm or a meal tray. If the door wouldn't budge, maybe she could get the slit open. Then at least she'd be able to warn Mender before she retreated to the safety of Raj's motel. Then it would be up to him to believe her or not. It was less than she hoped for, but at least she would've done what she could to save his wife and prevent more deaths like his son's.

She grabbed the door handle and pulled. Something latched on to her hand. She looked and saw tendrils of night wrapping around her fingers. She tried to pull away but the hand was stuck as more tendrils sprung from the door unaffected by her time-slowing warp. One touched her arm but she grabbed it before it could wrap around. She focused all her strength and yanked her hand free, leaving the glove liner, as her fingers snapped without the wet crack in the silence of the warp. She wanted to scream as she turned to run for the tunnel. She felt something tearing inside much deeper than muscle, sinew, and bone. It was as if her very soul was being torn away. Her teeth clenched to bury a shriek as she tumbled into the dark tunnel. She smelled ozone, and then everything went darker.

Fifty-Nine

Mary blinked several times as she dazed at the dark ceiling. Two lollipop silhouettes hung over her. They were speaking but everything sounded jumbled and fuzzy and slowly it didn't.

A flashlight blinded and her sensei's jeet-kune-do took over. She rolled and spun to a standing position. A roundhouse knocked one head out of sight and sent the flashlight tumbling to illuminate the hall to the RV. Kick-punch-OWW-wham-pow and she was gone.

She warped the way she came and didn't look back until she peeked from her room's window to see flashing red and blue in the otherwise dim direction of the containment facility. "Fuck," was all she said as her broken fingers throbbed and hastily healed.

Sixty

Late night, Monday, September 18, 2007, Ebola-Colorado Containment Facility.

Unit #9

The light returned and the door slit opened.

"What the hell happened earlier?" asked Ryan.

Since the transformer explosion, he'd been unable to return to sleep. Not that it mattered, since he was still having his usual nightmares as the strange woman's fingers ground deeper into his every thought, sleeping or awake. When the commotion outside his door died down, he felt like her fingers had turned to claws and he almost screeched as sudden searing pain tore through him. He also saw the old gentleman in the corner with his face lit up as if a flashlight had been held beneath it to make him look spooky. He was shielding his granddaughter's eyes as he pressed her head against his shoulder as he had in the apartment vision to hide the sight of her dead mother. His free hand was pressed to his cheek and his mouth was a terrified O like the man in the painting *The Scream*. Then they vanished.

"Come on, dude. Don't be a dick. Say something."

His doctor didn't answer and motioned for his arm.

"No man. I ain't doing shit. Fuck your samples and fuck the CDC. What's your fuckin' problem? You motherfuckers. I swear I'm gonna sue your ass and everyone attached to your bullshit lab."

His doctor said nothing and motioned for his arm again, more insistently.

Ryan laughed and punched the door.

The door slit closed.

Unit #1

Suzanne jumped then twitched some more. She preferred the darkness. Light only reminded her she wasn't dead yet. Somewhere in her mind, she wondered what had just shook her unit and about the earlier explosion but thought little more of it. Ryan was near but so was Alex, and she was torn and tired. She missed her dad and hoped Alex had found his way to the meadows and the house on the hill where his granddad lived in Heavenly Father's right hand.

The door opened. Her doctor, Johanna Müeller, stood there in her usual white hazmat suit with her creamy cappuccino complexion and her gentle smile shining behind the shield. Her eyes were full of sympathy for all Suzanne had suffered. She didn't want sympathy. She wanted her heart back. She wanted her Alex. And she wished Johanna would just go away and let her die.

"I brought you something to eat," said Dr. Müeller in her Dutch/German accent. "It's schnitzel. I made it myself. It was my mother's recipe. It was my favorite. I hope you like it."

Suzanne glared at her as she held the lid over the platter like a waiter at a fine restaurant. She extended her hands.

Dr Müeller giggled infectiously but Suzanne was well vaccinated and sighed as her doctor waited for her to eat. She cut a piece. It smelled wonderful, as much as she hated to admit it. She set it reluctantly on her tongue and flavor exploded as her taste buds tangoed like only a gourmet chef's could. She closed her eyes and savored the love as her lips began to quiver. A tear rolled down her cheek. Now this was worth living for, as was Ryan. They would have another child, or two or three or more, but Alex would always be there and in the world beyond.

"Is good?" asked Dr Müeller.

"Yes. It's good. Really good. The best schnitzel I've ever had. Thank you, Johanna."

Sixty-One

September 19-30, 2007, Mount Capitol Suites.

Mary's hand healed before morning but her attempt to contact Mender had sent four guards to the Grayson General's ER. The one whose head caught her wool sock would be in a coma for a week. *Hey, at least they're alive,* she thought. She also succeeded in having a dozen National Guard recalled to the town and stationed around the facility to prevent more breeches of security and vandalism.

On the news, there was also speculation that whoever had assaulted the CDC's containment facility had connections with the late Brigham Norsworthy's radical militia group which was known as BNM. She had no doubt that the General knew it was her, but was baffled that the Black Berets hadn't stormed into town as she feared they would. But she had plenty of time to ponder what game the mad General was playing. And as for further attempts to contact Mender… that would have to wait until the phony quarantine ended. She still couldn't figure out what the General had used to booby trap Mender's door. She hadn't seen or experienced anything like it at the lab and wasn't sure she could survive another run in with whatever it was.

By the morning after the close call, she had settled back into her temporary accommodations. She would make the best of the peaceful respite and try not to get an ulcer worrying about what needed to be done once Mender was released. She wondered if she could even get ulcers anymore, but decided not to ponder that any further.

In the coming days, Raj spent an inordinate amount of time cleaning room #12. It was nice and finally gave her the chance to get to know the sweet man who used to live in Portland, Oregon, after immigrating from India. This fact led to an initially awkward discussion about religion. She was curious about Hinduism and assumed Raj was an adherent. He was, and so he took no offense and was happy to engage in a deeper discussion than she expected. She told him that her grandfather, Thurston DeMure, was a Zen Buddhist. The meditation techniques he taught her had helped her escape the pain of an illness she no longer suffered from since the lab *cured* her. But that was before they gave her a touch that kills. Since then, she'd fallen away from Zen. Raj respected Buddhism and Taoism and promised to help her return to enlightenment. He brought her a Frespresso every morning and spent many hours meditating with her since he had little else to do. She still didn't see what was so special about the frosty beverage, but it was pretty tasty.

From discussions of philosophy and religion, they moved on to more important things, like sports. While Raj wasn't into American football, he loved baseball and, like Mary, was a big Seattle Mariners fan. And as he told her before the Mender debacle, he was passionate about snowboarding. For her, it'd been a few years since she'd put on a pair of boots and strapped into bindings. The sport wasn't cheap and she couldn't afford it after her grandfather died. But when she could, she won half-pipe and park competitions and almost made it to the Olympics. He was impressed but expressed that his joy was just to stand and carve black diamonds at Crested Butte without falling on his face too often. Mary had laughed.

When they finished talking snow, Mary asked Raj how he ended up in Packer City. The sad tale began in Delhi, India, one of the world's most polluted, smoggy, densely populated, and rapidly growing cities. Fifteen years earlier, he had immigrated to the United States with his wife, Riya, and their three-year-old daughter, Anaya, and moved to Gresham, Oregon, a suburb east of Portland. His daughter, Kyra, and son, Krish, soon followed.

After ten years in Gresham, Riya told Raj that she no longer loved him and wanted a divorce. He didn't go into details as to why things fell apart, but he lost half of everything and Riya won full custody of the children. When the divorce was final, Riya married a lawyer from Miami and moved the kids to southern Florida.

After a few months in the quiet house, Raj's mother and father had urged him to move back home. Home at that time was eleven-thousand-five-hundred kilometers away. As much as he loved his parents, he had no desire to return to India or his higher caste. Then he got laid off from his IT job. That's when Raj decided to take a road trip to see his kids. The visit didn't go well, and that was all he said about that.

On the drive back, he had searched for interesting things to do and places to see to take his mind off his miserable life. While surfing the web at a motel in Fort Worth, Texas, he found a photo of a beautiful lake in Colorado. The lake was located in one of the most remote counties in the lower forty-eight states. The county's only town, Packer City, which grew up around the lake, was home to only eight-hundred year-round residents. It sounded like Heaven.

Raj stayed one week at the Mount Capitol Suites in Room #12 around the same time of year. He absolutely loved the place and everything about the area, especially the *poverty of population* (as he put it), which was the antithesis of Delhi.

Several weeks later, after returning to Gresham, he learned that the motel was for sale. That very day, he put his house on the market and made an offer with the rest of his life savings. The former motel owner accepted.

Once his home was sold and closed, Raj packed up his meager possessions and returned to Colorado. That was almost five years ago. Though he'd spoken to his children, he hadn't seen them since the Florida road trip.

Mary felt sorry for the eccentric man who'd done so much for her and asked for nothing in return. She felt even worse one-upping him with her tragic life story. She told him she'd never known her father and continued with the story of her mother and grandfather's deaths. She droned on about the great potential her life once held, then told him about her abduction and the experimentation on her and ninety-nine others who were now dead. She told him about the guard who abducted her, and then fell in love with her and how he helped her escape certain death at the cost of his life. She also told him what she'd done to his killers—at least the parts she hadn't blackened out of her mind. What she revealed was enough to make Raj cringe and shift uneasily in his seat, so when she told him how Mr. Anderson died, she omitted the graphic details.

Sixty-Two

Monday, October 1, 2007, Mount Capitol Suites.
Mary peeked through the curtains and saw a gray 4Runner with a lightbar pull around the corner. Her head darted back, hoping she hadn't been seen. But if ruffling curtains in a motel without guests had been noticed, she'd be breaking for the room's back door, come what H.E.L. may bring. Then again, maybe there was nothing to worry about. Maybe it was someone coming to tell Raj that the quarantine was over. It'd been almost three weeks. That was about the same

period the lab waited before unleashing her and the other survivors on the orderlies to test the Touch. Why three weeks this time, she wasn't sure, since she'd infected Mender over a month before. Of course, it could've been longer or shorter than three weeks since there were no clocks at the lab and it was always daylight in the caverns. Still, she sensed the end was near, and she needed to be ready to move to catch the Menders when they exited the containment facility whether she revealed herself again or not. If she missed them there, the last hope would be catching them at home, but she knew Suzanne Mender would likely already be dead or dying.

Several tense minutes passed before she heard Raj's knock-knock-pause-knock-pause-knock-knock-pause-knock.

"May I enter?" he asked.

"Yes."

He entered carrying two black trash sacks. The laundry cart wasn't behind him. He closed and locked the door and set the bags on the ground.

"Who was that?" she asked.

"Oh, that was Pete, the Sheriff. He... he..."

"What? He, what?" It was bad news. She knew it and wasn't sure she could take it. She was too late. Suzanne Mender was dead. "Damnit Raj, spit it out. You're killing me."

"Pete... he came by to tell me that the lockdown is going to be lifted in the morning."

"That... that's great. Great news. You can reopen and I can get out of your hair," she said, though she wasn't ready for what would follow. For Raj, she buried her anxieties and asked, "Why are you sad?" as if she didn't know.

His lips trembled. He shook his head as his eyes glistened. "The bags contain all you need to restart your journey," he said without meeting her gaze.

She perused the contents. "Thanks. That'll do Raj. That'll do."

He sort of grinned and nodded but didn't lift his eyes. Then suddenly his face brightened as if his children had paid him a surprise visit. His eyes sparkled above a wide smile. "Tomorrow before dawn, I will take you to the Watchtower. That is the home of Ryan Mender. Then I will go with you to Arizona. I will not be a burden, I promise. And maybe I can be of help."

"Raj, you can't go with me. And anyway, I have to find the Menders before that. Look, I have no idea what's going down tomorrow. The lab has doctors here and even though the Black Berets didn't return after what I pulled on the nineteenth, I still think they're out there waiting for me to screw up again. Probably watching the facility, but I don't have a choice. Maybe I'm paranoid, but I doubt it. I mean, they're not just gonna give up and let me go without a fight. And if they find me, I'll be doing terrible things. And if you're with me, you'll have to do terrible things, if you wanna survive. But I know you're not a killer like me, and I'm not gonna be responsible for turning you into one… or getting you killed. Raj, today is goodbye. I'm sorry, but it has to be. I promise I'll never forget you."

Tears welled in his eyes as he chewed his lips. He looked as if he wanted to say something, but no words came. There was nothing left to say.

She gazed into swollen, bloodshot eyes as streams flowed down his cheeks. He remained silent, his face racked with pain far beyond a last goodbye. It was as if part of his soul had been ripped away in a storm that left his shell standing, bare, bruised, and bleeding, praying for someone to end its misery.

She hugged him and felt his warmth. She thought of Peepa's last embrace before she left for school. The last embrace before she found him cold and staring in his recliner when she got home.

Raj quaked and sobbed as if at a funeral. He held on a little longer then dropped his arms. He grabbed one of her hands and held on as if it were a rope that'd been cast to a drowning man. He wiped his eyes with his free hand and sniffed hard. He nodded and found the strength to let go and sink into sorrow. He turned, opened the door, and glanced back once. He sniffed and stepped out of her life.

Mary stood stunned, blank-faced. Her gaze remained on the door, hoping that Raj wasn't really gone and that he might step back through. She ran to the window, and watched him walk toward the office. She started crying.

Sixty-Three

Evening, Monday, October 1, 2007, Ebola-Colorado Containment Facility.

Unit #9

The door slit opened. Ryan didn't bother to fight, though he was ready to kill that sonuvabitch doctor who hadn't uttered a word in the three weeks he'd been in the cage. Nor had he let Ryan charge his phone so he could call his no-doubt-worried mom to let her know how he was doing. He guessed he didn't want him to inform her of the shitty treatment he'd experienced in the *care* of the CDC's *doctors*, so his dad could prepare for the lawsuit that was coming. He could only imagine how Suzanne was doing. It couldn't be good. He only hoped she was getting her Neuroxitine. He knew how she got without it, and it wasn't pretty.

He extended his arm for another blood draw.

His doctor shook his head.

"What the fuck, man? CDC cut out your goddamn tongue?"

He didn't respond and shoved in a tray. On it was a glass of water and a plate with a juicy looking filet mignon, mashed potatoes, three asparagus sprigs and a large dollop of chocolate pudding. Strange combination but it still looked good.

"Is this your apology for being such an asshole?"

His doctor didn't respond and closed the slit.

"I'm still suing your sorry ass," he yelled through the door.

He looked at the plate and wondered why the good grub now when all his host had been serving was subpar cafeteria food which he'd skipped the past two days. Didn't feel much like eating and hadn't been feeling well for the few days before that. In fact, he'd felt a little off since the nineteenth. And the dreams. Holy shit. He was going bat shit crazier and needed out of this cube. And soon, or he might tear his eyeballs out. He had suspected an ulcer, but at least his stomach felt fine now. He looked at the food. "Ah, fuck it." He grabbed the plate and chowed down.

Unit #1

The door opened and an unfamiliar female face in a standard white hazmat stepped inside. The new doctor held a tray with a delightful steak with sides and a glass of water. It wasn't Johanna's schnitzel but looked great all the same, though the chocolate mousse seemed a bit odd to be on the same plate.

"Where's Johanna?" Suzanne asked, feeling puzzled and beyond disappointed.

"Um, she was reassigned to the lab annex in Fort Collins."

"Why?"

"I wasn't told."

"Well, shoot. I liked her. I wish you guys would've told me she was leaving. I would've liked to have at least said goodbye... and thank her. Any chance I can get her supervisor's number? You know, so I can put in a good word. I'm still struggling with the loss of my son, and probably always will be, but she really helped me get through the past three weeks."

"We love to hear that. And I don't see why not. I'll see what I can do. Enjoy your meal."

"Yeah. Thanks. It looks amazing. I didn't..."

The doctor closed the door before she could get her name.

She shrugged. She didn't see her pill on the tray. "Hey, you forget my Neuroxitine," When there was no response, she knocked on the door. She called out several times but the doctor was gone.

She sighed and sat on her bed and inhaled swirling eddies of goodness. It smelled amazing. She cut a bite and enjoyed and followed with some potatoes and an asparagus sprig. She washed it down and took another bite of the filet. More potatoes. Drink. Another sprig. She'd eaten her meat so she figured it was time to try the mousse. It was heavenly. Absolutely to die for. She took a second bite and worked on the rest of the meal. Before she finished, she started to feel like Thanksgiving Day afternoon. She blinked, and exhaled. She felt… dizzy. She shook her head and blinked again. Everything was fuzzy, and suddenly double. She dropped the knife. The fork slipped next. Her eyes closed. The tray crashed on the floor. Her eyes sprang open, and then…

Sixty-Four

Suzanne sat in the waiting room, crying into her palms. All around, whispers of sorrow reminded her that Alex was gone. She looked up and around. The room was white with shades of browning gray and black, like vintage sepia with an old-western flare. Everyone was asleep and dressed as they were the day Alex had died. Ryan sat contorted in the chair next to her. Across the room, one elderly woman's head rested on her friend's shoulder. A small string of drool hung from a corner of the friend's mouth. Eugene Lee was in a wheelchair, his neck at an odd angle. Dr. Boyd, P.A. Tran, and Office Manager Marcy were spread around on the laminate floor and curled up like fetuses. Between them, a large black spot marked where Eugene nearly bled out. The wall that Ryan bulldozed with a guard remained broken.

Alex appeared, dressed in his Harry Potter pajamas that were one or two sizes too small—the same pair he was wearing when he died. He ran toward her from treatment. He smiled and yelled something, but no sound escaped. All she could hear was Marcy's snoring and the smacking of a grandma's tongue.

Alex lipped, "Mommy, Mommy, Mommy, I missed you," and soundlessly laughed as he continued barreling toward her from the hall that seemed much longer than she remembered.

She spread her arms and wrapped them around Little Clown. She gripped him tightly—almost too tightly.

Ryan opened his eyes and said, "Wake up, wake up, we gotta go."

She shook her head violently, held their son even tighter, and said, "We can't leave Alex again."

Suzanne opened her eyes. Ryan was shaking her shoulder. She saw empty arms. Alex was gone, and she was sitting in the waiting room. Everyone sleeping in the dream was now milling about in dim but colorful surroundings. Everyone was wearing the clothes they'd had on three weeks earlier, except Eugene, who wore blue surgical scrubs and slippers. His blood pool, smear, and polka dots that covered much of the floor had been removed, and the wall was repaired.

Her head pounded, but her worries had drained away. She felt an overwhelming sense of peace. In her mind, she held Alex's hand as they skipped through a rainbow-colored field of flowers while her daddy, Ira, watched in the distance.

"Seriously, Suzanne—shake it off! We need to get gone before the press gets here. I scouted outside. Wherever they were holding us isn't there anymore, but there're big rig prints in the field across the street. The lab must've dismantled the facility and moved out after they drugged us and dumped us. Oh, and it snowed last night." He paused.

She was listening but distracted by visions in her head.

"Suzanne. Suzanne! Are you okay?"

She didn't respond and continued gazing forward into Elysian fields. She saw her boy and felt his presence within her. Her lips fixed into a smile.

Sixty-Five

Before dawn, Dark Tuesday, October 2, 2007, Packer City Area Medical Center.

Ryan nodded at Dr. Boyd who looked as worried as he was about Suzanne. She wasn't right. Her eyes were glazed as if possessed and she had a joker grin that made him imagine someone wearing a strait jacket. He suspected the lab had failed to make sure she took her meds.

P.A. Tran and Manager Marcy left the room and returned with water bottles and blankets. They distributed them to the five in the frigid waiting area. Ryan covered Suzanne. He opened a bottle and put it to her lips. She drank but didn't take her eyes off a blank spot on the wall. He finished the bottle and left her sitting there while he looked for their keys. He saw them lined up with everyone else's on the reception desk by the phone. Ryan shoved them in a pocket, picked up the receiver, and heard a dial tone. He punched in his mom's number. She answered as if she'd been waiting.

"Mom, this is Ryan. You near town?"

"Oh, it's so good to hear your voice. But no, sweetie. I'm back in Grand Junction. I got word the lockdown's being lifted today. So, how're you and Suzanne gettin' along?"

"Not good. The lab drugged us, then dumped us in the waiting room, and bolted last night. We just woke up a few minutes ago."

"What? Why would they do such a thing? What is wrong with these people?" she asked, anger seeping through every syllable.

It was a question he'd asked more times than he could count and one he wished he could answer. "Is Dad home?"

"No. He left this morning before I woke up. He's on his way to Fort Collins to meet with Attorney General Russell Phillips. They're delivering a subpoena to Helix Eternal Laboratories. Russell wanted to make a statement, so he's delivering it himself. I'm sure it'll be on the news later. I'll call James and let him know what the lab did to y'all last night. I'm sure Russell will be very interested. Drugged and dumped in the waiting room. That is jus' pure madness."

Ryan heard his mother exhale through her nose. After a few furious seconds, she continued. "Anyhow, I just woke up, but I'm heading to Packer City this morning to help you and Suzanne any way I can."

"Thanks, Mom, but don't bother. I'm packing some things, then we're heading your way. I gotta get away from this place, or I'm gonna explode. I've been thinking long and hard these past three weeks, and I've decided to sell the restaurant and the Watchtower and move back to Grand Junction. I mean, unless Suzanne objects, but I can't imagine she will after what we've been through. There's nothing left here but bitter tears and fading memories. I guess I can go back to school and become a lawyer like Dad wanted me to be."

"That would make your daddy happy, but that's not important right now. We just want to be here for you and Suzanne. We're gonna need each other to get through this. After that, we'll support whatever y'all decide to do. We love you both and can't wait to see you and Suzanne this evenin'."

"Yeah. Can't wait to see you guys. I'd like to talk more, but I gotta get Suzanne out of here before the press shows up and starts hounding us for an exclusive."

"I completely understand. I'll see you soon. Bye, sweetie. I love you."

"Bye, Mom. I love you, too."

He hung up and regarded Suzanne. Her eerie, blissful expression remained unchanged. He helped her stand and adjusted the blankets around her. He held one arm as they stepped outside and were greeted by frosty pre-dawn air. They walked through the fluffy layer of white that covered the parking lot. His damaged truck and Suzanne's Land Rover were parked where they'd left them. He glanced up and down the quiet aspen-lined street. He looked at their Land Rover. He couldn't bear to look inside, but they'd have to pick it up sooner or later, or leave it. He leaned to the latter.

He helped Suzanne into the truck, as she stared forward. She was now expressionless and her lips were a straight line. He shook his head as livid mist blasted from his nose. The sight stoked a fire that'd been smoldering for weeks. He gripped the steering wheel until his brown knuckles turned white and the wheel molded to his grip. He relaxed and studied the permanent impression. He breathed deep and exhaled, trying to do as his granddad had taught him. *Breathe in the good. Breathe out the bad.* Shit wasn't working.

He tried to picture Alex's face but all he saw was his limp body as he handed his lifeless corpse to Lei Tran. *Where did they take him? Maybe Suzanne knows,* he thought in tones that were less than sound. But his mind was sound enough to know not to ask—not in her current state.

He had asked the doctor assigned to his containment unit but never got an answer. In fact, that dick never spoke at all when he slid his meals through the slit of his unit's ridiculous, over-the-top heavy door that might stop a charging elephant, or when he extended his arm through the slit for periodic blood draws. It seemed as if the lab wanted him to feel isolated, which made him angrier and intensified the nightmares about more than just the lady from the lake. His mind drifted as he turned onto Lake Hotchkiss Road. He fantasized about murder.

He rounded the bend where he'd rescued the woman one month earlier. His fingers tingled, and his arm hair stood at attention. Tingling became red-hot needling. Blue static sparked from his fingertips as the strange blue aura returned. He glanced at Suzanne. She was still in her stupor. The burning radiated down his arms and legs, until every muscle was on fire. Darkness engulfed him, consumed him, pushed outward, making him feel as if he might *literally* explode. He took a deep breath. *Keep it together. Keep it together. Keep it together*, he repeated in his mind until, like water over natural flame, the fire was extinguished and the darkness dissolved.

Sixty-Six

7:07 a.m., October 2, 2007, The Watchtower.
Suzanne entered the Octagon and went to the tall windows by Grandpa Edwin's rocking chair. She gazed at the panorama. It was oddly dark out—full dark—but she could still see shadowed peaks that would soon be dawn-colored then white with snow-covered aspens and pines. She started weeping.

She turned to the dining room where Ryan stood watching her with a kind smile and dry eyes. She knew he ached to hold her but was respecting her time with the view that she loved along with the happy, sad, and heartbreaking memories at their castle on Tower Rock. She thought about the last bitter words she spoke. How she agonized over them. It wasn't his fault Alex died or that he was unable to bring him back a second time. Yes, Ryan had the power of his ancestor, Healing

Hands, but it was a power he couldn't control. A*t least, I have my memories and dreams,* she thought. She smiled softly at her tall dark knight. She would apologize without words, but not yet.

She turned back to the view, sniffed, wiped the tears, and held back the ones that wished to follow. She wanted to remember the good and put the rest on the shelf which was about to break. After her eyes had their fill, she headed upstairs to Alex's bedroom. Ryan followed.

She looked at the unmade bed and the dried blood and vomit on the floor. Alex's toys and books were sitting where he'd left them. She went to his bed, crawled in, and wrapped his blankets around her. She placed her nose against his pillow, inhaled deeply, and closed her eyes.

Sixty-Seven

The wonderous illusion with Alex ended and Suzanne found herself alone in his room again. Strangely, she wasn't sad anymore. A lull in despair it might've been, but she'd just had the time of her life with Alex and her father in the land of dreams. She kissed Alex's pillow, got up, and saw that Ryan had cleaned the floor. She smiled, went to her bathroom, and took a long, hot shower.

She dried off and dressed in forest green sweatpants and a matching CSU sweatshirt. She snagged several photo albums from one of the two bookcases in the bedroom and carried them to the sectional by the fireplace.

The sliding glass was open. It was still dark out, like a solar eclipse if the moon forgot to move on. Or as if dawn forgot to arrive. Or like God had covered the area with his hand as far as she could see.

Ryan stood on the front deck in several inches of snow, looking over the black steel railing. He was dressed in warm boots, faded blue jeans, and the ugly Christmas sweater she'd given him as a joke.

"Ryan, come sit with me," she said loud enough to hear over the whistling wind. She turned on the lights to brighten the Octagon.

"The Fitzgeralds have company," he said as he stomped off the snow and stepped inside. He wiped his eyes. "I wonder how long it'll be before Jeremiah and Sarah come up. I really hope they don't. I don't want to see anybody today."

"Ryan, you know they only mean well. They'll want to know what they can do to help."

"I know. I know. Boy, it's dark out there. That seem weird to you?"

"Yeah, kind of."

"Uh-huh, kind of like there's a glitch in the matrix or something. And damn, it's cold."

"Maybe God's grieving as much as we are," she said.

Ryan glanced at her, nodded, and tried to smile. He stepped back outside, grabbed some firewood from the shed by the back door, closed the sliding glass, and started a fire.

When the pine was popping and the room was warmer, he joined her on the sectional. She scooted close, and for the next hour, they laughed and cried as they flipped through page after memory-filled page.

Ryan opened the last album and asked, "I hate to ask this, but I gotta know. Did anyone say what happened to Alex's remains? I asked, but no one would tell me anything. All I got was the silent treatment from my doctor and that made things so much worse."

"I'm sorry to hear that," she said. "I wish you would've had my doctor. Her name was Johanna Müeller. She was a sweetheart and had this pleasant Dutch or German accent, but nothing like that mean green-eyed bitch from the CDC. Yeah, Johanna always tried to make me feel better about Alex. Talking about how things are in Heaven. Like she knew. As if she'd been there. I think she even infected me with joyful dreams of Alex and my daddy. That's probably why I'm not more of a basket case right now." She released a melancholy chuckle as Ryan stroked her back. "I know, relatively speaking. I thought Johanna was a little crazy but, you know, nice crazy. I know I wasn't the best company, but she never stopped trying to get me to open up. I finally did last week. That's when I asked where they'd taken Alex's body. She told me they moved him to the lab facility in Fort Collins. When I asked if they were going to return him for burial, she said they couldn't risk spreading the virus." Suzanne glanced at Ryan.

He was staring forward with a thin line of lips.

She continued. "Well, after that, she looked really sad like she wanted to say something else. But she didn't. She just told me how sorry she was. I don't know what for. She didn't do anything to me. It was weird... like she was keeping a secret she was afraid to tell. Then she entered my unit and sat next to me. Again, she acted like she wanted to tell me something but stopped. I asked what was wrong, and she told me she knew what I was going through. Said she lost her entire family. Never got to say goodbye to any of them, and they were never buried. I think she'd seen some horrific things in her life. I really wanted to know what happened to them but didn't press her. I just couldn't—she was crying under her hood. I didn't know what to say. So, I hugged her. Last night, she was gone and I had a different doctor.

Look, let's take a break," she said and shut the photo album in his hands.

Sixty-Eight

Ryan set the photo album on the couch, and put his arms around Suzanne. The tingling and burning returned, but there were no sparks, and the burning was different, soothing, like steam from water poured over hot rocks in a sweat lodge or sauna. And there was no darkness—only intense light.

He leaned in to kiss her. She stopped him, stood, took his hand, and led him upstairs to the bedroom. Once there, she removed her sweatshirt and pants and stood wearing only pink underwear. She laid on the bed, removed the underwear, held them for a second, and dropped them on the floor. She eyed Ryan and smiled seductively.

He closed the blinds, stripped, and started tenderly kissing her navel. He inhaled lavender and peaches. Oh, how he'd missed it. His lips caressed her smooth skin and inched toward her flawless breasts. When they arrived, his tongue and a finger played ring around the rosy areola. He kissed her neck and nibbled an ear as she licked her lips and wrapped her legs around his waist.

She flipped him onto his back, positioned him, and moaned as he slid inside. She started slowly but soon her hips gyrated as he met every thrust with perfect synchronicity.

He rolled Suzanne and continued the rhythm as sweat dripped from his forehead. She smiled as her emerald eyes locked onto his, piercing his soul. There was a flash of blue, but he buried the errant thought in the passion of the moment. She moaned louder as he thrusted faster. Her movements became convulsive until the climax, her scream, and his collapse into her embrace.

When she caught her breath, Suzanne grabbed his chin and kissed him. Their tongues flickered and curled. She kept her legs wrapped around him and he enjoyed her warmth as they continued kissing. He'd missed her more than words could express and hoped a seed would take root and life would grow from the soil of tragedy.

Sixty-Nine

Suzanne released Ryan. He rolled onto his back, and they laid speechless for some time, sweat glistening in the dimness as steam rose from their bodies in the cold bedroom.

Ryan broke the silence. "Hey, let's move back to Grand Junction. I'm talking—let's leave today. I can't stay in this house or this town any longer. I just can't."

"I know. Neither can I, but let's stay the night. I just don't feel up to the drive today. And anyway, I want to have dinner here one more time. I'll make Alex's favorite: tortilla soup. Maybe his ghost will show up and bring us a smile and maybe a few laughs," she said with a soft lip curl that quickly faded. "We've been through so much, and I just... I just need to honor Alex and the good memories we had here, you know, before we leave this castle forever. And body or no body, he'll have a beautiful monument in Grand Junction next to where we'll be buried one day."

She kissed Ryan and went to the bathroom, showered, dressed in what she'd been wearing and went downstairs to the kitchen while Ryan cleaned up.

She searched the pantry and cupboards for missing ingredients, jotting several on a notepad. By the time she finished her list, Ryan was standing by the kitchen island. She tore off the sheet and handed him the list.

"You mind picking up a few things at Earth First?"

"Sure. I just gotta swing by the restaurant and call Mom to let her know we won't be coming today. I told her we were earlier. But, no biggie. She'll understand." He kissed her and headed to the garage.

She followed him to the truck and watched him back up and turn on the one working headlight. She waved with one hand and held the other against her womb.

Ryan returned the gesture as the garage door closed.

She staggered. She shook her head, then dragged herself through the dining room. She felt achy and wobbly. She studied the back of her right hand and saw a small red blotch. She touched it. The skin was numb. She hadn't noticed the spot when she took a shower.

She stepped into the downstairs bathroom, removed her sweatshirt, and noticed more blotches on her chest and arms. She touched them. Nothing. Her fingertips felt numb as well.

She put the sweatshirt back on, stepped into her bunny slippers, and went upstairs to Alex's bathroom. She grabbed the ear thermometer and checked her temperature. It was normal. She took a deep breath. *Don't panic. Don't panic,* she thought as she started to panic. She had no explanation for the strange symptoms that began an hour earlier. At first, she chalked it up to fatigue or a hangover from whatever the lab spiked her dinner with the previous night. Whatever was going on, Dr. Boyd would know how to help or send her someplace that could. But it would have to wait until tomorrow. The medical center was closed for the day, and she didn't want to bother Dr. Boyd or P.A. Tran, who'd gone through the same ordeal as she and Ryan. And she definitely wasn't telling Ryan. He would just call them anyway or rush her to Grayson or wherever in the world she needed to go. No. Nothing was getting in the way of Alex's dinner and their final night at the Watchtower.

With each passing moment, she felt worse. She breathed deeper to calm herself. It sort of worked, but would've worked better if she'd had her meds. She couldn't understand why the CDC had done what they did to her, Ryan, and the others. She didn't dwell on it; she had plenty of other things to keep her mind reeling. She felt cold. She grabbed Alex's blanket and wrapped it around herself. It helped, but it wasn't enough, either.

She headed downstairs, grabbed her heavy jacket from the closet by the front door, put it on, and sat in the rocking chair. She picked up the near completed Miller novel, leaned back, and lost herself in the final chapter.

Seventy

9:43 a.m., Dark Tuesday, October 2, 2007, Mount Capitol Suites.

Mary was shaken from her slumber by the din of vehicles driving up the steep hill into the parking lot. She heard voices outside the window. She looked at the alarm clock she forgot to set. It read *9:43* with a red dot by the *AM*. "No, no, no. Damnit!"

She hopped from bed, ran to the window, and peeked outside. It was still dark. Maybe the clock is wrong. She glanced again but her eyes hadn't deceived her. She peered back outside.

The night before, the parking lot was empty except for Raj's pickup. Now, every space was filled with news vans, cars, and trucks covered with a thin layer of snow.

She ran to the window overlooking the town. She could make out a crowd a few blocks away milling around the bridge over the river that dissected the town. The small bluff obscured the near part of downtown on the right. She thought about Raj. How she wished she could see him once more. She'd hoped to surprise him before she left, but now it was too late. It was probably for the best. She put it out of her mind. She had to focus. She had to find the Menders and warn them. *But how am I gonna do that now?* she thought.

She flipped off the TV that was playing an old movie she'd never seen. The night before, she'd planned to get to bed early for a pre-dawn start. That was before she checked the guide and saw *It's a Wonderful Life* was on channel nineteen. She'd felt sacrilegious watching it before Halloween, but she couldn't resist. Watching the classic on her birthday eve was a tradition she and Peepa had strictly observed for as long as she could remember, and a movie she'd been unable to watch since he died. But after saying goodbye and seeing Raj wrecked, she was crushed and needed a pick-me-up. So, she thought, *What could it hurt*?

She made it to the closing scene before her eyes drifted shut when Zuzu Bailey said, "*Every time a bell rings, an angel gets its wings.*" The voice in her head lied when it said her eyes would stay shut for only a few minutes. *Damn you, George Bailey!* But it wasn't his fault. It was her fault—everything was always her fault.

She looked at the clock again. It had to be wrong. Regardless, the direct approach was impossible with all the activity in town, but it didn't matter anymore. She had no choice. She had to find Suzanne Mender before her husband touched her.

Mary slowed time as she put on a Mountain Dew t-shirt, an aqua dryride, and a pair of long johns. She slid on loose-fitting jeans, cinched up a black leather belt, and pulled on boots over wool socks. She tucked her hair under a Seattle Mariners beanie and put on a southwest-patterned snowboarding jacket. She crammed the pockets with snacks and a bottle of water, then she slid on the large backpack, and adjusted the frame to fit.

She looked at the clock, still disbelieving. *9:44* and still dark. *Damnit.* She shook her head and flipped the hood over the beanie. With head down, she opened the door and stepped outside.

Two reporters stood by the next room, talking about an old man who was giving interviews at the medical center. They paid her no mind as she strolled around the side and down the hill to the main road.

She rounded the bluff, saw the medical center, and was surprised to find the containment facility gone. Across the street, several news crews had packed the medical center parking lot. Besides news vans and vehicles that didn't belong in the mountains, she saw an old red pickup and a green Land Rover, but not the white truck Mender was driving when he rescued her from the lake. She recognized the red truck since it had almost hit her head-on when she drove into town in Mr. Anderson's Jeep. The Land Rover gave her a glimmer of hope. She could see someone like Suzanne Mender driving something like that.

Maybe they're still there. I gotta walk faster. Gotta get past this. Then I can warp. Maybe I can even beat them home, she thought.

She kept her head down as she passed the clinic. Her hopes were dashed when she overheard a disappointed reporter say that all the patients were gone, except for a Vietnam veteran. The veteran had been shot by a Black Beret, almost died, and was currently ranting in the cold under camera lights. The lone patient was in a wheelchair by the entrance. His face was red and angry and he seemed unbothered by the frosty weather as he yelled and spat responses at the reporters. Unfortunately, little of the interview would remain after editing for profanity. If what she heard was true, there was little hope of saving Suzanne Mender now, but she had to try, even if chances were slim to none.

She took a step to run and felt a tap on her shoulder.

"Hi, I'm Julie Florid of WNN Denver. Would you be willing to answer a few questions concerning your experience during the lockdown, claims of harassment, and illegal searches by H.E.L.'s security force during the first two days of the lockdown?"

Mary looked into the rolling camera and lowered her face. She replied in a deep, masculine voice, "Uh, I have nothing to say. I, um, don't wish to be interviewed."

The reporter cocked her head sideways and raised an eyebrow.

Seventy-One

Julie Florid watched the warmly dressed boy or man or masculine-sounding female or… She wasn't sure as the face bounced like a pinball in her head. Her cameraman kept the video trained on the snowboarder for several seconds, then turned his attention to the next, hopefully, more agreeable prospect.

"Hi, I'm Julie Florid…"

"Darlin', I know who you are. You're that famous reporter from WNN," the woman said in an exaggerated southern drawl, unexpected in the middle of Nowhere, Colorado.

The woman was heavy-set, buxom-boobed, with an extra-body blonde perm. She was underdressed for the weather but overdressed for the morning as if she was waiting to be asked for an interview.

"Well, ma name is Charlotte Lee, and I would be honored to give you an interview about this sham of a quarantine and those terrible Black Berets, and most importantly, the loss of revenue at my coffee shop over the past three weeks. Oh, and also about my sweet Eugene almost getting killed. That's him over there, finishing up an interview." She waved at Eugene.

He didn't gesture back. He was in the middle of a tirade.

"Bless his heart. After he's done with this last interview, I have to take him home. But I can meet you in an hour for an exclusive interview at my coffee shop, *Charlotte's Espresso: Home of the World Famous Frespresso*. Would... would that be okay?"

"Um, that, that would be great. We'll meet you there in an hour."

"Lookin' forward to it, darlin'. I'll have a Frespresso whipped up for you and your crew. You will love it. I gawrantee."

Seventy-Two

9:45 a.m., Dark Tuesday, October 2, 2007.

Ryan went the back way to the restaurant, parked behind the building, and came in through the rear door. He stopped and looked around. He closed his eyes, and let good memories roll. He opened his eyes and they faded into the empty darkness. He bit his lip, and breathed heavier. The corners of his eyes moistened. He shook his head slowly, then went to the rotary phone by the register and dialed his mom's number.

"Ryan, have y'all left yet?" asked Norine.

"Mom, I spoke to Suzanne. She's not up to the drive today, but we're heading your way first thing tomorrow. She's making tortilla soup tonight in Alex's honor. We'll probably just sit around and go through more old albums and cry ourselves to sleep."

"Tortilla soup, huh? Little Clown just loved that stuff. Well, I hope y'all have a nice night. Y'all have been through… *too* much. It's probably for the best you come tomorrow anyhow. Your daddy won't be back from Fort Collins until late. He and Russell went there this morning to deliver a subpoena to H.E.L.'s headquarters."

"Yeah, you mentioned that."

"Yeah, that's right, I did. Well, can you believe that lab was cleaned out when your daddy and Russell got there?"

"Really? What the hell?"

"Yeah, what the H.E.L.? I told James about them drugging y'all and leaving everyone in the waiting room to sleep it off while the lab skipped town. I mean, how dangerous is that, especially with them old folks? Well, James was speechless. He told Russell and he was just as perplexed. He's already contacted the feds. James has his suspicions about what's *really* going on but he wouldn't give me any details. Said they need more evidence before they can proceed. But he did say they believe that missing woman is involved and that Uncle Mel's death was somehow related to the illegal searches during the lockdown."

Ryan's fingers tingled. His muscles burned. *What the fuck? I can't talk about this right now,* he thought. "Mom, I gotta go. I have to pick up a few things for dinner and get back to Suzanne. We'll talk more tomorrow."

"Okay, dear. You bring us some of that tortilla soup if you have any leftovers. We love Suzanne's as much as Alex did. Your daddy hates to admit it, but he likes hers even better than he did his mama's. Anyhow, I'll let you go. Give Suzanne a big hug and a kiss for me and we'll see you soon, sweetie."

"I will. Bye now." He hung up, took a last look around, and left.

Ryan pulled into Earth First Food Market two blocks away. He crunched through snow, stomped his feet, and stepped inside. After grabbing what he came for, he got into the only checkout line.

The male clerk looked up and glanced down when he saw who it was.

Ryan handed him a credit card and bagged the items.

"You need your receipt?" asked the clerk.

"Nah. I don't need one."

"Hey, I'm... I... I was really sorry to hear about Alex."

"Yeah. Yeah, thanks. I appreciate you," said Ryan, like he meant it. He grabbed the bags and headed for the exit.

Before he could crunch back into the snow, a spray-on-tan male reporter blocked his way. His cameraman was rolling a few steps behind him.

"I'm Kenneth Prattle from KNW News. You're Ryan Mender."

"Last I checked," he said with a *fuck-off* bite.

"Well, um, would you be willing to answer a few questions about the lockdown and your son's tragic death?"

"No. No, I wouldn't be willing to give a bloodsucker like you an interview," he replied as his fingers tingled.

Spray-On-Tan Man must've known better. Since the end of *Berets*, it was common knowledge that the former star of Nathan Miller's brainchild was no lover of the press. But his disrespect was cavernous for outfits like KNW and their tabloid shit they passed off as news.

Prattle made a cut motion. "I know you don't like reporters, but I really need this interview," he pleaded. "And I... and I can make it worth your while—really." He motioned for his cameraman to resume recording.

Ryan grit his teeth and took a deep breath through his nose. He wanted to punch the reporter in the face, but then Spray-On-Tan Man would have an exclusive that would make him famous. It would also complicate Suzanne's and his situation. His muscles burned, and his fingertips felt like they were being stung by angry hornets. He shook his head and tried to step around the reporter.

"Please. Just something. Anything," Prattle begged with a lightly placed hand on the ex-Ranger's chest.

Ryan's eyes went wide as he gently grabbed the man's wrist and removed the hand from his chest.

"Owww. Goddammit. What the... Cut. No, don't cut."

Ryan regarded the light weight rubbing his wrist like it'd been smashed with red hot iron. He scoffed, stepped around Spray-On-Tan Man, and bumped him on the way.

"Thanks for nothing, and you'll be hearing from my lawyer," spat Prattle as he continued rubbing his wrist.

Ryan set the groceries in the truck, got into the pilot seat, and cranked the engine. He flipped into reverse, spun around, and kicked up snow and mud, adding more brown to the white KNW van as he sped out of the parking lot.

Seventy-Three

10:25 a.m., Dark Tuesday, October 2, 2007, Charlotte's Espresso: Home of the World Famous Frespresso.

Charlotte Lee pulled up in a new black Lexus. She was ten minutes early much to the relief of Julie Florid and her crew. They were itching to get started, before calling it an all-but-wasted morning.

The big, buxom woman squeezed out of her luxury sedan and waddled toward Julie. She smiled and tried not to laugh. Since driving her husband home in his old rusty pick-up truck, she'd changed into something pink and flashy and one or two sizes too small. She wore so much makeup that she could've been mistaken for Tammy Faye Messner when she was still married to the disgraced televangelist Jimmy Bakker.

Charlotte waved as she rocked back and forth and said, "Welcome, y'all! Come on into my humble establishment." She unlocked and opened the door.

Julie, her assistant, Joni, and cameraman, Clyde, walked inside.

Charlotte followed. "Let me whip you up those Frespressos like I promised, then we can get started with my interview."

Julie smiled professionally and suppressed a chuckle. "It'll only take Clyde and Joni a few minutes to set up. I'd like to do the interview outside with the medical center and the snow-covered field in the background, you know, where the CDC's containment facility was located."

"Heavens, no. I think it would be much nighsah inside. It's so dark and dreary this morning for some God-awful reason. Yes, right over here, dear. That's the perfect spot." She pointed to the corner where an ornate wood-carved version of the sign outside hung on the wall. "Really captures the ambiance, don't you think?" Charlotte laughed in a hardy high pitch, then answered for her, "Of course you do."

Julie buried her annoyance and nodded at Clyde. He went to the van and brought in his equipment. While she waited, Julie walked along a wall packed with celebrity photos and autographs. Among the famous faces were Norine Jasmine Jones, Ryan Mender, Whitney Houston, Tupac Shakur, Snoop Dogg, Steven Tyler, Nathan Miller, Stephen King, Trey Parker, Matt Stone, Matthew McConaughey, and many, many more. She wondered why she'd never heard of the place.

Once Clyde and Joni were ready, Charlotte handed each a Frespresso, then sat in a chair across from Julie. Joni set her drink on a nearby table and attached Charlotte's microphone to her hot pink dress next to a bulging bosom.

"Are you ready?" asked Julie.

"Uhh, well, yes, but first, aren't y'all gonna try the Frespressos?"

"We will... after the interview."

Charlotte lifted one eyebrow and sighed deeper than necessary.

"Okay, here, I'm taking a sip. Mmmm. That... that's really good," she said. It was really good. *This thing is like crack, I mean, I haven't done crack, but I think this thing's spiked with a little,* she thought and continued sipping until her brain froze.

"Yeah, this drink's dope," Clyde said in a husky voice. "Starbucks doesn't have anything on you."

Charlotte smiled wide like a drug dealer and regarded Joni, who smiled back and picked up her drink. She sipped. She paused. Her eyebrows rose. She nodded, gave a thumbs-up, and kept sipping until the drink was gone, then made annoying slurping sounds until she'd sucked up every last drop.

After Julie and Clyde finished their drinks, Joni gave one more thumbs-up. Julie nodded, and Clyde pushed record.

"This is Julie Florid from WNN, bringing you an exclusive interview with Charlotte Lee from her café, *Charlotte's Espresso*, in downtown Packer City…"

"Ummm, darlin', please say the whole name."

Julie bit her lip and flipped on a smile. "*Charlotte's Espresso: Home of the World Famous Frespresso.*"

Charlotte nodded her approval.

She continued. "Earlier, I interviewed your husband, Eugene Lee, concerning his life-threatening injuries at the hands of the H.E.L.'s security contractors. Charlotte, how is your husband dealing with this traumatic experience?"

"Oh, he's doin' jus' fine, bless his heart. He's sittin' at home right now. Of course, this is nothin' compared to what he dealt with in the 'Nam when he single-handedly saved his whole platoon. Or when he stood shoulder to shoulder with that great American patriot Brigham Norsworthy. You know, he was my sweet Eugene's cousin, may the good Lord bless his soul," she said as she lowered her head to prayer hands and shut her eyes. She paused for a few seconds to show respect for the dearly departed, then raised her head and continued. "Terrible loss for our democratic republic. Brigham was a great man who stood up to our socialist government that is tryin' ta take away our right to defend ourselves. But I do digress. You asked me about my sweet Eugene. That man..." Her voice faux-faltered. She paused, feigned misty eyes, and continued, "... he jus', he jus' has amazin' fortitude. He'll pull through this jus' fine, especially after he wins that big lawsuit against that hor-ree-bull lab," she finished with a bright smile.

Julie fought to keep her eyes from rolling, her fingers fidgeting, and feeling irrationally more irritable. Charlotte failed to mention that Dr. Raymond Boyd and his Physician's Assistant, Lei Tran, saved her husband's life. And concerning Eugene's war record, she'd done her homework concerning Mrs. Lee's *sweet old man*. And this clown lady didn't want to get her started about Brigham Norsworthy, who was fifty-one cards short of a deck. Yeah. Eugene never saw *combat* and worked as a desk jockey during the war. And, and Brigham's so-called *militia* was nothing but weekend warriors who liked to play war. She'd lost an uncle in Vietnam and was tempted to call bullshit right there and then, but she wasn't there to debunk some old man's war fantasy or destroy the pretend patriotism of a second-amendment whacko. And, and, and... *What the hell was in that drink?* she thought.

Julie wrangled wandering thoughts, smiled, and asked the next question. "We've heard from your husband concerning his experience at the hands of, who many are calling, the *Black Berets*, but were you harassed in any way?"

"Oh, like everyone else in town, darlin'. Those Black Beret meanies forced their way into my coffee shop, ordered me to make them mochas, Americanos, and my specialty, Frespresso—which you must admit is a gustatory work of art. But anywho, back to my harrowin' tale. After I finished makin' all their drinks, they, they..." She sniffed, as her lips trembled. She appeared to mist up before continuing. "... they... they didn't even pay for the coffee and then grabbed all my biscotti before they walked out the door." She huffed. "It was jus' hor-re-bull, I tell ya."

Julie was sure Clyde caught her eyes rolling that time. She realized the interview was a complete waste and crossed out all but one question to speed things along. She was about to ask that question when she glanced at the bulletin board by the entrance. She had passed it several times while Clyde and Joni were setting up. Somehow, she failed to notice the wanted poster amongst flyers for local events on account of her star gazing the wall of celebrities. On the poster was a sketch of a woman's face.

She made a cut motion, and Clyde pressed pause. She went to the bulletin board as Charlotte sat nonplussed. Julie cocked her head to one side and examined the face on the poster. She read the description of the woman sought in connection with the murder of World War II veteran Melvin Anderson. She removed the poster, replaced the push pins, and continued examining the face.

"Ain't ya gonna ask me mo' questions?" asked Charlotte.

"Yeah. More questions. Sorry, I hate to do this, but we need to go. We'll let you know when you're going to be on TV. Thank you so much for your time." She reached over, removed Charlotte's microphone, and said, "Clyde, pack it up. We gotta go now!"

"Julie, I'll catch you in the van," said Joni. "I'm gonna grab another Frespresso."

"Yeah, get me one, too. That little concoction is out of this world," said Clyde.

"Might as well get me one, too," Julie anxiously added.

Charlotte folded her arms and smiled. "I told ya you would love it, but y'all have to pay for these. And before you go, if ya wouldn't mind too much, I would jus' love to snap a quickie of you for my little wall over there."

Julie sighed softly. "Sure. Why not?" she said with tensed lips.

Five minutes later, she and Joni sat slurping in the WNN news van, watching Clyde review an earlier video. He reversed the video to the teen or young adult who refused her request for an interview. Clyde paused a few frames before the teen looked up, then stepped the video forward frame by frame. He stopped when the face was clear. Julie looked at the poster, then at the screen.

"That's her, Clyde. That's her," she said, rubbing her lips. "Oh, my God! I gotta call Nate."

She grabbed her phone, punched in the boss's number, and glanced at her watch as the call connected. It was 11:06 a.m. Nate answered after two rings.

"Julie, how are things in Packer City?" he asked.

"Nate, you're not going to believe this. I have video of a dead ringer for the woman every police department in this state's been looking for since the Anderson murder. What do you want me to do?"

"Hmm. Well, we need to contact the Sheriff's office, but not quite yet. You know, once we do, every news station will have the same exclusive when the sheriff reports who you found. I can't imagine he'll be pleased, considering she's been hiding right under his nose. I trust you, so I'll let you run with this. I'll call Sheriff Maxwell after you go live."

Seventy-Four

10:27 a.m., Dark Tuesday, October 2, 2007.

Ryan passed Carson Horse Ranch south of downtown and saw a lone hiker heading the same way. Whoever it was wore a familiar-looking snowboarding jacket, jeans, boots, and a full backpack. He guessed it was Mount Capitol Suites' owner relieving some pent-up cabin fever. The man's name escaped him. He only knew him from crossing paths while climbing Gold Mountain.

He passed the hiker, whose hood was up and head down, as the elusive name tickled his tongue. He glanced in the rearview. It was too dark to see the man's face. Then he chuckled. "Oh, yeah, Raj... Raj from Portland." Cobalt eyes entered his mind. That wasn't Raj, but how could he be so sure? He didn't know, yet somehow he did. "Snip-snip," he said and chuckled again. He'd lost track of how many times he'd lost his mind in the past three weeks. And that lady from the lake—she was always there snipping the threads one by one—sometimes two or three. He wondered how many threads were left. He shook his head. "Nah, that's crazy. That was Raj. That girl's long gone... or dead," he said. The word sent a hot poker into his heart. He grabbed his chest with a shaky fist. He breathed faster. "Nuts! What the fuck!" The angina passed as his mind assured him that she was very much alive. "Yup. Snippy-snip-snip."

He turned onto Lake Hotchkiss Road and continued to the fork at the lake. He decided to turn left onto a dirt road that led around the southeast side to avoid anything that reminded him of the night he should've let that siren drown. He pressed the accelerator.

Seventy-Five

10:43 a.m., The Watchtower.

Ryan set the groceries on the kitchen island and stepped into the Octagon. Suzanne was asleep in the rocking chair in her snow jacket wrapped in Alex's Harry Potter blanket. Nathan's new novel was closed on her chest.

He let her sleep and put away the groceries. Once done, he sat on the sectional. The earlier fire was now dying embers that smoked on the hearth. He watched Suzanne's chest expand and contract as the book rose and fell with each breath. He thought how cute she looked in her CSU sweats and bunny slippers.

He laid back on a throw pillow and peered at the massive cedar beams and conical ceiling and through the skylight to the universe beyond. He sat up and glanced around at the paintings left behind by Brigham Norsworthy. His eyes focused across the room to the far dining room wall.

He chuckled under his breath. He couldn't fathom why this particular piece always seemed to capture his attention over the other equally bizarre canvases. He guessed it was the undulating, waving, flowing rivers and islands of surrealistic color that reminded him of Edvard Munch's freaky masterpiece *The Scream*. Yet, he was no art aficionado—quite the contrary. But who hadn't seen Munch's painting? His was closest in style to the Norsworthy with the mountain and the rook-shaped tower.

Around the tower, four massive ravens descended from four directions. Atop the tower stood a tall, bald, dark-skinned wizard in brown leather. His hands were raised out and upward. Cobalt light spiraled from his fingertips, wrapping around each monster bird. To the wizard's left stood a shorter pale-skinned woman with shoulder-length dirty blonde hair wearing gray-steel armor like Joan of Arc might've worn. The woman held an oversized, unbalanced sword, upright, ready to strike.

It was a strange piece, for sure, like the rest of Norsworthy's eclectic home décor left behind by his incorrigible children. Suzanne knew Ryan hated the paintings, but he never let on and tried to appreciate the whack-job's art. Whenever she asked his opinion for fun, he gave her a half-hearted grin and an unconvincing *"They're, uh, they're great, baby. Very unique."* But Suzanne and Alex loved the strangeness, and for that reason, he would miss the crazy old bastard's art collection when he and Suzanne said goodbye to the Watchtower in the morning.

He sighed, laid back, and joined Suzanne's slumber.

Seventy-Six

Suzanne's eyes grudgingly opened. Ryan was on the couch, snoring. She smiled and winced. She felt dreadful, far achier than she did when she read the final line of Miller's darkest novel to date. *"It was where I wished I was, and where I deserved to be."* It wasn't her favorite, but she knew it would do well like anything else with his name on it.

She looked at her hands. The blotches had grown, and there was no sensation in her hands. She unzipped the jacket, removed it, and dropped it to the floor. She felt her arms, legs, and chest. They were wet. At first, she thought it was perspiration, but her sweatshirt and pants were stuck to the underlying skin. She rolled up a sleeve, and her skin peeled off with it. *Ohhh, fuck. Oh, fuck. Oh, fuck,* she thought, wanting to scream, but not wanting to wake Ryan.

The blotches had grown and now extended up her arm. The center of each was ulcerated, moist, and necrotic. Blisters covered the remaining visible skin. She swallowed, tried not to cry, but failed.

She looked at Ryan, and an awful thought crossed her mind. *Uncle Mel. The woman from the lake. The first quarantine. Alex's death. Did you kill me too, Ryan?* No. No. The thought was too terrible to contemplate. Was Ryan infected with something the woman gave him that first night in September? All Suzanne knew was that she was dying. But from what? It was nothing like what Alex had. But if not Ebola, what was killing her so quickly? She had to know.

She shuddered as she struggled out of the chair, then staggered to the stairs, being careful not to wake Ryan. The stairs were dark. *My God, where is the morning?* she thought.

She flipped on the light, and took each step slowly, carefully, holding the rail. She barely managed to pull herself to the second floor. She stopped next to Alex's bedroom and turned on the game room lights. She fought for breath and felt like she'd run a marathon.

She swayed across the game room, tripping every few steps. She lost a slipper and shook off the other. Her green socks stuck to the hardwood, her every step making sickening pops as she dragged her feet to the bedroom. She turned on the light, went to the closest bookcase, and fell into a sitting position. She grabbed a dusty medical textbook from the bottom shelf entitled *Encyclopedia of Infectious Diseases.*

The subject once fascinated her when she still believed she'd one day be called Dr. Mender. She blew off dust and sneezed on the cover. She wiped the book clean with her sleeve, then flipped to the index to find pages concerning Hansen's Disease. It was impossible to think she was infected with *Mycobacterium Leprae* since the infection was rare in this day and age (especially in North America), and ninety-five percent of the world's population was immune to what was once called Leprosy. When it did occur, clinical signs took years to manifest. The disease had two forms. The more aggressive type was *lepromatous leprosy*, which caused disfiguring nodular skin tubercles (similar to what its bacterial cousins *M. tuberculosis* and *M. bovis* did to lungs). The less aggressive form, called *tuberculoid leprosy*, caused red patches, loss of skin sensation, and developed even more slowly. The end result, if improperly treated, was permanent skin, bone, and nerve damage, deformation of facial features, and occasionally death. A few of her symptoms resembled the tuberculoid form, but the rest made no sense because the disease was progressing exponentially.

Suzanne set the book on the cedar floor and tried to stand, but collapsed. With little strength to try again, she crawled to the bathroom and pulled herself up using the double sink countertop. She stood precariously on wobbly knees that wanted to buckle and gazed in the mirror as she peeled off her sweatshirt. She gasped. Her body was putrefying before her eyes. She wanted to scream. She wanted to cry some more. She definitely didn't want Ryan to see her like this. Whatever was killing her, she knew she wouldn't live long enough to reach help. Even if she did, it was too late.

She put her sweatshirt back on, gripped the walls, and staggered to the unmade bed. She laid down, and minutes later, the aching ceased.

Seventy-Seven

Suzanne smiled, happy to return to the delightful sepia-colored dream. Alex's face was above her. He was smiling, exposing the cute little gap between his teeth that matched his father's. Alex was still dressed in the pajamas he wore for the medical center dream.

"Mommy, you came back to see me again. I really missed you."

What? This is different. I hear his voice, she thought.

Alex hugged her. When he did, she saw an old man standing behind him by the deck windows. The man's hands were clasped at his waist. His eyes were dark and sad and his hair was yellowish silver in the strange light, unkempt, with hair poking out from under a black Stetson. Like his hat, everything he wore was black: trench coat, shirt, pants, and boots. That's when she realized she wasn't dreaming and that the Man in Black wouldn't be leaving alone.

She sat up and looked around as Alex held her tightly. To the left of the Man in Black were three black doors that blocked the one to the deck. She was unsure where the doors led but felt no fear to step through whichever was open as long as Alex was by her side.

Will I see Daddy soon? Suzanne thought hopefully and sighed with a melancholy smile. She turned to the Man in Black, and asked, knowing the answer, "Who are you? And... and what is this place?"

"Well, most people call me by my last name, Death, or since the great Plague several centuries back, the Grim Reaper. But those are just two of many. Can't say I like any of them. So, please call me by my first name, Morton. And this place," he said, spreading his arms, palms up, "It's called the White Room. It's part of the realm created for me, but I can come and go as I please. My job is to control this gateway between what is now your former reality and the place I'll take you and Alex soon—the land beyond the last breath known as the Afterworld." He pointed at the three black doors. "Through those doors is the so-called otherside. I'm here to guide you to a place where you won't have to deal with sickness and suffering and pain anymore. A place where you'll be happy forever in the paradise of your choice. Which, according to my sister Gladys—she takes care of my schedule. Well, according to her, you'll be headed to the Heavens of Christ—Mormon district to be specific. So please, if you could, walk to the door on the right, and I'll have you on your way to your final destination. I hear your daddy can't wait to meet his grandson."

Alex smiled. "I get to meet my other gamba. Awesome sauce!"

She laughed before the realization that she and Ryan would be separated smothered the joyous revelation. "Can I say goodbye to Ryan before we leave? I don't know what's going to happen to him once we're gone. I'm afraid of what he'll do, especially when he figures out what happened to us. I fear what he'll do to that woman who killed us. Somehow, I don't think she meant to."

Morton's expression was thoughtful but grim.

She watched him, said nothing, and waited for his response.

Morton went to one of the bookcases, took a book off a shelf entitled *Ghosts of Bosnia*, and flipped through the pages. He put it back with the rest of her Miller collection, sans his newest that was downstairs in a different reality. He picked up the next volume, and did the same. Still facing the bookcase, he said, "A fellow Nathan Miller fan. I love your collection, but I've never had the time to sit down, relax, and read any of his books. Still, I'm a big fan and have been since he was thirteen mortal years old. He's something of a curiosity to me... like your husband."

"Huh?" said Suzanne.

Morton set the book back on the shelf and turned. "Suzanne, I was in Almawt Lilkifaar when those suicide bombers hit Ryan and Nathan's convoy.

That day, I guided many on both sides to where they belonged, and some to places that they didn't. I've guided so many across these three thresholds, and I remember every mortal shell. How they died. Who they left behind. And of course, where I had to send them. People speak of cheating me as if I give a dang if they go on living in their reality. I'm happy Ryan was able to resurrect Alex and give you nine more months together. He's a great kid. No, when mortals no-show, it's less work for me, but Gladys always lets me know when an appointment's been missed. Your husband, Nathan, Travis Wright, John Smith, Maynard Coltrane... they weren't supposed to survive that day. While I have no idea why Travis, John, and Maynard are still alive, I suspect there's something big planned for Ryan and Nathan. I have my suspicions, but no one tells me anything. I'm just Morton Death—the one the Greeks called Charon. My one job is to guide underspirits to where they belong in the Afterworld. I'm not supposed to interfere with their affairs even though I know other Eternals do. Yes, like my younger brother and sister." He ground his teeth and sighed. *"But I won't delve into my family squabbles. Look—to move things along, I'll cheat a little and grant your wish. I have to say—you have one stubborn child,"* he said with a chuckle as he rustled a hand through Alex's curly hair. *"I see where he gets it, too. I gotta tell ya..."* He shook his head. *"That boy—when he died, he refused to leave his White Room. As you can imagine, I never have a slow day, and I wasn't about to argue with a seven-year-old who just wanted to say goodbye to his mom and dad."*

Alex looked up, grinned, and giggled.

Morton laughed and smiled with deep dimples that deepened wrinkles around his eyes and forehead. *"Yes, I had little choice but to leave him at the medical center. You see, mortals were created with free will to either move on with their afterlives or hang around in the White Room and haunt the living. But a soul can never leave the room where its mortal shell died except through a black door or by possessing another living shell, like Alex did to you this morning. What Alex did is frowned upon, and there are rules governing it..."*

he said, his aspect turning severe before his eyes gave his softer side away. "But... I'm gonna let it slide this time, you little clown," he finished with a soft smile. "Now that Alex is here with you, I don't want you both hanging around haunting this place 'cause you didn't get your way. So, let's head downstairs. But we need to move quickly while Ryan's asleep. That's the only time the living can see the dearly departed before they leave this reality. And, like I said, my workday never ends, and my queue is piling up as we speak."

Suzanne couldn't believe Death could be so kind. "Thank you, Morton. We won't be long. I promise."

She stood and gazed at her corpse. It looked horrific. She glanced at Morton, then back at the bed. The body was gone.

"Sorry about that. I usually tidy up my White Rooms so new immortals don't have to see what happened to their mortal shells. I just got distracted with your book collection. But hey, I'm only Eternal," he said with a wry grin.

"It's okay. I once wanted to be a doctor. It was just weird seeing my dead body."

"I can only imagine. I've never had one. Well, let's go."

She nodded, took Alex's hand, and followed Morton.

Seventy-Eight

Ryan felt warm fingers slide through his hair. He popped up and smiled at the sight of Suzanne sitting next to him with Alex standing by her side. The smile faded when he saw the old man in black who he'd seen once in a hospital waiting room moments before Alex died the first time. He ignored the meaning of the man's presence now as his smile returned. He extended his arms. Alex leaned in for the embrace, and Ryan kissed his cheek and forehead.

Alex opened his mouth, but no sound escaped. "I love you, Daddy. I'm going to miss you," he lipped.

Suzanne stood and took Ryan's hand. Alex took the other. The Man in Black led the way upstairs.

In the main bedroom, Ryan wrapped his arms around Suzanne and Alex between the bed and the black doors. He held on and didn't want to let go. From the corner of his eye, he saw the black door on the right creep open. The Man in Black tapped Suzanne's shoulder and Ryan's arms sank through her and Alex as if they were mist, leaving spiritual eddies as his arms wrapped in a self-hug.

Suzanne took Alex's hand and turned.

Ryan grasped at empty air as they moved toward the door.

The Man in Black entered first. Alex and Suzanne faced Ryan while the Reaper waited in the dark hall beyond the threshold.

Alex lipped, "Come see me and Mommy in Heaven soon. We'll be waiting for you."

Suzanne mouthed, "I will always love you, Ryan Bear Mender." She smiled softly as a tear trickled down her cheek.

They continued to the door. Alex looked back, and waved as they stepped into the hall to the otherside.

The door began to close.

Suzanne pushed it open and mouthed what looked like a warning.

Puzzled, Ryan said, "What? I, I don't understand!"

The Man in Black glared as he rocked a finger back and forth with eyes no longer gracious. He mouthed, "Stop!" The door slammed shut, and the black doors vanished.

Seventy-Nine

Ryan lurched up and cried, "Suzanne, Alex, don't leave me!"

He looked around. He felt confused, and then saw Grandpa Edwin's empty rocking chair. Suzanne's coat and Alex's blanket were on the floor. Her book was on the end table. He glanced around, then upstairs, and bounded to the second floor.

Halfway across the game room, he was greeted with the reek of rancid meat and saw wet sock prints. He gagged as he entered the bedroom. His eyes went wide when he saw Suzanne staring with once emerald eyes that were now spoiled and milky.

His shocked autopilot took control and checked for a pulse. There was none, but her wrist was warm. He tried CPR, but her sticky blue lips fell apart with each forced breath. Grief, confusion, and percolating fury churned as he thought about his latest nightmare. But there was no lying outside the subconscious. What he experienced in the dream was real, and he couldn't imagine a more sadistic joke than the one the Reaper had just played on him.

He took Suzanne in his arms and sobbed as he rocked back and forth. He prayed to Suzanne's God. He prayed to the Holy People whom his father and granddad believed held the answers. He prayed to anyone who might listen and give him one more healing miracle. One more resurrection.

Hope faded. Ryan laid Suzanne back on the bed and sat at her feet. He wiped his eyes, leaned forward, cupped his face, and seismically wept. Seconds passed as grief swirled into a wrathful maelstrom. A blue haze shimmered around him. He heard crackling like crumpling paper. Every muscle burned, compounding psychological trauma with physical torment.

He looked in the dresser mirror. The abyss of eyes was filled with flickering green flame and the whites were bruising dark blue. The veins on his head and neck rippled and pulsated the same cobalt as his body, the bed, and the floor quaked. His jaw suddenly unhinged and a bone-curdling roar blew out the windows. Suzanne's corpse shifted slightly.

Ryan flew to the wall. His fists started pounding like a jackhammer, leaving bloody smears. As sheetrock flew and timbers splintered, skin tore away, exposing flesh and bone. He paused to breathe and sob as skin healed without scarring. He screamed and resumed the smashing. He turned over bookcases. He tore the TV off the wall and threw it through a broken window. It clanged against the copper awning over the porchway and crashed on the rocks below. He shattered lamps and mirrors and pulverized end tables and chests of drawers.

He stomped into the game room, lifted the pool table like it was a feather, and threw it over the banister. It smashed against the sectional, breaking both into pieces. He twisted around, panting through clenched teeth, looking for something else to destroy. He saw Alex's open door and the rampage ceased like flipping a switch.

He stepped into his boy's room, sat on his bed, and thought of his silent words and his last wave goodbye. He looked at the nightstand where Alex had left a Harry Potter book on September 10. On top were his folded, round-rimmed and lens-less glasses. He ran a hand over the glasses and the book as he shakily held the other over his mouth.

He moved in a daze back to the wrecked room. He had no tears, though his eyes ached to cry. He stepped over debris from his bomb blast and sat at Suzanne's feet. He stared through a broken window and thought of the strange world with the three black doors. The door on the right led to where he, Suzanne, and Alex could be together forever. That gave him peace, but he knew he couldn't live another day in this reality without them.

He kneeled at Suzanne's corpse and held her purplish-red, clammy hand. It was colder now. "I'll see you and Alex soon," he said.

He kissed her forehead, then went to the walk-in closet, punched in the firearm-safe combination, and opened the heavy door. He surveyed his lethal options and eyed his Winchester shotgun.

Definitely would get the job done. Yeah. But kinda awkward. And really messy, too... He released a squeaky chuckle as thoughts bantered on the stormy seas of his fractured mind. *... Really messy. The Glock worked for the deer, but it's in the truck. And I don't want to leave Suzanne alone. Or maybe...*

He picked up the pearl-handled Smith & Wesson Model 27 he gave Suzanne years ago for self-protection. Since moving to Packer City, having it seemed silly and dangerous with a child in the house. She had locked it away in the safe and hadn't touched it since.

Ryan released the empty cylinder, opened the box of .357 Magnum cartridges, removed one, placed it in a charge hole, and closed the cylinder. He walked to the bed with the revolver dangling, and sat on the left side so he and Suzanne could sleep side by side one last time in this mortal world.

He laid the gun on the bed, lowered his head, and prayed. "Please forgive me for whatever I did to upset this universe. And forgive me for taking my life to escape this earthly Hell. And, and show me some mercy... Please... Let me be with Suzanne and Alex again in Heaven. Amen."

He picked up the revolver, inverted the grip, and shoved the grief-ending maw against the roof of his mouth.

Ding-Dong. Ding-Dong.

He snapped the gun from his mouth and threw it on the bed. "Seriously! Jesus Christ. What the fuck, Jeremiah?"

At least, he thought it was Jeremiah Fitzgerald, or maybe Sarah. Maybe it was Pete or Joe. Soon enough, they'd know about Suzanne's death and his suicide, but he didn't want to announce it like this.

He opened the deck door and yelled, "Be right down."

He went to the front door, glanced at the wreckage in the Octagon, then at the clock in the foyer. It read *11:13*. He rearranged his face to *everything's-great* and opened the door.

Eighty

To his surprise, the ding-donger wasn't the Fitzgeralds, Pete, or Joe. It was the hiker he passed less than an hour earlier at Carson Horse Ranch, ten miles away. Whoever it was, the hiker wasn't winded. But who was he kidding? He knew who it was.

The lady from the lake pulled back her hood.

He couldn't believe his eyes when he saw the face below the Seattle Mariners beanie. It was a face he'd seen only once and many times since in his waking thoughts and nightmares. It was the little girl in the dirty pink dress.

Before he could speak, the hiker introduced herself. "Ryan Mender, my name is Mary DeMure. I have to speak with you and your wife. Is your wife here? Is she well?"

His lips quivered as he trembled, searching for words. He finally found them filled with acid that could eat through steel. "She's dead, like my son and my granddad's best friend. What the hell are you? And what'd you do to me?"

Eighty-One

Mr. Anderson? Oh, fuck me, Mary thought and swallowed hard. Her voice broke as she said, "That's why I'm here. You need to know. May I come inside?"

"Sure. Why not? There's not much more of my life you can fuck up now, is there? So, come on in, answer my questions, then get the fuck out of my house. I'm a busy man. I have things to do, places to go, people to see," he said, stabbing her with every word.

Mary stepped inside, took off her backpack, and set it in the foyer.

Ryan crossed the Octagon and sat facing her in an old rocking chair.

She followed, stepping around the broken pool table and a scattered sectional until she was a few steps from him.

His fists were clenched and bitter contempt burned in his brown eyes. From where she stood, he could've easily bolted up and snapped her neck in one fluid motion. His eyes seemed to contemplate it. Part of her wished he would—end her suffering right there and then. She'd taken everything from him, and like her, he had nothing to live for except revenge. But the larger part needed to convince him not to exact that revenge on her. It sickened her to think of the mad General, Caine, and D'Amato getting away with what they'd done and were probably still doing. She needed Mender's help, yet regardless of her desire for justice that drove what self-preservation remained, she needed to test a theory. If wrong, Mender wouldn't have to break her neck and it would end here... at least for her. Whether or not Louis died for something would no longer be her concern, nor would anything else.

She stepped forward, knelt, and grabbed Mender's hand. She held it firmly.

Eighty-Two

"What the fuck!" Ryan scowled. He tried to withdraw his hand, but the lady named Mary held on tight.

Relaxxx. Don't fight thisss, said a seductive whisper from somewhere inside his head.

He obeyed as his eyes rolled back. He closed the lids and savored the sensation. It was better than the morphine after taking a 7.62 Soviet round in a shoulder. His fingers tingled, but the burning was gone. All fight had drained away.

Mary stroked his thumb with hers.

His eyes creaked open. He gazed hopelessly into those magical blues and asked from bottomless sorrow, "Why Alex? Why Suzanne? Why Uncle Mel?"

Eighty-Three

Mary's throat tightened. Her heart ached. She didn't answer. What could she say?

Mender lowered his head, gripped his forehead with his free hand, and shuddered as he wept.

Seeing him like this... justice no longer mattered. She only hoped his touch would end her life in some gruesome, agonizing way. *It's more than I deserve, but what if I'm right? What if he did do more than cure me?*

That was the thought, the theory, the epiphany that hit her on her warp to the Watchtower. What if those cured by these special healers were immune to whatever made them sick? It was a devilish concoction of pestilent ways to die that created the Touch within her and the others. What if Ryan consumed all that genetic baggage, incorporated every bit of that nastiness into his being, and somehow created a stronger, completely resistant Mary? What if Ryan fixed inside her the one quirk about Dr. Caine's formula that caught the General's attention? The one quirk that gave that sadistic fuck the idea to back Caine and D'Amato's sick experiments in exchange for assassins to carry out his take-over-the-world scheme. Nowhere in the book about Mender's family did the *Indestructible Nathan Miller* suggest a permanent curing effect. He only wrote that those healed were *"stronger than before being sick."* But what *if* that meant immunity? If she were wrong, it would be a terminal what if. She only wished Louis had told her more before he died. Either way, she would know soon.

Minutes passed, but her hand never burned. She felt only natural warmth and the wetness of Mender's tears. An intense burning was the first thing a victim felt, or so they screamed. Caine and D'Amato tried to correct the problem—to make the Touch imperceptible for the General's purposes. They failed. It was probably why he ordered the execution and disposal of her and the remaining lab rats. She thought of Louis's sightless stare behind the shield and the two black holes in the suit over his heart. She chewed her lip and her grip tightened. "We have to leave here, now," she said.

Ryan withdrew his hand and glared. "What's this *we*? You haven't even answered my questions."

"There's so much I need to tell you, but you have to trust me for now. A reporter saw me in town, and her cameraman caught my face. It's only a matter of time until they figure out who I am. When my face hits the news, Black Berets will come straight here to capture us both. And, uh, they won't be as nice as they were the first time they came into town."

"Who are these Black Berets?"

"They're private contractors—ex-Rangers, Seals, Marines, soldiers of fortune. They do security for the lab that ran the bullshit quarantine."

Ryan's face was pensive and severe.

"From your look, I take it you didn't hear what they did during that bullshit quarantine."

"I heard about 'em," he said, "but the ones I came across were dressed in hazmat suits. Real assholes."

"Yeah, they're all real assholes. Look, I promise I'll tell you everything once we get somewhere safe. For now, know this—Albert Caine and Antonia D'Amato's experiments are responsible for your wife's death and the death of your son and Melvin Anderson. And, I... I'm responsible for infecting you with what they put inside me. And like you, or, or me before you cured me, every living thing you touch will die..."

Mender sighed, closed his eyes, and gripped his forehead.

"... It's even worse if you're frightened, angry, or hate somebody. Even emotions like love and joy can do it. Your touch releases something into the victim—infectious diseases, cancers, or whatever else Dr. Evil and his whore bitch crammed inside me during their fucked up experiments—but the symptoms progress like wildfire. And after somebody dies, their body decays so fast it removes any trace of what killed them. Mr. Mender... I... I am so sorry..." Her eyes watered as she continued, "I wish I'd let the lab put me out of my misery and I wish you would've let me drown. But I can't change what's happened, and I can't bring back those you lost or replace anyone or anything the lab has taken from you... or me..." She sniffed. Her lips trembled. "... And they've taken everything. Please, let me try to make this right." She shook her head as tears trickled down. "I don't want these bastards to get away with what they've done or find out they've hurt anyone else. Come with me to Arizona. My friend Louis told me there's an old shaman there who lives near the Canyon de Chelly. He's a... he's a healer like you. Louis said he could cure me before you saved him the trouble. Maybe the shaman will know what to do with you, or teach you how to control the Touch. Until then, it's not safe for you to be around anyone except me, since I'm not dead... at least not yet."

"Who's Louis?"

"Damnit. We have to go."

Ryan's glare didn't waver.

"We—don't—have—time to talk about this right now. We have to get out of here unless you're dead set on taking our chances with our army of two. Like I said, I'll tell you everything later."

Mary strolled to the foyer, hands shaking.

Ryan stood. "Okay, I'll go with you and help you find this healer. My family knows a Hataalii. That's what the Navajo call their medicine men. But I'm not exactly sure where he lives. I just know he lives somewhere around Chinle on the rez. Who knows? Maybe he's the one your friend Louis was talkin' about. I gotta distant cousin in Crownpoint, New Mexico, who can contact him. If he's not the right guy, she'll know who we need to see. I hope your friend Louis was right about this healer, and I hope he knows what he's doing—unlike me—or this curse might pass right into him and make him into another monster. Mary, I want these sons of bitches to pay for what they've done to my family… and you. But you're right—I can't do anything when I don't even know what I can do, and everyone around me dies because of what you, I mean, that lab, did to me."

"Don't worry," she said, "I have faith Louis knew what he was talking about. Once the healer cures you, we'll need all the help we can find to take these bastards down 'cause these monsters are worse than you can imagine."

Eighty-Four

11:18 a.m., Tuesday, October 2, 2007, Helix Eternal Laboratories Main Complex, Undisclosed Location.

The Benefactor sat inside the Horseshoe Lab above the meeting hall. His eyes (or at least the eyes he was using) were glued to Reality

Windows tuned to mortal airways and breaking news from Packer City, Colorado, in Reality 313. It always felt good to get away from his Prison, even though as its Warden and Curator he could make it as nice or hellish as he desired. But it wasn't the same as the power he once wielded that had been stripped of him, lowering him to a status beneath his lessers. Now, even the mortal shell he dwelled within was prohibited under the laws of the Council of Thirteen, as was crossing the River Styx into any of the many realities.

He examined Albert's weedy arms and bony fingers. He was less than pleased with the puny mortal shell who loaned itself to his exalted essence—he, the Lord of Lords, Lord of Heaven and Storms, Greatest of the Fallen, Marduk of the Original Three, Bēl, Horus-Ra, and the Fifty Names of countless more. But it was the mind within the shell that pleased him and had allowed him to complete the formula Antonia D'Amato's grandfather nearly perfected. But like all who fail him, that angel of death was now suffering for a season in the prison, which in Hell was quite longer than mortal minds could conceive and could last forever, or so it seemed, if he chose.

He continued watching the unfolding public outrage over the behavior of Adamson's clandestine Black Berets. It was concerning that Plan A failed, but not due to any potential carnage that Plan B might bring. Mortal shells were a dime a billion or less. Also, Adamson was a good acolyte. He would no doubt muscle through and redeem himself before the successful harvest. And though War had informed him of Adamson's desire to know more about the greater plan, Mr. Fire and Brimstone knew better than to ask the Greatest of the Fallen what wasn't voluntarily divulged. No. What bothered him was Delores Destiny's sudden and unforeseen Eye problem and the fog that formed over Mary's present and future (and everyone around her for that matter) after the foreseen *accidental* healing. He hated surprises and hoped this was a temporary failing of sweet Delores.

Eighty-Five

Darkness dissolved and Dr. Caine wondered where he was until he saw his surroundings. He was in the lab and had no memory of walking there. His last recollection was getting out of bed and pouring a cup of coffee and adding a dash of Light Ethereal.

He looked at his RW. It was tuned to WNN. Reporter Julie Florid was in the middle of a report about the sighting of someone he knew well. The popular reporter speculated that the unnamed murder suspect was headed toward Silver City. Caine knew better. Mary had a good heart. That made her weak and predictable. That's why she was chosen. No doubt, her next move would be to warn Mender, hoping to save his wife. General Adamson had his finger on the Plan B trigger, ready to fire when he was sure Mary and Mender were together. His assets were in position and had been for three weeks. Unbeknownst to anyone outside he, D'Amato, and those directly involved in the op, the Black Hawks (code-named Raven One through Four) had never left the area. They were parked in the high mountain valley near a long-abandoned ghost town. The pilots and forty Black Berets were camped nearby on Greenley Mountain.

Since then, there'd been one security breach, but the two hikers hadn't been declared missing yet. That same day, four Black Berets secured a home at the base of Tower Rock to watch for activity at Brigham Norsworthy's Watchtower and await Mender and Mary's arrival after the quarantine was lifted. General Adamson mentioned a mishap while securing the location, but only said that the incident was *"appropriately handled."*

Oh, and then there was the little incident at the Ebola-Colorado containment facility when Mary learned about the back up security system Adamson designed for Mender's cage. Adamson had wanted to move on Mary and Mender then, but according to Dr. D'Amato, the Benefactor didn't feel the time was *right*. He felt that Mender wasn't yet ready for harvest, even though it'd almost been three weeks since Mary infected him with the Touch. That was ample time, based on all the lab studies, for Mender to manifest his powers which he'd already displayed when he killed his son. Whatever the Benefactor was doing made no sense to him.

Caine sighed, left the lab, and headed downstairs. He passed through the black steel gate into the sizeable half-oval meeting hall. He glanced at the second story observation window, panned to the massive turquoise skin of a small portion of the iron cross shaped Terrarium, and then craned his neck up to appreciate the enormous cavern's ceiling. He regarded one hundred empty chairs that would soon be filled with the next group. *What a shame. So much work. So much promise*, he thought.

He hoped tweaks to his formula would correct issues which had plagued Mary's group but wondered if his frequent passenger and General Adamson would allow him to test it on any of the incoming rats. He doubted it. They only seemed interested in the old batch, which brought him disgrace and led to his deal with two devils. Still, he had signed the Man in White's contract with his own blood and it plainly stipulated that, *"The Demon, known as the Benefactor, promises to provide all necessary resources for Dr. Albert Caine to complete any and all research in exchange for occasional use of his mortal shell and mind within the confines of Helix Eternal Laboratories main lab complex and associated caverns."*

It was more than *research*. What he was working on was paradigm shattering and would hearken in a new era of human evolution that would justify the hideous things he'd done in the name of science for the betterment of humankind. But would it matter? For his efforts, he would be remembered as a monster for the things that the Benefactor and General Adamson had done and would continue doing in his name. His only consolation was that his work was greater than himself, the lives of his test subjects, or the demons he was forced to work with. He only hoped Cassandra and the kids would someday understand.

He crossed the meeting hall and headed down another, much longer, flight of stairs. He saw Dr. D'Amato in the distance across the River Styx. She was sitting in a lotus pose on a large rock just inside the west half of the Terrarium's north section. He passed over an ornate ivory bridge in the central dome and continued to where D'Amato was seated. Her eyes were closed, but he knew she was seeing everything. At least, he hoped she was seeing everything. He waited and thought about the wonders around him like the rain falling on her that revealed everything beneath her white blouse. But her body was now a forbidden fruit he longed to taste again or at least remember tasting when the Benefactor feasted on her with his shell. It was just another torment he was forced to endure in the name of science.

The rain. Yes. Oh, how Dr. D'Amato loved the simulated rain and gray clouds. It gave her the much-needed illusion of being above ground during the long months of research below the earth. Of course, soft rains and autumn skies were just one of the settings. The Terrarium's weather and reality controls could create simulations for every imaginable environment—even fantastical ones. Within this artificial mini-world, each of the five sections was individually controlled. When inactivated, the Terrarium floor was pearl white and the ceilings were starless night. From the outside, the center section was a circular dome. It was the smallest and opened into the other sections in four directions with four additional entry/exit points between the sections that led to other areas of the titanic complex.

Unlike the central dome, the other sections were triangular and longer than three football fields. The River Styx split the north and south sections. Each half was connected by several ivory bridges. The north section was bounded by a massive waterfall and the south by what seemed like a bottomless pit. The wide ends of the east and west sections were built flush with the cavern wall. The west wall exited into a large hallway, which gave access to more of the expansive miracle of underground engineering. The east expansion was never completed. The exterior shape of each section did not affect the interior's illusion and reality controls could expand the deception to cover a space ten to twenty times greater than the exterior would fool one into believing.

He still remembered his awestruck elation eighteen months earlier when he first laid eyes on what he'd believed was an urban legend—another fantastical tale ascribed to the world's richest and most well-known psychopath, Lester Ackerman. But what impressed him even more than the copious volumes of eye candy was the inexhaustible energy source housed within the central dome. Four thirty foot columns had been erected around the central bridge. Each was filled with a cold burning fuel that gave the inactivated dome a shimmering blue ambience one might see in an aquarium. It also produced a light blue powder with mind enhancing benefits similar to the air that filled the caverns beyond the Terrarium complex.

Whatever the inexhaustible fuel was, it had kept the installation illuminated since the fallout shelter for the elite of the elite was abandoned after Ackerman's Christmas Massacre in 1964.

Caine shook his head. Referring to it as a fallout shelter was an injustice. The sprawling complex was carved from the cavern's variable colored granite or sculpted from the caves. Along the lengthy, wide corridors were mind-boggling works of art which included statues of every imaginable and unimaginable deity, kings and queens, and other world leaders, many of whom he didn't recognize. The corridors led to more meeting halls, sculpted luxury apartments, restaurants, and activity centers with swimming pools and tracks. There were large wheat and cornfields, orchards, woods, parks, and ponds. It was a virtual paradise covering several square miles, of which he'd only explored a fraction.

Built in secrecy between 1949 and 1965, Ackerman attempted to create a place where humankind could survive until it was time to rise from the nuclear ashes. No doubt, the underground city's construction must've required a massive workforce. And what they constructed was arguably the most magnificent wonder of the world the world had never seen, since almost no one knew it existed. The Benefactor and General Adamson meant to keep it that way. And like the workers who built the wonder, it was a stipulation of his and D'Amato's blood contract that they never speak of its existence to anyone who didn't also have a soul-binding contract with the Benefactor. That wasn't a problem since he'd never been allowed to see the outside of whatever mountain housed Ackerman's Fallout Shelter. And sometimes, he wondered if he was dreaming, as he often fell asleep somewhere else and woke up in his bed or in the lab, like he did three weeks earlier when he fell asleep in Fort Collins after Plan A failed.

D'Amato's eyes opened. She dispassionately regarded him with the Farseer's deep blue eyes. As present awareness returned, the ghostly cobalt phased to a dazzling swirling green.

"Did you see Mary?" he asked.

Her expression remained frigid to match the harsh accent. "I still cannot see Mary or Mender or any lives near them, but north, south, and east of Packer City, the fog has lifted. Only the southwest, beyond the big lake, is hidden from the Farseer. Mary is either with Mender or very close. Call the General and initiate Plan B."

He pressed his comm button. "General Adamson, sir. Dr. D'Amato believes Mary DeMure is near or already with Mender."

Adamson replied. "I'm one step ahead of you. Our sweet little Mary was spotted passing the outpost three minutes ago. The Ravens are in flight."

Eighty-Six

11:30 a.m., Tuesday, October 2, 2007, The Watchtower.

Ryan threw an eighty-liter pack in the back seat by Mary's pack while she fidgeted and chewed her fingernails up front. He would have to ditch the truck soon, and wanted to be ready for the long hike to follow. He climbed in the cockpit.

Mary opened her mouth to speak.

He raised a finger to his lips. He heard chopper blades.

THUMP...

A few seconds passed...

THUMP...

There was another THUMP...

Then one more.

He pointed a finger gun at the glove box.

Mary opened it and handed him the Glock and holster.

He grabbed the gun, set the holster on the seat, and checked the magazine. It was still missing two cartridges. He reinserted the magazine, racked the slide, and got out. Mary was already standing by the driver's side.

He aimed the pistol at the door to the dining room hall as he stepped backward toward the breaker box by the garage door along the south wall. He wanted to take advantage of the night that wouldn't go away in case the intruders forgot their night vision goggles for what was supposed to be a day operation. Darkness would be their only friend when the boots above breached the Watchtower.

He opened the panel and went for the main power breaker. He was about to flip it when he saw a small red switch below. Beneath the switch was an old message written in black: *when ravens descend, flip the red switch.*

"Huh?" slipped from his lips. He'd never seen the message before, but then he'd never had reason to open the breaker box until then. He regarded Mary and glanced at his hands and thought of the painting with the four blackbirds, the tower, the black wizard, and the Joan of Arc. *No fuckin' way*, he thought. *How could Norsworthy have known?* He shook his head as his mind raced with possibilities, shrugged, and flipped the sticky switch.

The main power breaker switched off, and the garage plunged to black. A second later, a sheetrock section near the water heater at the wall's opposite end slid away without a sound, illuminating the garage with shimmering blue like one might see at an aquarium. The opening led into a short passage that ended with a stairwell. On the left was a knee-high conduit that radiated aqua blue like heat signatures but the hall was chilly. The conduit continued to a stairwell and down.

Ryan entered and glanced back at Mary's boo-berry face. He motioned for her to follow, and then moved toward the stairs. Halfway there, he glanced back as the door slid shut as silently as it opened.

He moved down two long flights, dropping what must have been at least a hundred feet. At the bottom, the conduit wrapped around the corner and continued along the left wall, delicately but sublimely lighting a long tunnel to an end beyond sight. A shorter hall to the right was lit by six comparatively harsh white incandescent fixtures and led to a heavy gray door. The white smothered the blue like a line in the sand.

Mary went to the door and grabbed the knob below a deadbolt keyhole, glanced at Ryan, and turned the knob. It was unlocked. She stepped through the threshold.

He followed and gawked at the control room. He had no foreknowledge of any of this being beneath the dream castle from Hell. Before him were rows of numbered monitors and a panel of switches corresponding to each display. Each black-and-white monitor showed different feeds from cameras throughout the Watchtower and outside from the base of the switchback drive to the woods above the fire pit and solar panels.

Mary stopped at the monitors.

He left her there and continued through another unlocked gray door. He turned left down a corridor, stopped, and stood even more nonplussed by the next thing he saw.

Eighty-Seven

Mary watched as three fireteams of four Black Berets in formation arrived at the Watchtower's three entrances. The contractors were dressed in camo which blended well with the snowy landscape. Each wore a backpack and helmet with night vision attachment and had a hip holstered sidearm. All but one held carbines with laser scopes and suppressors. The exception at the living room's glass sliding door held a shotgun. Attached to each vest was a pair of grenades.

The lead at front entry and bedroom set charges while the third lead with the shotgun waited at the living room's sliding glass. The first two stepped back from the doors and crouched, facing away. Silently, the doors blew from their hinges and shotgun blast splintered the sliding glass, showering the living room with shards. Each group threw multiple grenades through each breach. They discharged and whited out the monitors for a few seconds. The groups moved inside.

The contractors in the bedroom appeared to be gagging. Mary saw Suzanne Mender's body on the bed, looking as terrible as she expected. She noticed numbered switches on the panel below the monitors. *Wonder what these are for?* she thought.

The three fireteams moved with rifles ready as black laser dots danced on the upstairs walls, halls, and in the kitchen and dining room. Each group checked the rooms and closets for signs of life. A contractor in the garage lipped something Mary couldn't read as he peeked in the truck's backseat. His lips continued moving, but she didn't need to read them to know he'd found the backpacks.

She checked the outside monitors.

Two more fireteams headed into the house. Two others held their positions outside. One was in the terraced garden below the porch next to a broken television. The other was behind the Watchtower by a fire pit and the solar panels.

Twenty-eight Black Berets, she thought. She and Mender had little choice but to hide and hope they didn't find the secret door.

The contractors in the garage knocked along the south wall then headed inside.

Her gaze shifted to monitor 1. It had a bird's eye view from the top of the octagon-shaped living room. Two fireteams were walking below, searching for seams and stomping on the floors. The other teams checked the upstairs, kitchen, and dining room walls. A few Black Berets paused to examine the paintings. One contractor seemed to puzzle over a phantasmagoric masterpiece of a mountain and a tower on a rock being attacked by four massive blackbirds. She saw two figures standing on the tower but couldn't make out the details.

She eyed switch 1 and glanced at the door Ryan went through. She paused, rubbed her mouth, and flipped the switch.

An explosion followed, unheard this far beneath the tower. Monitor 1 went to static. The other monitors showed nails raining on the eight Black Berets. Several mouths gaped in various expressions of surprise and pain. *"Get out! Get out!"* was read on the lips of another.

"What was that?" asked Ryan.

She hadn't noticed his return to the monitor room. She didn't answer as she watched eight contractors grab their necks, foam at the mouth, and fall convulsing to the nail-peppered hardwood.

"That motherfucker," spat Ryan. "My wife and son used that room." His hands were shaking and crackling like static.

She grinned and started flipping switches for every display showing breathing Black Berets. The strange paintings on the Watchtower's mountainside slid away, exposing metal doors. The doors slid open. Inside the hidden wall cavities were mounted heavy machine guns on swivels. Faint muffled rapid-fire cracks followed as the guns panned back and forth and large cal bullets blew holes through everything in their path.

Outside, two pill-shaped towers erupted from the ground. One was between the solar panels and fire pit and the other in the driveway next to the front porchway. Metal sides opened skyward, and spring arms flipped up with heavy machine guns.

Mary watched the heavy guns pivot as the contractors dove for cover as plate-size holes replaced walls and bodies and made craters in the floors. Flesh shredded and exploded in black and white and sprayed the house and outside with coal-colored gore. In no time, the twenty not dead from the poison nails lay mangled and dismembered.

The guns continued pivoting and firing for several more seconds, further tenderizing and scattering the mounds of flesh and pulverized bone. When the machine guns stopped, smoke poured from the barrels.

She watched three black choppers hovering from a few different angles. Three monitors were trained on each. Unlike the other monitors, there were three corresponding thumb joysticks with safety covered red buttons. She raised the covers and reticles appeared on each screen. She moved the reticles over the three hovering Black Hawks, then pressed each button.

A third pill tower burst from the driveway. The machine guns on the other towers flipped down, followed by the sides. In unison, all three tower tops slid open, and three rocket-propelled grenades streaked toward the choppers.

One took a direct hit to its fuel tank and exploded over the edge of the driveway. More screens displayed the flaming fuselage rolling down the tiers. What remained came to rest between the first and second switchback.

The helicopter over the Watchtower careened away, then spun as black smoke poured from its engine. It smashed into the tower's face, exploded, shattering the tall windows. Cedar supports split, and a blade spinning like a throwing knife stuck in the wall above the stairs. The Black Hawk's carcass landed on the cedar deck and exploded again, knocking out several cameras. Other monitors showed a large portion of the tower's face turning into flying splinters. The front deck tumbled down the rock wrapped in the flaming fuselage.

The last rocket clipped the third chopper's rear rotor and sent it whirling. It barely missed the other two Black Hawks and crashed out of sight, northwest of the big rock and its burning tower.

Mary grinned with shaky giggles. *Fuck yeah,* she thought.

Mender was speechless.

She continued watching the monitors until Mender startled her with an arm tap. "Follow me," he said. "I gotta show ya something."

She followed into a wide hallway. Inset to the right was a massive weapon collection that continued for at least a hundred feet. The deceased aficionado's toys were meticulously arranged and included legal and illegal firearms, attachments and modifications, knives, and grenades of every variety. It was like a museum, or more likely, a weapons cache for a very eccentric, wealthy extremist.

"Did you know any of this was here?" she asked.

"Hell no. I didn't know about any of this shit. Brigham Norsworthy owned this place before us. No doubt this was his weapons cache for his Goddamn militia. Fuckin' Eugene Lee."

"Who?"

"Nothin'. Previous caretaker. Norsworthy's nephew. I guess the rest of this was his uncle's home security system."

"Shit," she said and continued down the corridor. She stopped at a metal door halfway down the wall of weapons. She opened it and descended another flight of steps.

At the bottom was a firing range with dozens of lanes on each side. Easily read, chiseled into the rock at the far end and lit up in red, white, and blue, was:

Amendment II
A well-regulated Militia,
being necessary to the security of a free state,
the right of the people to keep and bear Arms,
shall not be infringed.

Ryan glowered and shook his head. "I can't believe that crazy motherfucker had all this shit, and his Goddamn kids sold us this house without telling us. We are so fucked no matter what happens now. Hell, I don't even give a shit anymore. I mean, damn, I was about to paint my bedroom red when you walked up," he said with a humorless chuckle. "Fuck yeah, I'm glad you slaughtered those motherfuckers. Hell, I guess I should thank you for giving me something to live for 'cause I'm gonna kill every one of those sons-of-bitches before I'm locked up or put in the ground," he finished in a growl.

"We will, but we're not ready to attack them head-on. For now, we just gotta get out of here. I'm sure your neighbors and the surrounding counties heard our, uh, little fireworks display. We gotta be gone before the cops get here. But I'm not that worried about the lab. These dead guys and their choppers probably never left the county. I'm not sure where the lab's located, but it's pretty far north. I counted twenty-eight dead. If that's all they sent, it'll be a while before more arrive. By then, everyone will be here."

Ryan rubbed a thumb over his upper lip, then wagged a finger. "Hey, why don't we watch the monitors for a few minutes, you know, just to be safe? They arrived like airborne and airborne travels in chalks of twelve. That means there's at least two more fireteams nearby, and we don't know how many were here during the lockdown."

"True. But, uh, we don't have a choice. Staying here isn't an option."

"Shit. Then fuck it—let's go. Grab whatever you need from the wall, but don't grab anything you can't handle."

She went to the wall of revolvers and pistols and grabbed a Smith & Wesson Model 29 long barrel. She grabbed two boxes of .44 Magnum cartridges from a drawer below the inset counter.

"Seriously?" he asked, raising an eyebrow.

"You don't think I can handle it?"

"Hmm. Okie dokie, Dirty Mary. Whatever. Let's move."

She found a chuckle as she loaded six chambers. She shoved the rest of the box in a coat pocket.

Mender grabbed a shotgun and a box each of 12-gauge slugs and buckshot shells. He loaded four slugs in the magazine and one in the chamber.

Mary attached a hip holster to her belt, put the nine-inch cannon in its place, and went to the wall of knives. She grabbed a large Bowie and its sheath, and attached it opposite the revolver.

Mender set the shotgun on the counter by his Glock. He grabbed a modified automatic rifle and threw the strap over his neck. He inserted a full magazine and pulled the charging handle. He set the forward adjustment to ready the first cartridge. He grabbed four more magazines, squeezed them into his jacket, picked up the shotgun, and left the Glock.

Eighty-Eight

Ryan checked the monitors once more. He saw a growing fire filling the living room with smoke.

He followed Mary up the steps and hit a red button on the hall's left side. The garage wall slid open and closed as they exited the secret passage. He jumped in the truck and slid the rifle between the front seats and wedged the shotgun and shell boxes under the packs in the back.

Mary got in front.

He inhaled and exhaled and pressed the opener on the visor. When the garage door was up enough to squeeze through, he stomped the truck into reverse.

Pulsed rifle fire erupted along with the bullet clangs on the tailgate. The back and front windshields shattered, as more bullets zinged past Mary's head and dotted the utility room wall.

She ducked as Ryan shifted into drive, punched the gas, and hit the garage door button as more trios zipped through the missing windows. The door scraped the truck-top. Ryan crashed into the wall, flinging Mary forward.

Bullet pulses peppered the garage door. A rapid-fire torrent followed from what Ryan recognized as an M249 Squad Automatic Weapon (SAW). It added holes to the bathroom's sheetrock and punctured the water heater, sending fifty gallons gushing onto the concrete.

He noticed the shooters were now only firing on the garage's left side. They were either trying to flank or corral them, but it made no difference since he couldn't get to the breaker box to open the wall. Ready or not, he and Mary would have to face them head-on. At least now, the odds were better, but they had to move fast.

He eyed the shotgun but grabbed the rifle instead. He turned the selector from safety to auto, then back to single fire, drew a deep breath, and let his training take hold.

The firing stopped and was followed by the faint sound of the SAW's cover assembly opening.

He jumped from the truck and ran for the door, adjusting the buttstock on the move. He glanced back as Mary slid across the seat. She was right behind him, revolver ready for business as he opened the door. The hall was clear.

Mary took the lead before he could protest. He followed, peering down the iron sight.

She peeked through the utility room to the office and foyer beyond, then turned to the bathroom. She nodded at Ryan and moved forward.

He checked again as a Black Beret stepped into the office. **CRACK-CRACK-CRACK**—two in the chest, one in the head. The man dropped on the white marble.

Mary moved into the dining room and rounded the corner.

Ryan saw another contractor.

Mary didn't hesitate. **BAM-BAM.** The contractor reeled into the flaming living room as Ryan's ears rang. Smoke and a collection of nastiness filled his nostrils. He coughed.

They crouched below the smoke and moved through the dining room, maneuvering around and over body parts as their boots sloshed and sticky-popped through blood soup seasoned with casings.

Mary checked the foyer.

TEWT-TEWT-TEWT.

"OWW!" she spat.

Ryan spent most of a mag forcing the crouched contractor to roll off the porchway. He checked Mary, unsure if she was grazed or took the full pulse. "You okay?" he asked.

She grimaced and waved him off as she limp-crouched past the fireplace over broken glass and nails stuck in the hardwood. He moved backward with his muzzle trained on the front door until they reached the shattered slider. He released an empty mag and let it splat on the floor. He clicked in a freshy and pulled the charging handle.

They exited the Octagon, crossed the deck, and began ascending the steps. Ryan saw movement and pressed the trigger three times.

"Oomph," was all the contractor said before tumbling down the mountain stairs.

Suddenly, silence fell and several things happened at once. A crack of light found its way through the clouds and lit up the stone stairs to the tower top. It made him think of a stairway to the heaven where his heart was. He looked back. The black and gray smoke was billowing and flames were curling and licking in extreme slow motion. He looked forward. Mary jumped at normal speed an impossible fifteen feet in the air and landed at the first bend of the rocky stairway. Discharge vapor exploded and fanned out twice from the long barrel without a noise. Mary winced before firing a third time. She dropped the Model 29, and withdrew her right arm. She unsheathed the Bowie, and leaped out of sight. Several seconds later, two bodies sluggishly rolled down the steps. One landed face down with a fist-size hole in its skull. The other landed face up with eyes fixed and a black hole in the forehead turning red to match the trail down.

Dawn arrived and sound returned as a head in a helmet bounced down the steps at normal speed. Ryan moved and let it pass, then ran to where Mary stood. Blood covered her face and the front of her jacket. Her knife was re-sheathed, and she was holding her right arm. At her feet was a headless contractor surrounded by ruby snow sprinkled with brain and bone. Her eyes flickered with furious madness as blood dripped from her chin.

"You're shot."

"No shit, Gomer," she growled through her teeth. Her tone softened along with her expression. "Hey, um, I'm sorry. I didn't mean to snap at you. It… it'll heal. Bullets just hurt like a bitch when they hit bone. Anyway, that's thirty-four. If you're right, there's just two more assholes left. I really hope that's it."

Mary strode down the steps, let go of her arm, and picked up her snow-covered revolver. She grimaced as blood dripped from the jacket sleeve. She sat, reached into a pocket, and removed four cartridges. She reloaded as crimson trickled down the barrel.

Ryan looked again to the way they came up. Flames had engulfed the deck. He ran up the steps to the tower top and peeked over the parapet to the driveway. He saw movement in the rocks near the top switchback. He fired several times and sent stone chips flying, but missed his target as the Black Beret rolled out of the way and left the SAW. He watched for movement then pulled back from the parapet.

He returned to Mary. "Follow me."

He led her toward the fire pit and solar panels, and glanced back and around while trudging through more gore in the wine-colored snow.

A pistol discharged with a slightly different sound.

Ryan's head darted forward. He fired into the woods, sending splinters flying.

"I'm hit," cried Mary.

He grabbed her and pulled her behind the solar panels as several air pistols discharged and the metal backing clang-clang-clanged. He flipped the rifle to auto and emptied the mag in a blind arc. He loaded a freshy and returned to single-fire mode. He saw a bullet-size dart stuck in Mary's shoulder and removed it.

"I feel… sleepy," she said. "You gotta leave me, uh… Go, see your cousin… find the, uh… the healer…" She smiled and grabbed his face.

"Like, hell. I ain't leaving you. We do this together, or we die together,"

She closed her eyes.

He slapped her.

"Oww, you fuck-nut!" she spat as her eyes shot open.

"Sorry."

"No... no problem. There is something you can do, um... It's... It's a lil' trick I learned, um... When... when they get close, uh... uh... focus your hate... your rage... your... your whatever, um... anything that really pisses you off... makes you wanna... makes you wanna kill... Imagine it's a... it's a ball of fire... like the sun... Yeah, picture it... picture it going... going booom..." Her voice trailed off and her eyes closed.

Ryan slapped her again, but she was out.

The situation was hopeless. There were several more contractors. How many? He didn't know. But he did know they were likely as well trained as he, had the high ground, and that there was no going back to the Norsworthy's secret lair. Saving Mary was impossible, but leaving her wasn't an option with her grandfather's spirit lurking in his thoughts reminding him of a promise he never actually made but felt compelled to honor. But that didn't matter. She could've left after the lockdown, but she stayed to warn Suzanne and tried to save her life. She was too late, yet, Suzanne's death wasn't her fault, nor was it his, and neither was Alex or Melvin's. Like them, he and Mary were victims.

He chewed his lip. There was no option except Mary's trick if he could pull it off. He would have to find that pit of darkness that nearly consumed him at the lake and again in his bedroom. He would have to embrace it and hold it in this time. There was nothing left to lose.

He watched sleeping Mary. Her lips were curled for what must've been a pleasant dream. There was no other way, but could they survive him going nova? *Probably not. It's probably best that we don't*, he thought. The decision was made and now he had to draw the fuckers out for one big bang. *The more the fuckin' merrier.*

He laid his rifle in the snow. He raised his hands and headed toward the woods. He shouted, "Hey, we give up. What do you want from us?"

Four air pistols answered.

He staggered, dropped to his knees, and fell sideways next to one of the two snow-covered benches by the fire pit.

Four Black Berets exited the woods with pistols holstered and rifles trained. Before everything darkened, he felt a kick in the ribs that revived him long enough to see a familiar face before it blurred to nothingness.

Eighty-Nine

"Fuck, ow!" said ex-Army Sergeant David Eubanks, grabbing his side as he crouched. The pain served as an ample reminder of his first encounter with his fellow ex-Ranger. The contractor checked for a pulse with a gloved hand and spoke. "He's alive. Raven Four, we got 'em both. Let's bag 'em and get 'em back to HQ." The nearing sound of chopper blades made further words pointless. He stood, let his rifle hang, pulled his air pistol, and shot Mender again. Then once more.

Ex-Army Lieutenant Wayne Stiner grinned. His misshapened nose was still surrounded by the light brown-yellow from recent bruising. He removed two black body bags from his pack. He unfolded and unzipped them.

Raven Four landed in the wide driveway, its blades almost clipping Greenly Mountain.

Two more contractors emerged from the woods. They stripped weapons and ammo from Mender and DeMure, and then helped Eubanks and Stiner lay the limp bodies in the bags. They zipped them up, secured each bag with a padlock, and then the four carried the bags down the steep, snowy trail as the buffeting blades challenged each slippery step.

After loading the bags, Eubanks sat on the bench, strapped in, and spoke loud enough to be heard over the chopper's blades. "General, sir. Operation complete. Typhoid Mary and Pestilence are alive and sleeping like babies. We're moving out. Should be back at HQ around 1330."

"Very good. How many casualties?"

"Repeat, General, sir?"

"HOW MANY CASUALTIES?"

"It's bad. They killed thirty-four of ours, but the house was booby-trapped. We didn't expect that kind of firepower."

"Yes. Quite unexpected," said the General. "It's unfortunate we lost so many. I'm just glad you were able to capture Mender and Mary. The Benefactor will be pleased. Tell your men good work. See you back at base."

"Yes sir, General sir," Eubanks said as Raven Four lifted off.

Ninety

Ryan's eyes opened. He gasped but the sound was muted by the vibrating roar. Darkness smothered him. He was cold but he didn't dare shiver. He focused on Melvin, Alex, Suzanne, Mary, and his life's obliteration. There was no sorrow. No tears. Only venomous spite. The throbbing, stinging sensation returned, but rather than releasing his wrath, he internalized it as instructed.

The din of the chopper slowed, then went silent. Time stood still as he floated in raging hate. He pushed and pushed, feeling the pressure build until every cell felt ready to explode as he burned inside. Melting. Molten. He saw the power of the sun. Its birth. Its life. Its death. The sun shrank.

Sound returned and his body crackled and convulsed.

Ninety-One

Eubank's eyes widened at the sight of the vibrating bag. "EVERYONE, GET OUT NOW! JUMP!"

Eubanks and Stiner made the thirty-foot ankle-breaking drop. Eubanks limped fast as he glanced back. Cobalt rays tore through the chopper's skin. Fire engulfed Stiner as Eubanks jumped from the edge of the driveway. He rolled and cartwheeled and felt more snaps and cracks as he took the short cut off Tower Rock and down the switchbacks.

After what seemed like a lot longer, he came to a stop. He felt nothing below his screaming neck. He tried to breathe but his spine was broken too high up. He knew he wouldn't be waiting long for death's embrace.

He couldn't see the Black Hawk in the driveway but he could see it explode again into an orange, yellow, black, and blue fireball. *So pretty*, he thought as flaming pieces of metal and his fellows blew in every direction, showering the area around him. A hand bounced to a stop and remained propped up, reminding him of Thing from the Addam's Family. If he could've breathed he would've chuckled.

The fire ball continued expanding like napalm sending out swirling blue tentacles hundreds of feet in every direction. Everything it touched erupted into eerie blue flame including Eubank's paralyzed body. Then, as if God inhaled, the fires were extinguished.

The last thing he saw was the snow—the cobalt colored variety he'd seen before. It sparkled like diamonds in the sun's late arrival. Then his world turned sepia. He would be in Hell soon.

Ninety-Two

Ryan's breaths were shallow. Everything was dark.

His eyes sprang open. He was back in the dream that Suzanne and Alex had just left. He sat up and looked to the room where Suzanne's corpse lay rotting—the room where the Reaper guided his green-eyed goddess and their little clown out of his ghoulish reality to a better place. He was ready to join them.

He glanced around. He saw no man in black, and there were no doors. He was alone except for Mary who lay unconscious several feet away in a melted body bag. Or was she dead? She had to be. He was unsure how this sepia world worked or if his visions of Suzanne, Alex, and the Man in Black hadn't been a hopeful, cruel illusion.

Sepia faded, and darkness returned. He felt nothing. Saw nothing. Heard nothing. Smelled nothing. Tasted nothing. He couldn't even breathe. Then, there was light, a blurred blue sky, and clouds above. And falling snow. Dark blue snow. Smell and taste returned. Sulfur. Burnt flesh, oil, and iron. A sickly hint of rose? Then came the pain. His vision improved and he tried to blink but couldn't. Discomfort grew, rising rapidly into a raging river. He tried to move but couldn't. Then a finger twitched as more nerve endings found their friends. Strength to breathe returned and he screamed, "JUST LET ME DIE!"

He sat up and saw what remained of a twisted Black Hawk fuselage. Around him, associated debris and charred body parts poked from the accumulating layer of cold ash. He saw a fuzzy Mary through lidless sockets and blurry vision. She was wrapped in a melted vinyl coffin.

He crawled through sparkling blue ash, ripped open the bag, and didn't bother checking for a pulse of what remained inside. Driven by some deeper instinct, he picked her up. His knees wobbled and he almost collapsed. He willed himself to take a step. Then another. And another. Slowly stepping, dragging his raw feet through the icy powder.

Gunshots erupted from Crown Lake or the Fitzgerald's place. Wherever they'd come from, he didn't give it a second thought. He had to heal himself, and quickly, then perform a miracle. But who was he kidding? He wasn't a healer anymore. He'd failed to save Alex and Suzanne. All his hands could do now was kill. Nevertheless, the old gentleman's eyes prodded him on. *"You must save my Mary,"* said the voice in his head.

Ryan made it to the outside stairs to the bedroom. His arms ached. He stopped, took several labored breaths, and adjusted his hold on the little girl in the pink dress. He continued on, legs trembling, nearly buckling, with every step to the second floor. He limped across the deck, his soles slicing on broken glass from his earlier, less dramatic explosion. He entered the bedroom through the ruined door. The flames hadn't extended that far, but he sensed the fire was no longer burning in what remained of the Watchtower.

Floating dark ash had left a frosty coat over everything including Suzanne. Her eyelashes sparkled and the rest of her reminded him of someone from the Blue Man Group. He laid Mary next to Suzanne as the aroma of decay overwhelmed his heightened senses. He retched once, twice, then turned his head and vomited blood. He crumbled to his knees and curled on the floor. He rocked back and forth, moaned and shuddered from splintering agony, the likes of which he'd never thought possible. He needed it to stop. It had to stop. He wanted it to stop, and with that thought, the pain vanished, and he felt... stronger—much stronger than before his explosion. Stronger than ever before. Stronger than all. Hell, he felt superhuman, like a god. Perhaps, he could save Mary and bring her back from the off-yellow world before she crossed over.

He got to his feet, regarded her corpse, and then began peeling off the melted vinyl attached to remnants of clothing, loose skin, and muscle that slid off bone. He regarded her face. One eyeball was missing and her nose was gone. Her jaw bone and teeth were exposed on the left side. He closed new eyelids and ran his hands over what remained of her breasts, ribs, and blackened heart and lungs. Nothing happened. He concentrated. Still nothing. He focused harder. It wasn't working. He felt panic seep through cracks of doubt. He paused and removed his hands and opened his eyes. He breathed in and out. In and out. In and out. He relaxed and cleared his mind of everything but his earnest wish. He closed his eyes, and placed his hands on her chest once more. He thought of how the pain stopped when he willed it to do so. Now, he wanted Mary to live. He wanted her to heal. He wanted her to be whole. And with that commanding desire, he felt a surge of adrenaline and her chest rose.

He opened his eyes and watched her wrist. An artery pulsated between exposed muscles and bones. Tissues began to bleed and the color of life washed over the blue and blackened skin that hadn't burned away. Her nose and eye reformed as he re-sculpted her former beauty. Soon, he felt warmth as skin regrew and spread over exposed flesh, bone, and organs, merging with spontaneous grafts without scarring.

When the healer had finished his work, Mary lay naked with the skin of a newborn. Ryan left her and went to the closet. He picked out an outfit, and grabbed some bedsheets. He found a pair of underwear and long johns among the clothes lying on the floor that weren't covered with blood. He shook off ash, frost, pulverized sheetrock, and splintered wood. He set the clothes at Suzanne's feet and kicked an area clear of books and debris. He moved Mary onto the floor, spread the sheet over her blood and gore print, then picked her up and returned her to the bed next to Suzanne.

He dressed then returned and regarded his handiwork like one would a work of clay. *Why can't I do the same for Suzanne?* He knew the answer because he had watched the door close. What he saw wasn't Suzanne—it was just a shell.

He sat between the reanimated and the dead and stared out the same window as earlier. He laughed, then cupped his face. He wept for a minute, then looked at Mary's change of clothes that he'd left at Suzanne's rotting feet. *I can't let that girl wake up like that. That wouldn't be proper,* he thought or said in a hollow voice. He wiped his eyes, then respectfully dressed her, and went out to the deck.

His gaze drifted east beyond what could be seen. He glanced at his left hand. He turned it over and released a grunting chuckle. The P-shaped scar was gone and the palm felt smooth as a baby's bottom. He removed his coat and sweatshirt and studied his arms. His bullet wound and his tattoos, including the names of his fallen brothers, had burned away with his old skin leaving soft, unblemished brown. He put his shirt back on and continued staring in the direction of the dawn that had finally come and gone.

Ninety-Three

Mary stirred, rolled over, and felt cold steel. She opened her eyes and saw a revolver and then Suzanne Mender's Ethereal blue corpse. "Shit, shit, shit. Oh my God, oh my God," she screamed, pulled away, and sprang from the bed.

She felt dizzy and disoriented as she scanned the room. Her gaze was drawn to the deck where Mender stood. She looked at the clock on the wall. It was the only thing still attached. It read *11:57*. She remembered saying something to Mender as she dozed, but nothing after that. *The clock has to be wrong,* she thought as she glanced again at the corpse on the bed. Oh, how she wished the earlier one had been wrong. Like that one, this clock was correct. *But how?* She'd experienced Caine's sleepy time darts before and should've been out for hours or days.

"Ryan," she said.

He didn't respond.

"Hey, we need to get gone."

Still nothing.

She noticed she was wearing a different snow jacket, a Pike's Peak sweatshirt, a pair of blue jeans, and a new pair of boots. The outfit must've been Suzanne's, who conveniently wore almost her same size, like Raj, except looser around the chest and tighter around the waist. She looked out at Mender and uncomfortably pondered why she was wearing his wife's clothing.

Her gaze returned to the wrecked room. She looked down and gasped. Burnt remnants of Raj's clothing and jacket were on the floor next to part of his Mariner's beanie. It was stuck to a large piece of blackened, crispy skin with spotty clumps of melted hair. She rubbed her forehead as if she could still get headaches. Her face tensed. The scar from September 1 was gone and she had no eyebrows. Her hand drifted to her scalp. It was smooth as a cue ball.

Recollection of her *stellar* whimsy returned. *What was I thinking suggesting the nova option?* She scoffed. Of course, she knew. And Mender had done it. He'd self-combusted, and she was caught in the blast. She didn't think they'd survive and believed it best that they didn't. It was the only way to prevent the mad General from getting his hands on Mender or her. But Mender was different than her fellow lab rats. No doubt, Mender had full control of his healing abilities. How else could he have healed her so fast after the crippling pain of rapid regeneration? Her last near-life-ending injury had taken days to heal, and the agony was epic. This time, she felt like she'd awoken after a long nap, but she'd only been asleep for a few minutes. She looked at the fried shards of clothing, plastic, and skin. She was lucky to be breathing.

She stepped toward the door, disbelieving of the cobalt hellscape coming into view. She stood next to Mender. He seemed dazed as he gazed toward the horizon. His face and head were as hairless as hers.

Her attention returned to the driveway horror show. No doubt, she'd gone beyond sleep since there was no way anyone could've survived the frosty inferno she was trying to comprehend.

"Ryan, snap out of it. We gotta go now," she said.

He returned a blank stare, nodded, and said flatly, "Yeah, I'm ready. Let's get the fuck out of here."

She turned and headed inside and navigated gore, and plate-sized holes in the game room. She ducked under a helicopter blade stuck in the wall, then moved down the charred, creaking staircase. A step broke under Mender halfway down and he nearly tumbled into the pantry.

Everything on the lower floor was blackened and blue frosted. A frigid breeze blew through a gaping hole in the living room as the sagging ceiling groaned above. Mary maneuvered to the garage and went to the truck, taking care not to slip on the now ice-covered cement. She grabbed the backpacks, Mender's holster, and the shotgun and shells, and set everything on the slick surface. She shoved the shell boxes in Mender's pack and made for the red switch as he grabbed his stuff. She flipped it and entered the glowing passage, bounded down the steps, and continued to the Hall of Weapons.

Ryan grabbed his Glock and holstered it, and attached the belt holster. He searched for a shotgun case while Mary grabbed another Smith & Wesson revolver, fitted a holster harness, and selected a more conservative version of her favorite blade. She packed all the ammo she could cram then slid on her anvil-heavy pack. Ryan did the same and slung his shotgun case over a shoulder. Without small talk, she exited, passed through the monitor room, and moved quickly into the long tunnel beyond.

She glanced back. Mender had stopped and was gazing up the stairwell with longing in his eyes for something that was gone forever—something she took from him. She sighed as her reanimated heart ached. They had to find Louis's healer. Then, at least, she could reverse the curse she'd given him. After that, they would bring down Helix Eternal Laboratories together and kill Dr. Evil, his whore bitch, and the mad General.

She caught Mender's eyes. He nodded and looked at his feet as if they were rooted to the ground. He lifted his face, nodded once more, and took his first step into the shimmering unknown.

Ninety-Four

12:13 p.m., Tuesday, October 2, 2007, Helix Eternal Laboratories Main Complex, Undisclosed Location.

D'Amato sat with Caine listening as Adamson delivered grim news from the Reality Window on his desk at the Pentagon. Caine's aspect was as grave as she felt since they might soon be sharing one.

"My men saw everything from the outpost..." said General Adamson. He went on to describe the disastrous failure of Plan B. "From Captain Rice's description, it was definitely a Blue Nova—the largest ever produced by your guinea pigs. Of course, we'll wait for confirmation from the Benefactor, but I believe Mender and Mary were lost and so are we."

Caine looked paler than usual.

"I assume your men at the outpost are searching the Watchtower for Mender's and Mary's empty shells," D'Amato said without a telltale trickle of terror. "If so, the Fog of Mary would have been cleared, but it still lingers and blinds the Farseer's eyes. No. I refuse to believe that they are dead until I hear it from the Benefactor."

"That is, uh... reassuring," said Adamson, sounding shaken like she had never heard him sound before. "Oh, and my men at the outpost... they are on the way to the Prison. And if by chance you are wrong about Mender and Mary—we can only hope that the Benefactor likes his new toys. If not, we will be seeing each other very soon in Hell."

Caine retched and ran from the room.

D'Amato rolled her eyes.

"Antonia, there is something I would like to know," said Adamson.

"What might that be?"

"Just a curiosity. Before the Ravens left for their date with Fate, the boots on the ground reported a strange darkness as if morning never got to dawn. Does Destiny have an answer for this?"

D'Amato closed her eyes and opened them seconds later. "She has no knowledge of any such anomaly. I will ask the Benefactor when he returns, if he does not tear off my head off and eat it before I have the chance," she said, oozing annoyance.

"Yes, of course. Well, if this is our last farewell in mortal shells, I will be quite sad not being there to relish of your brutal death. I have no more to report. All we can do now is wait." Adamson disconnected.

D'Amato closed her eyes again as Destiny searched far and wide around the Watchtower. She saw no futures, presents, or pasts. Her eyes spread their webs further. Still nothing. And further again, stretching, stretching, before finding something, but no Mary... or Mender. It was as if her fog was growing, not contracting. D'Amato smiled inside, and Destiny agreed. *Mary, you are still alive. But where are you taking Mender now?*

Caine returned smelling like Scope and Polo. She hated that cologne. He stopped in his tracks and appeared lost. He closed his brown eyes, inhaled, and took D'Amato's breath away. The Benefactor was coming. She could feel it and now she wanted to vomit. She resisted the urge and observed as Caine was shut away and the Benefactor returned.

Blue shimmered around Caine's shell and stole the air from her lungs. With his every breath, the air thinned until there was little left for her. She gasped as her chest seized up.

The aura faded. The Benefactor folded his arms over his chest and stood tall like an ancient god on a stone relief. His eyes crept open as if awakening from deep sleep.

She groped her throat and starved for oxygen. She usually loved the change. It was terrifying and exhilarating and fed the asphyxiophilia which she loved to give and receive. But she was tense and trembling this time as death closed in. Yet if Destiny could convince the Demon that Mender and Mary were still alive, she might survive his wrath.

The Benefactor's gaze fell upon her. Caine's awkwardness was gone, replaced by supreme confidence and arrogance. Her Lord had returned to his temporary temple.

Black polka dots filled her vision as darkness pushed inward to the center of unconsciousness. She tried not to faint or cower.

"Well, that was fun," said the Benefactor as oxygen flooded into the lab.

D'Amato sucked in with a violent, throaty rattle.

The Benefactor's lips drew into a satisfied, wanting grin. "All the General's Ravens and all the General's men are dead, but Ryan Mender was magnificent. And still breathing, I might add, as is Mary," he said in a voice that was deeper and sweeter than Caine's meek and mild. He stroked her hair as her vision cleared. He continued. "Mender is everything I hoped for, and soon he will become what I need to win this game once and for all. You must understand, I never believed Adamson's Black Berets had a chance, even if it'd been a fair fight." The smug smile didn't falter. "Ahh, old Brigham and his Watchtower. Why, that sly little devil. How did he know and why didn't Delores see? Well, no matter. Had Plan B succeeded, I would've killed Mender and Mary and started over."

"Great One, exalted above others, I, I do not understand."

The Benefactor laughed. "No you don't, and there is much you never will. This wouldn't have been the first time things didn't work out. Just have to keep my ancient eyes on the prize. Once the massacre is discovered, Mender will be isolated, and his thirst for revenge will draw him closer to Mary and then to me when they are ripe and ready for the harvest."

"I, I thought Mender and Mary were ready."

"No. Not yet," he said as his hand slid from her hair to her lips.

She shuddered, felt flushed, and squirmed in her seat. She kissed and sucked one finger and another and a next. Her face rose to meet her Lord's eyes. "Oh, Great One, exalted above all others, may I ask a question?"

"Yes, of course, my sweet Antonia. And please just call me Great One."

"Yes, Great One. General Adamson reported something strange, and Destiny did not know the answer. He spoke of a darkness, like a great hand, covering the Watchtower this morning, but her eyes had seen nothing like it in previous visions. Was that you?"

"No, that wasn't me. I don't have that power, but there is one who does."

"Who?"

The Benefactor's eyes narrowed and no longer matched his grin. "Dear, some things are best not to know or ask of again."

She nodded, dropped her face, and continued loving his hand.

The Benefactor kissed her head and drew in her essence. "Mmmm." He continued, speaking softly, each word caressing. "My sweet Antonia, don't worry yourself with such things. Concentrate on Mender and Mary. And know this—they will come to me, whether or not your passenger can break through the fog surrounding their destinies. My purpose here was only to test them, unite them under fire, and make them inseparable. That mission was accomplished—spectacularly. Now, what does not kill them only makes them stronger for what I have planned for Heaven and your earth.

End
of
Book 2

Coming Soon
just in time for Halloween
a tale of terror and two detectives
in
Mortal Shells
Tales from the Afterworld Book 3
Coming October 16, 2024

Also check out:
Accidental Healer's prequel novella,

Suzanne and the Menders' Son

Now Available at Amazon
https://www.amazon.com/dp/B0D1P5CGX4/

If you enjoyed this novel, show your love and leave a rating and a review on Amazon. For those who wish to continue this journey, subscribe to my website for a free gift with more to come.

www.vkpasanen.com
v.k.pasanen@vkpasanen.com
v.k.pasanen@talesfromtheafterworld.com

For upcoming books
Amazon.com: V. K. Pasanen: books, biography, latest update

Spotify saga playlist: Tales from the Afterworld
https://open.spotify.com/playlist/0zqW1pSnwzjzzuhtCw0QCC?si=cf13b4a2ad6e4fdf